PRAISE FOR
A TESTAMENT TO WIND AND STONE

"An intriguing tale of identical twins, separated at birth, eventually finding each other. Beyond the engaging plot, the true heart of this book lies in love and appreciation—for families, faith, nature and the power of music. Reading *A Testament to Wind and Stone* is a healing experience, reminding us of the beauty around us in these troubled times."

—BETTY SUE FLOWERS
PAST DIRECTOR OF THE LBJ PRESIDENTIAL LIBRARY & MUSEUM
EMERITA PROFESSOR OF ENGLISH AT THE UNIVERSITY OF TEXAS
AUTHOR AND FUTURIST

"A lovely and timely rumination on the ties that bind, the tensions that strengthen us, and how we are knitted together by faith, decision and destiny. Kudos to Max Sherman on a wonderful journey."

—STACEY ABRAMS
AUTHOR AND POLITICAL LEADER

"What a remarkable and original novel. Historically rich and deeply compelling, it tells a story few would ever imagine—and does so in a way that completely captivates the reader. As both a rabbi and a Texan, I found this book profoundly meaningful and one I will cherish for years to come."

—RABBI BRIAN STRAUSS
SENIOR RABBI AT CONGREGATION BETH YESHURUN, HOUSTON

Continued on next page

"Max Sherman has employed his vast and meticulous knowledge of politics, religion, music, and international affairs to create a novel that both captivates and inspires. He creates believable figures from the Texas Panhandle culture and puts them on a world stage to exemplify an ecumenical spirit sadly missing in the world today. It's a heart-warming story of two gifted young men who use their exceptional talents to pursue and fulfill their dreams."

—GREGG RAMSHAW
FORMER PRODUCER OF *PBS NEWSHOUR*

"A book for musicians and music lovers of all stripes, Max Sherman's novel is a touching statement on the power of music to create and strengthen the bonds between us."

—DR. ADAM KERRY BOYLES
DIRECTOR OF ORCHESTRAS AT MIT AND
ASSISTANT CONDUCTOR, HARTFORD SYMPHONY ORCHESTRA

ALSO BY MAX SHERMAN

Releasing the Butterfly:
A Love Affair in Four Acts

❧

Barbara Jordan:
Speaking the Truth with Eloquent Thunder

A
TESTAMENT
TO
WIND
AND
STONE

MAX SHERMAN

Palo Duro Press

Published by Palo Duro Press

Contact: maxshermanauthor@gmail.com

Printed in the United States

FIRST EDITION

Paperback ISBN: 979-8-9939964-1-7

Large-Print Paperback ISBN: 979-8-9939964-2-4

Ebook ISBN: 979-8-9939964-0-0

Book Editing by Katherine Moore & Cyndi Hughes of Booktique Consulting

Editing & Proofreading: Booktique Consulting and Melanie Bonner Thomas

Book Production by Booktique Consulting / www.booktiqueconsulting.com

Cover Design by MIBLart / www.miblart.com

❀ Formatted with Vellum

For Gene Alice
The love of my life who continues to whisper in my ear

CONTENTS

PART I

THE BIRTH

NOVEMBER 1952

1

DANIEL

AMARILLO, TEXAS
NOVEMBER 5, 1952

DANIEL JAMES SAT IN HIS LEATHER-LINED CHAIR, ITS FAMILIAR comfort doing little to settle the turmoil inside him after the last few hours. His dark brown hair was receding, just a bit, at his temples, as he ran his hand through his curls. His office in Amarillo, Texas, was evidence of his up-and-coming career, with its dark wood panels, shelves brimming with legal volumes, and a stately mahogany desk anchoring the room. He had inherited the office from a retiring partner, and its gift signified his new partners' confidence in his abilities as a lawyer. As one of his steady new streams of legal work, Daniel had taken on private adoptions for a local doctor, Dr. Thomas Brewer. Daniel had come to admire the doctor, whose dedication to unwed mothers and their babies was a testament to a truly good man.

Daniel mulled over what Dr. Tom had just asked him to do: The unwed mother Dr. Tom was caring for was not having just one baby; in the delivery room, the doctor realized that she was having twins. Because the original adoptive family had already declined to take twins in their vetting interview, Daniel would need to line up a family for the second baby quickly. He had an idea—a couple who had a ranch outside Canyon, Texas, had been on the adoption list for almost a year. So Daniel made a call to Joe Bob Mueller to ask if they could take the baby on short notice. Joe Bob asked for time to talk with his wife. Twenty minutes later, he called back to say they would be thrilled to adopt the baby. Daniel had just finished drawing up the paperwork for the Muellers to sign when they arrived to pick up the baby.

The paperwork Daniel had prepared for the mother of these twins was slightly different, as she, at thirty-four, was not in her teens nor without her own wealth. When the doctor told Daniel about her a few months before, he had spoken with a unique reverence. "She's not young; no, not at all. She is a mature woman, a revered pianist famous in some circles, and she found herself in a situation that I could help her with. I agreed, of course I did. I helped her find a place to stay where she could be comfortable as she awaited the birth."

Daniel wondered why she ended in the Panhandle under Tom's care, but Dr. Tom never explained that, and Daniel decided it was not his to know.

The mother's lawyers from New York City had worked with Daniel on the closed adoption, requesting copies of the paperwork and providing language to protect their client's identity. It was the first time Daniel had worked on an adoption with a mother who had access to her own counsel.

Once the twins had been delivered, all Daniel could do was listen as Dr. Tom struggled to decide where to place the two infants. "Against my better judgment, I must separate these identical twins. This goes against my principles, but the situation dictates that it must be done. Which baby do I give to which family? One family is Jewish, the other is Christian. Both will provide good homes, both babies will be well cared for and loved, of course. But will those different religions provide a different life? How can I know?"

Daniel said nothing while his friend was juggling five balls in the air—the mother, the two boys, and two expectant families. It was obvious that it was a conundrum.

Now, with two chosen families, two sets of paperwork, the decision as to which baby went to which family was left to Dr. Tom. Daniel swigged from a crystal tumbler of single-malt Scotch and thanked his lucky stars it was not his choice to make.

His gaze shifted from the Scotch to the latest edition of the *Amarillo Daily News* on his desk, its bold headline declaring, "Eisenhower Defeats Stevenson: First Republican in 20 Years." It was 1952, and the country was at a turning point. But Daniel's mind was not on national politics; it was on his friend and the empathy he felt for him having to play such a massive role in two children's lives. *It must be knotting his soul,* Daniel thought as he took another swig. Dr. Tom had to make not one choice but two, and two lives—and families—would never be the same.

The high-end Scotch offered some warmth, albeit a fleeting solace. His thoughts wandered back to eighteen months before, when he first met Dr. Tom. The doctor had reached out to his law firm to handle the paperwork for the adoption of a baby born of a sixteen-year-old unwed mother. Daniel, as the newest attorney in the firm, was given the job. Once the adoptive parents headed home with the new baby, Daniel asked Dr. Tom to join him for a drink, and they hit it off immediately. The two men discussed the rising conflict in Korea, then their conversation turned to the doctor's service in World War II. Dr. Tom's face, normally wise and welcoming, turned stormy. Quietly and with purpose, he told Daniel there was an evil in the world that he had witnessed firsthand as part of the Allied forces that had liberated Germany. What they discovered in the concentration camps haunted the doctor every day: the shattered remnants of those human beings, the haunted eyes of Jews who had survived the unthinkable, the burned remains of the corpses. As he told Daniel about the emaciated children with their skeletal hands reaching for the chocolate bars he handed out, tears welled up in his eyes. The memories of those camps were forever seared in the doctor's mind. Silence fell between them as the doctor sat with his demons, then he quoted from *Hamlet*:

> *What a piece of work is a man!*
> *How noble in reason, how infinite in faculties,*
> *in form and moving how express and admirable,*
> *in action how like an angel, in apprehension how*
>   *like a god!*

When they parted that evening, Daniel concluded in admiration that the doctor was the most erudite of men. Since that time, he had drawn up paperwork for nine other adoptions involving Dr. Tom's patients. This, however, had been the first set of twins.

As he sipped his Scotch, Daniel thought it was no wonder that Thomas Brewer was so devoted to helping unwed mothers and their babies. It was as if he was trying to save those Jewish children, the ones he could not save in Germany, by making sure these Texas babies went on to have the best lives possible.

Daniel also knew that helping the doctor with his mission to find loving homes for the children was only one small service he could provide. But he was willing to do anything to make his friend's choices easier.

Dr. Tom's story was intriguing to Daniel, and the two men often compared notes on their upbringing. Tom had been raised by a single mother in rural Mississippi. Luckily, he'd had a father figure named Amos, a Black man who taught him to respect nature and the mysteries of all the natural world. It was

Amos who showed Tom that nature itself was a realm of choices —the strongest survived, the weak perished. Tom often reminisced about the countless conversations he'd had with Amos about the nature of chance, the cruelty of life, and the power of a single choice.

Daniel's own childhood in Texas had been similar. He, too, had been raised by a single mother in a bookish household, and that led him to consider becoming a teacher. Ultimately, however, he had opted for a career in law, a path shaped by mentors and circumstances, and he wondered how different life might have been if he had taken another turn along the way.

From his work on the adoptions, Daniel admired how Dr. Tom always honored the mothers' hearts in his choice as well. Most of the mothers were just young girls—alone, bereft, pregnant, with no options. He, as their doctor, did his best to offer those girls a way to go on with their lives, secure in the knowledge that their babies were taken in by loving families. It was a small comfort, but one Dr. Tom was committed to providing.

Yet, Daniel thought, no matter where you placed a child, life would happen. Tragedy would strike and hope would endure. He had only to look at Dr. Tom's life to see that fate has its hand in all lives. When Tom was in medical school in New Orleans, he had fallen in love with a young Jewish woman studying to be doctor. They eventually married, despite both of their families opposing their nuptials, and were blissfully happy until she was tragically killed in a hit-and-run accident. After her death, Tom found himself wandering the world, from Native American communities in Montana to small villages in Palestine, delivering babies, seeking some sort of redemption through acts of service. He had been so distraught by the loss of his wife he never remarried or had children of his own. In a way, his choices determined his own life's purpose of making sure babies came safely into the world and found loving homes.

Daniel knew his friend would be thinking of the circumstances of his own life as he decided which twin would go to which family.

Whatever Dr. Tom decided in the quiet solitude of his office would ripple outward, affecting lives, and not just those of the babies. Daniel looked down at the two folders offering two starkly different paths. Whatever happened next, it was just another step in the labyrinth of choices that would make up two lives and the lives of their new parents.

Daniel glanced down at two folders sitting before him, one marked "Rosenbaum," the other "Mueller." Two paths, two variations of a life. Twins separated at birth. One to a Christian home, the other to a Jewish home. Daniel was certain Dr. Tom would make the right choice.

2

THE TWINS

Amarillo, Texas
November 1952

A soft hum, a chorus of delicate breaths, and occasional soft cries filled the nursery at Amarillo General Hospital. Thomas Brewer stood by the window, a tall, imposing figure with his broad shoulders slightly hunched as he gazed at the rows of tiny swaddled infants. His dutiful charge nurse walked past. "Another busy day for you, Doctor," she said, her voice tinged with both weariness and warmth. "So many lives you've brought into this world, and we have seen far too many tear-stained pillowcases from our young mothers. You do good work, you know that. Today is just another day in that work."

Dr. Tom was not surprised with her intimacy with him—together they had delivered countless babies in the Panhandle. But late last night had been unusual, with the surprise of a second baby delivered by an unwed mother. Ethically, Dr. Tom was bound to finding them the best homes, and since none of the prospective adoptive families he was working with were open to accepting babies of multiple births, he knew he would have to separate the twins. He thanked his stars for his friend Daniel James, who had set off on a last-minute quest to find another worthy family for the second twin and succeeded with the Mueller family, assuring Dr. Tom that both babies would have good homes. He left the nursery with a glance at the last two bassinets with blue blankets labeled "Baby Boy 1" and "Baby Boy 2" and headed to his office down the hall.

Now that they had the two families, it was up to Dr. Tom to decide which twin would go to which family. He brooded over separating these twins, identical ones at that. Identical twins come from one egg fertilized by one sperm, then split into two embryos, and it's a miracle of science as to what causes the split. After sharing the same womb for nine months, the twins would now be sent to different homes. As a doctor, Tom knew that these twins would be bound to one another like no two humans could be.

On his desk sat a mason jar with two pieces of paper. All he had to do was draw out a slip marked either "Rosenbaum" or "Mueller," give it to the nurse, and say, "Baby Boy 1." Then he would hand her the other slip and say, "Baby Boy 2," and the die would be cast. He couldn't help but think about the magnitude of the moment—each tiny life cradled in that nursery held a future filled with endless possibilities. What would happen to these boys?

The nurse knocked softly on the door and entered with an expectant look on her face. She had seen too much weeping when the mothers were taken out of the delivery room. She knew their pain, and she knew Dr. Tom's.

He nodded to her, but kept his expression inscrutable except for his soft, brown puppy-like eyes that betrayed a glimmer of melancholy. "It's never easy, Nurse," he said with a sigh.

It wasn't just the reality of twins that had the doctor mulling over this decision; it was also the creeping feeling that perhaps he had let his feelings for the mother be more than a doctor should have for his patient. Karolina Strapovic was nothing like the normal unwed teenage mothers Dr. Tom usually cared for—no, nothing like them at all. She was not only a stunningly beautiful mature woman who spoke with a mesmerizing Czech accent but also an internationally renowned concert pianist, with her own money and stature. When she came to him begging for his help, he went out of his way to find her the perfect place for her to wait out her pregnancy, then agreed to be her liaison with the outside world. Over the weeks, he began visiting her at the remote cabin in Palo Duro Canyon, with food and drinks, a record player, records, and, eventually, a small piano. On those evenings, the widowed doctor sat companionably with this gorgeous woman as they watched the sun set over his favorite place in the world, and they would speak of music, always of music.

Somewhere, in those shared moments, Tom knew he had crossed a line, and now here he was, invested in this choice, both for her and for her babies. A choice fraught with the idea of the nature of chance.

As her pregnancy progressed, Tom had suspected Karolina might be having twins, but there was no way to know for sure until she gave birth. When he had entered the recovery room, she turned her head to him and asked, despite the drugs in her system, "Did I have two babies, or did I dream that?"

He reached down to gently wipe the tears from her eyes. "Yes, Karolina, but it is for the best if I do not tell you if they were boys or girls. Only that they are both healthy and thriving." He desperately wanted to hold her and tell her all would be well, but he kept his composure as she begged him to somehow help her keep in touch with her babies.

How could he resist this woman he had already fallen for? He knew he shouldn't give her that hope, but he said he would ask the lawyer handling the adoptions if he would agree to be the recipient of some sort of correspondence with Karolina. Of course, because of the closed adoption, the communication would not be delivered to their babies or their adoptive parents

He made a note to ask Daniel about the letters. And his attention returned to the mason jar. It was time to make a decision: Which baby boy would go to the Muellers? Which one to the Rosenbaums? As the nurse waited patiently, Dr. Tom reached into the jar, drew out a slip that he didn't read, and handed it to her, announcing, "This is the family for Baby Boy 1." With that, it was done. One boy would have a life with a loving Christian family, the other with a devout Jewish one.

Tom poured himself a dram of golden Scotch from the bottle he kept in a drawer in his desk and sat back heavily in his chair. Fate had been decided.

ON THE DAY THE BABIES WOULD LEAVE THE HOSPITAL, DANIEL bounced into the doctor's office with the energy of the young. As the lawyer for the adoptions, he would do what he had done several times before: meet the charge nurse in the nursery, take his seat in a wheelchair, have a baby placed in his arms, and be rolled out by the charge nurse from the hospital into the parking lot, where he would meet the prospective adoptive parents for them to sign legal documents previously explained to them. He always had to remind them that the adoption would not be final until a court approved the adoption six or more months from now.

Tom rose and shook Daniel's hand. "Daniel, please have a seat." He motioned to the chair in front of his desk. "There's something else I need to discuss with you."

Daniel raised an eyebrow, curious about this uncharacteristic request from his friend. "What is it, Tom?"

"It's about the mother." Tom's voice, normally strong and confident, hesitated. "She has a special request. She wants to write to her children. Not for them to see, but she wants some-where to send a letter every year on their birthdays. I don't think I can be a keeper of that confidence. I know this is not the normal course of business for you, but would you consider it, letting her write to her children through you?"

Daniel was thrown. Normally, Dr. Tom was completely by the book, totally in control and never veering outside the lines of propriety. This request was definitely outside the lines. For the previous closed adoptions, Daniel had drawn up the paper-work, vetted the families through the legal channels, taken the babies to the family in the parking lot, and then filed the signed papers. Once the new families left with their babies, he had no other communication with them. He'd often been left to wonder what happened to the mothers and their babies. Maybe receiving these letters from a mother could make his work more bearable. He didn't see any ethical issues or legal problems with him receiving and keeping the letters, so he said, "I'd love to be of help, but she will need to ask me herself."

Tom breathed a sigh of relief and asked the nurse to take Daniel to Karolina's room. She paused at the door to put her hand on his arm to steady the lawyer, sensing his anxiety. "She's had the twilight sleep for the birth, so she is still recovering from that, tired and groggy. Don't overtax her; she needs her rest."

Daniel crept in. The woman in the hospital bed wasn't like the other young mothers he had dealt with in other adoptions. He was expecting a mature woman, but not such a beautiful one. Karolina had raven-black long curls, porcelain skin, and Slavic cheekbones. Daniel stared down at her from her bedside, reminded of Elaine, his own wife, who'd recently given birth to their first son, and how completely beautiful she had appeared to him. How sad it was for this woman that the father was not there to bear witness to her beauty and power as a mother. He coughed, lightly, and Karolina opened her eyes. "Hello there, I'm

Daniel James, the lawyer handling all the paperwork for the adoption. Dr. Brewer said you had a special request?"

Her eyes shimmered with unshed tears as she nodded. "Yes. Yes, I do." Her accent was Eastern European. "Of course, I know this is a closed adoption. My lawyers explained what that means, no contact whatsoever. I know this, but … is there any way I could write to my babies? Every year, on their birthday?"

Daniel sighed, torn with both empathy and struggle. "Because this is a closed adoption, the families may decide not to tell the children they are adopted. It's their choice. You understand that, right?"

She bit her lip, tears spilling over. "I understand. But please, I would like to know where I can send the letters for them?"

Daniel couldn't help but feel the weight of her despair. "I will be happy to receive the letters. But I can't promise your babies will ever know who they are or who you are."

Karolina's face softened as a faint smile formed. "Thank you. Just knowing the letters will exist in the world is enough." Her voice took on a passionate note as she added, "Music has been my life. It saved me, gave me purpose. I hope they can find something like that too. I pray they find music." With that she drifted off again.

Daniel left her to rest and walked back to Tom's office, wondering what gate he had opened with this acquiescence.

"How was she?" Tom asked.

"Fine. Sleepy, but fine. I agreed to let her send the letters to me via my office, and I will hold the letters for her. I explained again that it is up the families to tell the child, so there is a chance the letters will never be read, and she seemed okay with that. I'll bring a letter with my contact information for you later today to give to her before she's discharged. Oh, and she mentioned music? She wants them to be musical or at least have music in some form in their life."

Tom smiled at this. Surely, these two identical babies would carry her genius for music. They had to; her talent was just too strong for it not to carry on.

"Oh, good. Many thanks, my friend. The nurse has tagged the bassinets with the family's names. I think the Rosenbaums are first." He looked down at his calendar.

"Tell me again why you want me to do this for you," Daniel said. "I mean, I absolutely don't mind doing it, but I am just wondering what is different about this adoption than the rest of them. Is it because of the twins? The two families?"

Tom lifted his gaze to meet Daniel's. "As you know, the twins were a surprise. And having to separate them is hard for me, as a doctor." What he didn't tell Daniel, was that it wasn't the two babies or the separation. It was Karolina. How could he admit to his friend she had awakened something in him? She made him hear music again—whenever he was with her at the cabin, watching the sun set, with her playing the piano he'd found for her at a garage sale. Even out of tune, she made it sound like angels' harps. His fingers had itched again to play his cello. She had inspired him to pull it out of the attic and practice. Eventually, he rustled up the courage to take his cello to the house overlooking the canyon. Karolina was delighted and suggested some duets they could play together. No, this was not merely a doctor-patient relationship; he'd let himself slip, and he would not let it go further. "It's because … well … I'd be too invested in the outcome of each boy's life. I need to maintain some professional distance."

Daniel reached out for his friend's arm and embraced him lightly. "I would do anything you ask of me in these situations, as I trust your process completely."

The nurse appeared at the door. "The Rosenbaums have just arrived."

Daniel rose and shook the doctor's hand again. "You have my word—all will go smoothly."

Ten minutes later, Daniel was in a wheelchair, being pushed

out of the hospital with Baby Boy Rosenbaum in his arms, wrapped in a light-blue blanket. Jacob and Ruth Rosenbaum and the baby's prospective paternal grandmother were waiting by their car in sincere anticipation.

The baby's grandmother, a formidable woman with a commanding presence, asked many questions of Daniel, mostly about the six-month waiting period until the official hearing that would finalize the adoption. Daniel explained that because the judge had always approved Dr. Tom's decisions about adoptions, her family should have nothing to worry about. By the curt nod she gave him when her son took the baby from his arms, Daniel sensed she had taken his measure and approved of him. Both new parents had tears of joy in their eyes. Then the grandmother said to him, almost under her breath, "This child will be loved beyond measure. I assure you. Thank you for all you have done for us."

Daniel hoped she was right.

Half an hour after the Rosenbaums left, Daniel repeated the procedure with Nancy and Joe Bob Mueller. Again, this new mother and father had tears in their eyes as they welcomed their new son. Daniel rarely saw their kind cry, but this was a day to celebrate.

Tom watched from his office window as each family drove away with a piece of Karolina's heart. Then reality settled on him. This separation of twins, the unknown futures they faced —it was a ripple in the vast ocean of life. He whispered a quiet prayer, "May they find what binds them, even if they never know."

3

THE BRIS

THE MONDAY AFTER BABY BOY 1 HAD BEEN PLACED IN THE HANDS of his new parents in the hospital parking lot, Tanya Rosenbaum made an unannounced appearance at Daniel's law office. She waited in the main reception area for twenty minutes, twisting her many gold rings impatiently. Once Daniel was free, she charged into his office. Dispensing with any cordiality, she stood in front of his desk, all five feet three inches of her dazzling in gold and an immaculately tailored pantsuit. "Mr. James, I was impressed with your candor and legal skills as you explained the adoption procedure and guided us through the early stages of the adoption of my grandson. I would like to hire you and put you on a retainer for myself and for our family business, which is growing day by day. We started in scrap iron and metal when I was only seventeen, and now we have expanded into the largest pipeline and steelworks company in the Panhandle. We need a lawyer on retainer to handle all our legal issues in Texas as well as our expansion into Oklahoma. I hope you'll take us on as a client. It would be a pleasure to work with you."

Daniel had learned the Rosenbaums were a wealthy family when he did the paperwork for the adoption. This, though, came as a surprise—the grandmother was in charge, not her son? He looked her over, taking in her resolute stature, and saw a future with this confident woman. He was well aware that pipeline businesses in general had been growing and growing because of the boom in the oil and gas industry. "Please, take a seat, Mrs. Rosenbaum. May I offer you some coffee or something cold? I'd like to hear more about your business and how you think I can be of service."

Borger Pipeline and Steelworks had been founded four decades earlier, when a pregnant Tanya moved with her ambitious young husband to Borger, Texas, at the crossroads of two railroads. The small Panhandle town helped give birth to the oil-and-gas development of the area. Her husband's unexpected death left the company in her small son Jacob's hands, but it was Tanya's leadership and fierce intelligence, not to mention her formidable contract negotiation skills, that had turned Borger Pipeline and Steelworks into one of the biggest pipeline operations in Texas. Now, she explained, her company was hoping to expand again, and she wanted to find reliable legal representation.

After they discussed the business, Daniel happily agreed to work with the company. He then inquired after the baby. "How are your son and daughter-in-law settling in with the new baby?"

Tanya looked down at her hands and took a breath before answering. "For as long as anyone can remember, I have been the keeper of our family's history. Our Jewish history, our family, what we have endured, what we have overcome. What we have achieved is deeply entrenched in our bloodline. I came to the Texas Panhandle as a young bride, with only one other

Jewish family, the Eberstadts, to welcome us. I made sure we had a Jewish life, a Jewish soul. It is through my dedication to our past, to our faith, that our company and our Jewish community thrives here. But the fact that my daughter-in-law was barren, well, that has been weighing heavily on my soul." She twisted her weathered hands with thick ropey veins that seemed to trace the branches of her family tree. "Jews must continue the bloodline; this you must know."

Daniel nodded to encourage her to continue, sensing that he was going to be not just her lawyer but also her confidant. "The Rosenbaums are known for their wit, their endurance, and their ability to adapt and thrive. As well as our thick black curls. How can I know what the baby will take on and what he will inherit from being in our house? And what is already in his blood?" Tanya paused. "I realize we have to wait for the adoption hearing to formally confirm the adoption, but our faith requires a bris within eight days of a male baby's birth, so we are moving forward as our faith dictates. I have spoken with my rabbi, and he has agreed that the child can undergo both a bris and then a conversion ceremony that serves as a symbolic rebirth to remove all legitimacy concerns. He has assured me that Talmud gives rabbis permission to convert a child before the age of consent, based on the principle that we can act to someone's advantage even without their permission." She took another moment, as if she was trying to convince herself of something. "So ... the child will be a Jew, by our laws, if we proceed with this ceremony."

Daniel waited for her to keep going, but Tanya was deep in thought. "I think you are a force of nature, Mrs. Rosenbaum. And from what I've learned, in our very short conversation, your intelligence, your faith, but most of all your confidence will be passed down, with or without the genes. I also know that Dr. Brewer always picks the right families, and he wouldn't have chosen yours if he didn't think your family would completely love that boy. By the way, what are you naming him?"

Tanya raised her unflinching gaze to his. "His name will be Ari Nesanel Rosenbaum, after my great-grandfather. Would you and your wife like to come to my home in Pampa to witness the ceremonies on Wednesday? The other Jewish families in our community will be attending. I've also hired a cantor for the music. It will be a lovely celebration. There, my grandson's name will be written in the book."

Daniel, sensing a deepening friendship and partnership with this indomitable woman, accepted her invitation.

With that, she removed an envelope from her purse and handed it to him. "I hope you'll forgive me for hand-delivering this, but I wasn't sure you would receive the invitation in time."

"That is not a problem at all, Mrs. Rosenbaum. Thank you for coming and for allowing me to represent your business."

DANIEL'S WIFE, ELAINE, WAS SURPRISED WHEN SHE READ THE engraved invitation. "Why are we being invited to a Jewish ceremony? What is this?"

"The Rosenbaums adopted one of the twins, and they are welcoming their new baby with something like a baptism. Tanya Rosenbaum is my newest client; I'll be representing her pipeline company. It's an honor she has bestowed upon us, so I think we should go," Daniel replied.

"Love, I know your choice in clients is impeccable, but this is unusual, isn't it? Pampa is forty miles away, and I'll have to find a babysitter."

"Mrs. Rosenbaum is not going to be an ordinary client, Elaine. Something tells me that she will be a friend as well. Besides, it will be interesting to see her home and meet her family."

"What does one wear to a ceremony like this?" she asked, smiling.

"I suppose we wear what we normally wear to church. And our smiles! It's going be a cultural experience for us both, but I feel like we are at the start of learning something we are meant to know." Daniel planted a quick kiss on his wife's cheek. "What's for dinner, sweetheart?"

WHEN DANIEL AND ELAINE ARRIVED AT TANYA ROSENBAUM's elegant mansion in Pampa, the house was abuzz with excitement as Jewish relatives and friends gathered for baby Ari's ceremony. They waited behind several other guests to greet the new family in the foyer. Ruth cradled their seven-day-old son as a beaming Jacob gave Daniel a prolonged handshake as his way of saying thank-you. Daniel then introduced Elaine to Tanya, who clasped her hand with both of hers and gave a soft smile. "Welcome, Elaine. It is so nice to meet you. Please help yourself to some food. We'll be starting the ceremony soon."

Rabbi Klein, from Temple Shalom in Dallas, cleared his throat, signaling the start of the ceremony. "Today, we welcome this precious soul into the covenant of Abraham and the Jewish people," he began, his voice warm and inviting.

Jacob and Ruth took their place in front of the rabbi, with Ari asleep in Ruth's arms. The rabbi placed his hands gently on the baby's head and recited the blessing:

> *Baruch atah, Adonai Eloheinu, melech ha-olam,*
> *asher kideshanu bemitzvotav vetzivanu le-hachniso*
> *bivrito shel Avraham avinu*
> (Blessed are You, Lord our God, King of the
> universe, who has sanctified us with His
> commandments and commanded us

to make our sons enter the covenant of Abraham
our father)

Tanya watched with a conflicted heart. She loved her son
and wanted life's every happiness for him, but the absence of a
biological connection gnawed at her. The rabbi announced the
baby's Hebrew name, "Ari Nesanel ben Rosenbaum," then spoke
about its significance, explaining that Ari meant "lion" and
symbolized the courage and bravery of the Tribe of Judah. "This
child is indeed a gift," he said, smiling at Ruth and Jacob, "a gift
of love, a gift to your family, and a gift to our community."

Tanya felt a pang of loss for the traits that could not be
passed down genetically. She thought of her own mother's gift
for numbers, her father's iron will, and both of their stories—
their families coming to America and how strong they all were
to survive. Would this little boy have those traits, or were they
traits she could show him, breathe into his life with her
willpower to make him her Jewish grandson?

Tanya looked over at Daniel and his lovely, willowy wife.
She had struggled a bit over inviting Gentiles to such a private
ceremony, but she felt the lawyer's openness and true curiosity
when she described in his office what the ceremony would
entail. She hoped he had warned his wife about the next part of
the ritual.

Ruth's father, Eddie Eberstadt, serving as the *sandek*, took his
place next to the Chair of Elijah, holding the baby on his lap.
Then with the swiftness of a surgeon, the rabbi circumcised Ari.
The baby cried out, but just briefly. Elaine grabbed her
husband's arm and took a brief inhale of breath, as if to stop
herself from crying out herself.

The rabbi recited the blessing again:

Baruch atah, Adonai Eloheinu, melech ha-olam asher

kideshanu bemitzvotav vetzivanu le-hachniso bivrito
shel Avraham avinu

He then spoke the blessing for the circumcision:

Baruch atah, Adonai Eloheinu, melech ha-olam
asher kideshanu bemitzvotav vetzivanu al ha-milch
(Blessed are You, Lord our God, King of the
universe, who has sanctified us with His
commandments and commanded us regarding
circumcision)

The rabbi announced the baby's name again, adding, "May he grow to study Torah, to marry, and to do good deeds."

The family signed the paperwork, and the baby's name was engraved into the family's sacred Torah.

Then Eddie Eberstadt pranced forward, despite his years, to lead everyone in the recitation of the Shehecheyanu blessing, his voice cracking with emotion:

Baruch atah, Adonai Eloheinu, melech ha-olam
shehecheyanu, vekiyemanu, vehigiyanu laz-man hazeh
(Blessed are You, Lord our God, King of the
Universe, who has granted us life, sustained us,
and brought us to this occasion)

Tanya felt that after this ceremony, no one would dare question Ari's true heritage; anyone who did so would have to answer to her. She watched Ruth's parents, whom Tanya had loved as her own when they took her in as a young widow. They embraced the baby, kissing his head, their eyes glistening with tears of joy.

Suddenly, Tanya felt ashamed of her reservations. This was

her grandson, regardless of biology. She resolved there and then that he would be hers, in all ways and forms.

The ceremony concluded with the cantor leading the song "Siman Tov u'Mazal Tov," accompanied by Tanya on the piano. Everyone in the room except Daniel and Elaine joined in. The cantor's voice was otherworldly, as if an angel had descended from the heavens.

Elaine leaned over and whispered to Daniel, "I have goose-bumps; this is the most beautiful thing I have witnessed. It's so real and tangible."

As the song ended, Tanya stood up from the piano, her legs shaking. Playing the piano and singing always moved her, because music was the way to a Jewish soul. She approached Jacob and Ruth and held out her arms for her grandson.

Tanya and baby Ari joined Daniel and Elaine as they filled their plates. The proud grandmother explained the significance of each dish on the table for the feast. Bagels and lox symbolized the continuity of Jewish tradition. Round challah represented the cycle of life. Hard-boiled eggs signified the renewal of life and mourning for the Temple. Chickpeas or fava beans were a traditional food for mourners, acknowledging the pain of circumcision. Honey cake represented hopes for a sweet life for the baby. Finally, fish symbolized fertility and the blessing of "Be fruitful and multiply."

Tanya was pleased when Elaine asked for the honey-cake recipe and then told Tanya, "You are truly blessed to have such an amazing faith, such honest and real traditions. I was moved to tears. I'm honored you invited us."

"You are welcome in our home again and again." Ari inter-rupted the conversation by starting to fuss. "Please excuse me, Mrs. James."

Tanya returned Ari to her daughter in-law, who took him upstairs. She then turned to survey the crowd of her new friends, her family, and her Jewish community, all there for her new grandson. In that moment, she realized that family was about more than shared DNA—it was about shared love, shared values, and shared traditions. And her grandson would never lack for any of them.

4

THE CHRISTENING

CANYON, TEXAS
MAY 1953

JOE BOB AND NANCY MUELLER HAD TRIED FOR MANY YEARS TO
have a child, but were not so blessed. Too many times to count,
Nancy had knelt in the First Baptist Church of Canyon, her
head bowed, hands clasped, and a prayer rising fervently. "God,
bless me with a child, and I will walk with thee all the days of
my life."

She knew of her husband's devotion, despite his taciturn
ways. The couple's love was a quiet, understated kind of love,
like that of tree roots, and they deserved to be parents.

When it was clear that she would never have the baby she so
longed for, Nancy decided to dedicate herself to her music
students at the local college and the high school and those she
gave private lessons to. Perhaps if she gave to the Lord every
day by sharing her musical gifts with every child, she might be
blessed in other ways.

Joe Bob had long been aware of her yearning for a child and
knew the blame was his. As a child, he had suffered a severe case

of the mumps, and the doctors warned there was a chance he could be left sterile. Joe Bob never told his wife about it; he thought this would make him less of a man in her eyes. So he kept to himself his fear that their childless situation was his fault. It was this burden that led him to visit Dr. Brewer to discuss the possibility of adoption. The doctor's reputation in the Panhandle of making sure babies found their way into good homes was well known.

A year after their names had been added to the adoption waiting list, Joe Bob was surprised when Daniel James called him out of the blue and said there was a baby who needed a loving home as soon as possible. Joe Bob saw the situation as nothing short of a miracle, and since he had taken upon himself to make Nancy happy with a baby, regardless of its origin, it was his miracle to take. Joe Bob promised God then and there that this child, his child, would be a child of God.

When Joe Bob hung up, Nancy asked, "What is it, Joe Bob? Did something happen?"

"It's a miracle," he whispered.

"What kind of miracle, honey?"

"Well, there's a baby that'll be needing a good home"

"A baby?" she interrupted. "Where?"

"Amarillo," he said, still in shock. "I've been asked if we can take it."

"WHAT?!" Now it was Nancy who was stunned. "How? I mean, who thought of us?"

"Daniel James, a lawyer over in Amarillo. There's something I haven't told you."

Nancy just stared at him.

"I meant to tell you at some point, and now's as good a time as any. My heart has been aching for you all this time, seeing your sadness that we couldn't have a child. So I asked Dr. Brewer if we could be considered for a baby needing to be adopted."

"You didn't!"

He worried that Nancy was angry with him, but suddenly she hurled herself at him and kissed him again and again. "You wonderful, silly man! I just wish I had more time to be prepared."

"Well, we can't pick him up for two days. Can you get out of school on Friday?"

"Of course I can! I'll call Mr. King right now and make arrangements for my leave. I can't believe it—a baby! I'll need to run to Amarillo tomorrow and shop for baby goods so we'll be ready. Did he say if it's a girl or a boy?

Joe Bob paused. "I forgot to ask. I'll call Mr. James back. But first," he took her delicate hands in his, "let's give thanks for this miracle!"

Together, they knelt to give the happiest prayer either of them had ever spoken.

After a whirlwind day of shopping and organizing the room Nancy had always hoped would be the nursery, they drove to Amarillo, signed the adoption papers, and brought their new son home. They named him Archer, after Nancy's grandfather.

Nancy spent the six-month waiting period tending to Archer, marveling over his daily growth. Every now and then, however, she would catch herself fretting that their adoption might not be approved. At those moments, she would say a simple prayer: "Thank you, God, for bringing us this little miracle!"

The day Daniel James called to tell them that the judge had approved the adoption, Nancy decided a celebration was in order. Something to mark the importance of this child of God, this miracle, to their family and to their close-knit community. Her Baptist faith did not believe children could make the choice to commit themselves to God; only adults could be baptized in their church. Debra Hamilton, one of Nancy's friends and a fellow music teacher, was married to the priest at Canyon's

Episcopal church, where Nancy occasionally helped out with their choir and musical arrangements. After conferring with Debra, Nancy sent him a letter asking if he would host a ceremony to christen her child, not just in the name of one religion but in respect to all religions:

Joe Bob and I have tried and tried to have a baby, and we thought we'd never have a child. This baby was conceived by parents whose faith and culture we'll never know. Archer's christening ceremony should pay tribute to the miracle of the birth of a child as well as the miracle of an adoption.

She wanted to show how committed she and Joe Bob were to ensuring that baby Archer would walk with God the entirety of his life.

Reverend Hamilton agreed to host the christening and offered his own church. But Nancy wanted the ceremony to be in their own church, the First Baptist Church, where her choir could sing for her new son. When Nancy met with their new pastor, Reverend Griswold, to see about using First Baptist for a christening conducted by the Episcopal priest, it did not go well. In fact, the young egotistical man fresh out of Bible college proved to be more set in his ways and old-fashioned than any one she had ever met. His inability to be open to their miracle and be happy for her and Joe Bob left a bad taste in her mouth.

Being the proactive woman she was, Nancy had an idea. She asked her best friend and neighbor, Seraphina Walker Ross, to come with her to visit the semi-retired Pastor Campbell, to see if he could talk some sense into his upstart replacement. Seraphina was set to inherit the biggest cattle ranch in the Panhandle, she wielded an immense amount of power for her father, and everyone knew she was in charge. Seraphina pointed out to Pastor Campbell that Griswold wouldn't have a choir or as many congregants if it wasn't for the talented and revered

Nancy Mueller. Through Seraphina's formidable power of persuasion, the pastor agreed to put in a word, and after a couple of days, he called to tell her that the First Baptist Church would host the christening.

Archer's christening was a party the town of Canyon would never forget. Everyone was invited—all of Nancy's music students and colleagues, every rancher she and Joe Bob knew, their friends, and every member of their church. For the ceremony, Nancy had done something out of character for her: She asked Daniel James to stand as godfather for her son. The two had become close friends during the six-month waiting period. Nancy hoped that her son would be a man of letters, not just of the land. Daniel was one of the smartest men in the Panhandle, and Nancy wanted him to have a presence in her son's life. At the christening, the lawyer sat in the front row with his wife and their young toddler.

The First Baptist Church bell tolled, calling the congregation to worship. Inside, the simple wooden pews were filled with familiar faces. The air was thick with anticipation and the scent of well-worn hymnals. Nancy chose the hymns herself—as choir director it was her duty, but today it was her pleasure. She selected hymns that reflected her desire for her son to be a warrior for Christ, a beacon of hope, and eventually a man who saw God in all the faces of the world. The choir walked in, singing "There Is a Balm in Gilead":

> There is a balm in Gilead, to make the wounded
> whole,
> There is a balm in Gilead, to heal the sin-sick soul.
> Sometimes I feel discouraged, and think my
> work's in vain,
> But then the Holy Spirit, revives my soul again.

Nancy had trained every singer in the choir herself, and they lifted their voices up for her, for her new son, and for the future he would have with their community.

Reverend Hamilton, dressed in his black cassock, stood behind the pulpit, and Pastor Griswold was seated next to the choir pit, trying—and failing—to look as beatific as possible. The priest began the service with a prayer: "Dear Heavenly Father, we gather today to witness and celebrate a new life joining Your flock," followed by the congregation singing "Shall We Gather at the River?"

After his brief sermon on the importance of the acceptance of community and devout faith in family, Reverend Hamilton announced, "Brothers and sisters, we are here to witness the baptism of Archer James Mueller, adopted son of Nancy and Joseph Robert Mueller. For years this family has been a cornerstone of this church and this community, and we welcome their new son into our family with open arms."

He moved to the baptismal font, a simple stone basin filled with water that had been blessed earlier that morning. He motioned for the family to join him. "Nancy and Joe Bob," he said solemnly, "do you present this child for baptism, willingly undertaking the responsibilities of Christian parents to bring him up in the nurture and admonition of the Lord?"

"We do," they responded in unison, their voices trembling slightly with emotion.

The priest turned to the congregation. "And do you, as members of this church, promise to guide and nurture Archer James Mueller by word and deed, with love and prayer, encouraging him to know and follow Christ?"

"We will," the congregation affirmed.

"Who will serve as the child's godparents?" asked the priest.

Daniel rose and approached the baptismal font, along with tall and gangly Seraphina, dressed in an ill-fitting prairie dress, loads of turquoise jewelry, and cowboy boots. She glanced over at Pastor Griswold and smiled broadly. The lawyer and the rancher's daughter agreed in front of God and everyone to watch over Archer, to guide him in the way of the Lord, and always stand for him in times of love and crisis.

The priest asked Nancy and Joe Bob to profess their faith by reciting the Apostles' Creed. Then he took the baby in his arms. "Archer James Mueller," he said, dipping his hand in the font, "I baptize you in the name of the Father," he touched water to the baby's forehead, "and of the Son," again, "and of the Holy Spirit." As water trickled down his face for a third time, Archer squirmed but did not cry. The priest then etched the sign of the cross in anointing oil on the child's forehead, saying, "Archer, child of God, you have been sealed by the Holy Spirit in baptism and marked as Christ's own forever."

He carefully handed Archer back to Nancy and presented the family with a small white candle, lit from the church's paschal candle. "Receive the light of Christ," he said. "Parents and godparents, this light is entrusted to you to be kept burning brightly."

The ceremony concluded with a prayer and a final hymn. As the last notes faded, the priest presented Archer to the congregation. "It is my joy to introduce the newest Christian, Archer James Mueller!"

The church erupted in applause and a few heartfelt "Amens" as Nancy and Joe Bob, beaming with pride, turned to face their community, with their son cradled between them. The entire congregation walked out into the hot Texas sun to the hymn "How Great Thou Art." Nancy was filled with a true sense of purpose, a desire to make sure this baby, her son, learned all he could, played every musical instrument, and became the kindest soul in the world.

The Mueller ranch bustled with activity as trucks and cars kicked up dust along the long driveway. The sprawling farmhouse, its white paint gleaming in the afternoon sun, stood as a beacon of hospitality. On the expansive front lawn, tables draped in gingham cloths were laden with food, while bales of hay served as rustic seating.

Nancy's mother, Eleanor, presided over the kitchen, directing a small army of helpers as they carried out steaming dishes of green beans with ham hocks, macaroni and cheese, potato salad, and peach cobbler. The aroma of barbecue wafted from the pit where Joe Bob and his cousins tended to ribs, brisket, and steaks—all from a butchered steer from Seraphina's father, Mac Walker Ross, who stood over the barbecue pit like Henry VIII holding court. His large belly jiggled when he laughed and called out to Nancy and Joe Bob, "There's our little cowboy!" Mac reached for Archer and held him as delicately as a newborn calf. "Welcome to your first ranch party, baby boy."

Friends and family gathered around, cooing over the black-haired boy with huge dark-brown eyes. "He's gonna be a heart-breaker one day," Mac predicted.

There was a table filled with gifts, handmade and store-bought, and so many books. Everyone knew that Nancy Mueller was the finest teacher around, and it was just natural that she would teach her son everything she could. Nancy's cousin Lisa presented a handmade quilt to the boy. "For Archer's first bed on the ranch," she said, misty-eyed.

A few older kids had set up a small petting zoo with gentle calves and piglets, much to the delight of the younger ones. Children darted between the adults, their giggles mixing with the twang of country music played by some of Nancy's students. Even though almost everyone in attendance were Baptists who were not allowed to dance, a makeshift dance floor of old barn boards appeared as if by magic. Young and old danced with each other, and almost all took turns holding baby Archer in their arms. The child was never upset, instead, he stared into each person's face thoughtfully and reverently. The baby would smile and giggle until finally, he was exhausted.

As the sunset cast a golden glow over the pastures, the celebration continued. Older couples swayed to slow songs, while the younger folks engaged in lively square dancing on the impromptu dance floor. When darkness fell, lanterns were lit, fireflies danced at the edges of the lawn, and the distant lowing of cattle provided a gentle backdrop to the festivities.

Joe Bob invited everyone to raise a glass. "Dear friends, you know I am a man of few words, but I feel like you being here today with us to celebrate warrants me breaking my silence." His voice was thick with emotion, "Nancy and I can't thank you enough for being here today. Archer may not have been born into this family, but he was certainly born for it." Here Joe Bob struggled to continue, and Nancy took her husband's callused hand and said, "Your love and support mean the world to us. We promise to raise Archer with the values that have kept this community strong for generations—faith, hard work, and love for the land and each other."

Cheers erupted, followed by a cry for Nancy to sing. She went over to the band and grabbed a guitar, sat down, and belted out a heartfelt rendition of "Amazing Grace" with tears in her eyes. As Daniel listened to Nancy sing and play the guitar, he knew that Karolina's wish for her sons to have music would be fulfilled in this family as well as the Rosenbaums.

Daniel and Elaine felt entirely at home, as did their small son Danny Junior, who ran around with the other children, chasing lambs and petting pigs. Texas Panhandle ranchers are the most loyal of folk and also some of the best partiers around. The beer was cold, the brisket moist, and the ribs perfectly cooked. When barbecue sauce dripped on Elaine's gorgeous pink dress, she was embarrassed, but to Daniel she looked perfect. As she dabbed at her dress, Elaine told him, "I was a bit hesitant when Nancy asked you to be godfather, not knowing what to think of you being involved in another boy's life other than our own, but I'm glad you said yes. These are wonderful people, and this is a wonderful home. That boy is going to have the best of both worlds, with her knowledge and his father's love of this land. Archer will be a force of nature, I am sure."

Daniel smiled and took Elaine in his arms for another dance in the perfect evening. His limbs were warm from dancing, and he was happy. The Mueller family had needed a son, and he was proud to have helped to facilitate it for them. He just knew that the Muellers would be the best of parents.

As Daniel and Elaine, who had Danny tucked against her shoulder, went to the porch to say their goodbyes to the Muellers, they saw a group of ranch hands presenting their gift to Nancy and Joe Bob—a tiny, hand-tooled leather saddle with Archer's name engraved on it. "For when he's ready to ride," they explained, to Joe Bob's delight.

Daniel went up to Nancy, who was holding a sleeping Archer. "Thank you for inviting us to this amazing celebration."

Nancy clasped his hand. "I'm so grateful to you, Daniel. You helped bring us this miracle. And I'm so glad you brought your family. You're welcome to come visit anytime."

Elaine laughed. "I think Danny fell in love with the calves and the piglets! I'm sure he'd love to come back. Thank you again, Nancy."

Afterward, Nancy and Joe Bob paused for a quiet moment amidst the celebration. They looked out over their land, at the friends and family who had come to welcome their son, and felt a profound sense of gratitude and belonging.

"Welcome home, Archer," Joe Bob whispered, placing a gentle kiss on his son's forehead. "This is your legacy now."

PART II

THE YOUNGER YEARS

1957–1958

LETTER FROM KAROLINA
NOVEMBER 1957

My dear babies:

One of the blessings of my life was to bring you into this world, and one of the heartbreaks of my life is not to be with you every day and hold you and tell you how wonderful you are.

You are now five years old, and this wonderful man, the lawyer who handled your adoption, has allowed me the chance to speak to you, even if you might never see my words, I want to tell you that every night I say a prayer of gratitude to God for you being in this world, wherever that may be.

Every time, before walking onto the stage to give a performance, anywhere in the world—be it Cairo or Beirut, Madrid or London, Tokyo or Beijing, or New York—I thank God for my love of music, its gift to me, and its power to unite us all. I pray for you to know that love, its power, and the gift. For it has guided my life. I hope it guides yours.

The performances I have had this past year were booked over two years ago, long before we knew what would be happening in the world. I had no idea when I walked on stage in Tel Aviv, a city in the relatively new country of Israel, that the country would be at war with the country of my most recent performance in Cairo.

But it is the power of music, the love of it, and the gift of it that allow me as a performer to transcend the violence and the aggression. I hope one day you will know music's power as I do. May it bring peace.

I know you each are in a home with music, because my friend, Dr. Tom, who delivered you, played beautiful music whenever I was in his office. The same with Daniel James, the bearer of these letters; he too played beautiful music every time we met.

Music was there when you were born, and I just know it is in your life now. May it be your guiding light.

I love you, forever.

Your loving mother

5

DANIEL AND DR. TOM

Sitting across from Daniel at his law office, Dr. Tom was a bit dusty but tanned, fit, and more relaxed than Daniel had ever seen him. His latest trip—this time to Cairo to see a famous pianist perform with a North African symphony at the base of the Great Pyramid—seemed to have done the hardworking doctor a world of good. Tom had brought Daniel a bottle of arak, an aniseed liquor from the Levant and immediately poured it into a pair of crystal tumblers before offering an Egyptian toast: "*Fe sehetak*, my friend—to the liars and the cheats." He chuckled at his own joke before correcting it. "It actually means 'to your health,' which of course I always wish you and your family."

Daniel couldn't believe how congenial his friend was. Something interesting must have happened on that trip. He took a tentative sip and was glad he hadn't slammed his drink back. Noticing how Tom savored his drink, he didn't have the heart to say that it reminded him of cold medicine. Instead, he prompted, "So, tell me about your travels."

"It was ... marvelous. You know how much I love the desert. Maybe it is how humble one feels, maybe it's the light—I don't know. But the desert gives me purpose."

Daniel set his glass down and asked the question that had been on his mind from the moment Tom had told him he'd be seeing the pianist Karolina Strapovic. "So, Tom, when did you and Miss Strapovic become such good traveling companions? I mean, I'm assuming she was the reason you went to Egypt, or am I wrong? Something has put that smile on your face."

Dr. Tom reddened a moment. "Well, yes. Karolina and I have become quite close. Aside from you, she knows more about my life than anyone else, and she especially understands my strong affinity for the desert and the mountains. As you well know, seeking out those quiet places has been the only way I can face the cruelties of so many aspects of our daily lives, especially isolation and mistreatment of the unwed young mothers I help, not to mention the tragedy of the many wonderful couples who desperately want something they cannot have—a baby of their own blood and DNA. So what else could I say when Karolina invited me to join her in the Sahara Desert, one of our cradles of civilization? How could I turn her down? The pyramids ... my God, Daniel, they are breathtaking. And to have the chance to hear a concert featuring Karolina against such a wondrous backdrop ... well, let's just say, I'm really glad I went."

As his friend talked, Daniel looked out his window at the vast expanse of the Panhandle and the views that never disappointed him. That was something these two unlikely friends shared, their love of this terrain and its emptiness. For Daniel, too, appreciated the solace that nature's silence provided.

Tom then took one of those turns that Daniel had come to love—he reached into his wallet and pulled out a worn piece of folded paper. "One of my favorite books is *The Prophet* by Kahlil

Gibran. I brought my copy with me and read a page or two each evening as Karolina and I sat looking out over the desert. Here is one of our favorites that seems to capture our relationship at this time in our lives."

> *Love one another, but make not a bond of love.*
> *Let it rather be a moving sea between the shore of your*
>   *souls.*
> *Fill each other's cup but drink not from one cup.*
> *Give to one another of your bread but eat not from the*
>   *same loaf.*
> *Sing and dance together and be joyous, but let each one*
>   *of you be alone.*
> *Even as the strings of a lute are alone though they*
>   *quiver with the same music.*

Daniel caught a faint smile creeping up on his face as Tom turned away. He had disclosed something close to his heart, and again, that was not at all like him.

Whenever he was in Texas, Tom worked himself to the bone, never really socializing with anyone except Daniel. His life was devoted to delivering babies and tending to the overall maternal health of his patients. If he had to leave Texas from time to time to find some happiness, then who was Daniel to say anything? Plus, Daniel was pleased to see that Tom was showing the telltale signs of falling in love.

Daniel rubbed his hand along the top of his filing cabinet, where Karolina's most recent letter sat in the folder with the birth records of the two boys who now belonged to the Muellers and the Rosenbaums. He wished he could tell Karolina how well her sons were loved by their new parents and how each boy had music in his life, so much music. But Daniel was bound by his oath of confidentiality and could say nothing, not even to Tom. He made a mental note to speak to Elaine about that; she always eased his heart every year when the birthday letter arrived.

Daniel changed the subject. "Tom, the Chamber of Commerce has decided to nominate me as the Panhandle's Man of the Year."

"My God, my friend, what an honor!" Dr. Tom smiled broadly. "I am very pleased for you."

"Well, it comes with some strings attached. It appears I'll have to make a speech, not so much to talk about myself but, rather, to focus on the issues we need to work on. I'm at a loss as to whether I should raise some of more controversial matters you and I have kicked around the last few years. There's so much to say these days about our world, how can I even attempt to bring up even three or four of the tougher issues?"

"By all means, Daniel, seize the moment. The chamber chose you for who you are and what you have done as a young lawyer. It is the perfect time to also let them know of some of your concerns."

There was a reason the doctor chose to keep working with Daniel on the private adoptions: The young lawyer had a heart. He cared deeply for his fellow man, regardless of race or creed or income level. He also saw the value in women doing the same work as men and being treated with equality. Many a night over whiskey, the two men shared their despair over how unfair it was that the girls of the Panhandle were left alone to sort out their pregnancies, with no accountability of any kind for the fathers, and then have to face a lifetime judgment that was unfair, unfounded, and unwarranted. Both men had been raised by hardworking single mothers, probably the cornerstone of their close bond, almost as a father and son. And both had no doubts that a more equal and fairer world was possible.

Tom opened his briefcase to pull out a book. "I think this might provide some insight for you as you struggle to choose two or three issues important to you."

Daniel walked around his desk to accept yet another gift, *Profiles in Courage,* by John F. Kennedy, the charismatic United States senator from Massachusetts. He profiled eight senators who had defied the opinions of their party and constituents to do what they felt was right and suffered severe criticism and losses in popularity as a result.

"The chamber's members respect you and will hear you out, even if they disagree. Remember to get people to let their guard down and acknowledge the other side of each issue. For example, I know that you believe racial strife is tearing this nation apart, but you also realize reconciling Black and white men may cause more of an alienation of white men rather than their brothers. You'll have to comment on that feeling of alienation." Tom paused to take a drink. "There you have it, advice from a tired but content doctor. By the way, keep the book. I'll pick up another from Brown's in Amarillo next week."

Dr. Tom was one of the best-read men he knew, and Daniel took his advice to heart. "Thank you, my friend. I will read this tonight. And you are right—it is our actions that speak louder than our words."

"I was struck by the section on Sam Houston, a history I did not know about Texas. As a senator from Texas, Houston voted for the Missouri Compromise, making him so unpopular that he lost his bid for reelection. Two years later, he was elected governor, but he wanted Texas to remain in the United States and not break away as a part of the Confederacy. When the Legislature held a special session and decided to do just that, Houston refused to be inaugurated as governor. Amazing! I never knew! It's something they didn't teach me as a schoolboy in rural Mississippi—that a hero of the Texas Revolution was so opposed to slavery and breaking up the Union that he jeopardized his own political career. Now, that is what I call courage."

Daniel knew the story, all too well, as his oldest son was named Samuel Houston James. It was a small victory that

Kennedy included Houston's story in his book for all the world to know.

Dr. Tom motioned to refill Daniel's glass. When Daniel shook his head, the doctor smiled, "Yes, I know—it's an acquired taste. But just in case you find yourself wanting to try it again, this bottle is for you. I promise, it does grow on you."

THAT EVENING DANIEL DID NOT START READING *PROFILES IN Courage.* Instead, he found himself thinking about his speech, a subject he pondered for the next few weeks.

Daniel knew from reading a book on speechmaking that he should not exceed fifteen minutes, preferably thirteen or fewer. He'd open with praise for the God-fearing, friendly folk of the Panhandle, then he'd tell the Sam Houston story as an example of an issue important to his heart. The other two issues he intended to touch on were racism and the growing factions within the churches of the area, to bring attention to the way controversial issues could divide churches, communities, and even families.

Soon after his conversation with Tom, Daniel had been touched by an anecdote that Martin Luther King, Jr., told in his "Loving Your Enemies" speech delivered in Montgomery, Alabama:

> Sometime ago my brother and I were driving one evening to Chattanooga, Tennessee, from Atlanta. ... And for some reason the drivers were very discourteous that night. They didn't dim their lights. ... My brother A. D. looked over and in a tone of anger said: "I know what I'm going to do. The next car that comes along here and refuses to dim the lights, I'm going to fail to dim mine and pour them on in

all of their power." And I looked at him right quick and said: "Oh no, don't do that. There'd be too much light on this highway, and it will end up in mutual destruction for all. Somebody got to have some sense on this highway."

Somebody must have sense enough to dim the lights, and that is the trouble, isn't it? That as all of the civilizations of the world move up the highway of history, so many civilizations, having looked at other civilizations that refused to dim the lights, and they decided to refuse to dim theirs. ... [and] have found themselves in the junkheap of destruction. ... [I]f somebody doesn't have sense enough to turn on the dim and beautiful and powerful lights of love in this world, the whole of our civilization will be plunged into the abyss of destruction. And we will all end up destroyed because nobody had any sense on the highway of history. Somewhere somebody must have some sense. Men must see that force begets force, hate begets hate, toughness begets toughness. And it is all a descending spiral, ultimately ending in destruction for all and everybody. Somebody must have sense enough and morality enough to cut off the chain of hate and the chain of evil in the universe. And you do that by love.

Daniel hoped to work that in as well as recount his own indelible first-time encounter with racism. Actually, he would start with that, by talking about his first job as an eight-year-old shop boy at the drugstore across the street from his mother's beauty shop. Each day Daniel was tasked with scooping rock candy into small plastic bags, tying each bag with a colorful ribbon, and attaching a sticker that read "10 cents." He planned to start with that, hoping his audience would all identify with him, since most of them had probably been working from a young age. That would make the next part of the story easier for them to hear.

Then, he'd tell them about Dorothy, the beautiful teenage girl who worked behind the soda fountain and always gave him free ice cream cones. Surely every man in that crowd had had a crush on an older high school girl at some point, and he hoped he would have the whole audience on his side.

Next, he would talk about his second job of doing chores for his auntie and her neighbors—mowing, washing windows, and emptying trash—in nearby Borger. To get there, he had to take the bus for the two-mile trip. That's how he met Evangeline. They became close and laughed a lot. Their friendship was not predicated on anything other than mutual jokes and a shared experience. But then, one very hot day, waiting for the bus to Borger outside of the drugstore, Evangeline offered to buy Daniel an ice cream cone, and she dashed across the street to the drugstore.

At that point in his speech, Daniel would pause to give the chance for the crowd to anticipate having an ice cream cone on a hot Texas Panhandle day. Then, he would tell them what happened next.

When Evangeline returned, her face was crestfallen. "Daniel, don't they serve coloreds in your drugstore? That girl behind the counter wouldn't even look at me. It was like I was a ghost." He had never heard of this, so he walked over to drugstore to talk to Dorothy, who was working the counter that day. She smiled at him, then gave him an ice cream cone and a hug.

Again, he would pause for effect, hoping the audience feel what he had felt that day when he first encountered racism—two young women, both of whom Daniel had a deep affection for, divided by skin color.

He would follow up by asking the audience how that translated to 1957. Did that same feeling apply to the Mexican workers coming into the Panhandle in 1957? And what about school integration in the Panhandle, where white and Black students were studying together, singing together, playing in band and orchestra, competing on athletic teams, and developing friendships? How could they grow into becoming brothers and sisters with those whose skin is a different color or who speak a different language?

Daniel knew his speech could make a difference. Even though they faced a long road to equality in the Panhandle, he would lead by example. He hoped others would follow.

6

ARI

DESPITE THE ROSENBAUM FAMILY'S VAST BUSINESS HOLDINGS AND wealth, Jacob and Ruth's ranch-style house was modest. The only sign of their financial status was Tanya's gleaming pearl-white Cadillac Seville parked under the carport next to Jacob's Ford truck, dirty from driving the dusty roads of the Panhandle. The aroma of freshly baked challah wafted through their home as Tanya set the table for their Shabbat dinner while listening to the latest radio reports about the Israeli attack on the Suez Canal. She couldn't stop thinking about her brother Yacov, an engineer who had worked on the canal and lived in Jerusalem. Although he was thousands of miles away, they stayed in touch through letters, and she anxiously awaited his next one. She took a deep breath and said yet another prayer for his safety, then brushed aside her worries about her brother and the survival of the new nation of Israel. The table was perfect, and dinner was almost ready. Outside, the sun was about to drop below the western horizon, readying the sky for the distinct hues of orange and purple of another spectacular sunset.

Ruth peeked out from the kitchen. "Tanya, Tommy Johnson just called to see if Ari can go over to his house to see his new puppy." Ruth had a hint of hope in her voice.

Tanya paused before answering. "You know what to do, Ruth. It is Shabbat. Once the sun sets, Ari must be with our family."

Ruth pressed her lips together briefly. "I don't see the harm in letting him go down there until after sunset and it's time to eat. Ari loves that puppy, and Tommy's parents are happy to have Ari at their house, unlike some of the other families in the neighborhood. Ari needs to be accepted; you know that better than I do."

As if on cue, a knock echoed through the house. Ruth opened the door, and little Tommy Johnson, freckled, blond, and lisping, asked, "Can Ari come play with the puppy, please? I wanna show him the new trick I taught Maverick. Please, please!" His wide-eyed innocence and his love of her son always melted Ruth's heart.

"Of course, but just until suppertime, after the sun goes down, okay? I will come get him then. Ari! Tommy's here." Her gap-toothed son with his dark curly hair appeared, delighted to see his friend. The pair of them rushed out the door and down the cul-de-sac to the Johnsons' house. Ruth sent up a prayer for the Johnsons and their open Christian hearts.

As she closed the door behind them, her mother-in-law lit into her with steel in her voice. "How dare you let him out of the house on Shabbat!"

"I'm sorry, I know, I know. It's important for Ari to be with us tonight and tomorrow too. But I cannot say no when Tommy asks him over. Ari will have it hard enough being the only Jewish boy in town. Plus, the sun hasn't set yet."

"It's Shabbat. We light candles, we eat challah, we say

prayers. It's our special time with God." Shabbat had always been important to Tanya.

She thought of her father, who had been forced to change his name as he fled from the czar's military conscriptions at the age of twelve, never to see his family again. He had to live off roots in the forest and scoop cow dung for farmers along his way to Germany, where he met and married Tanya's mother. After some years, he left his wife and young daughter behind to board a ship for America.

Once in America, he made the trek west and settled in Trinidad, Colorado. Eventually, various Jewish organizations helped Tanya and her mother flee from Bremen, Germany, and reunite with her father in Trinidad. There, they rarely had the opportunity to honor Shabbat, because they were so poor that work always came first, even on Shabbat.

Yet her family had been sustained by her father's never-ending faith as well as by the town's small temple. The synagogue and its members were connected by the marrow in their bones, Jewish bones. It was there that Tanya perfected her English; it was there that her parents learned to speak it. It was where Tanya met her own husband, another Jewish man of great faith, God rest his soul, and then moved to Texas.

When Tanya became a young widow running her husband's company, the Jewish faith and culture was what drove her and her family to excellence and kept them sane in a very unsane world. Now that her family was in a position to honor Shabbat regularly, Tanya felt she owed it to her faith to make sure they did so.

Ruth, however, had other ideas. She feared that being so rigid with their Jewish practices and culture made the Rosenbaums—one of two Jewish families in Pampa—stand out even more. It wasn't that Ruth wasn't a believer; it was that she worried what such devotion would mean for Ari as he got older, especially in a town that worshipped football every Friday night.

Ruth didn't reply, instead returning to the kitchen just as Jacob came in. He sensed the tension between his mother and his wife and retreated back to the garage, where he had set up his newest train engine for his model train set. But when he saw Ruth's tight-lipped expression, he knew immediately his wife needed his help in the face of his mother's double-edged sword glare.

"Mother, what seems to be the problem?"

Before Tanya could respond, Ruth told her husband about Tommy's invitation to Ari. "Jacob, you know, as well as I do, how important it is for Ari to have friends and be accepted, even if it's just by one family. That will help him as he grows up. We can't afford for him to run the risk of being ostracized. You and I are devoted in our love for God and our faith, but isn't our son's happiness just as important? I'll go and get him when the sun is completely down. Let him have the next twenty or twenty-five minutes to just be a normal boy."

Jacob nodded his agreement. "Mother, give Ari a break. Let him be a boy, a boy who must grow up here. You forced me to miss so many chances to have friends with Gentile families, and in the end, that alienated and isolated me. Surely you remember how that made me feel?"

Tanya focused on twisting her hands and didn't answer.

"Ruth will make sure Ari comes home for Shabbat. Please, don't let my son be singled out like I was." He put his arm around Ruth and gave his mother a pleading look.

Of anyone in their family, Jacob knew all too well what it was like to grow up Jewish in the Panhandle. It was a lonely existence. Jacob remembered in particular his mother's insistence on observing Shabbat and every Jewish holy day during his high school years. Jacob had never gone to a football game, and because of that, none of his classmates ever invited Jacob to a party or a dance. He did not want the same for his son, of this he was certain. Even as an adult, if it hadn't been for Morris Silverstein and Jack Bergman in Amarillo, he wouldn't have any close friends.

Tanya was torn inside, for she did realize how their faith had set her son apart from his peers. Sure, everyone was nice to them, not only because she and her son were some of the biggest employers in the area, but also because folks genuinely liked them. If anyone knew how hard it was to preserve a Jewish identity in a world that wanted to erase it, she did.

"This is how it starts," Tanya snapped. "A small compromise here, another there. Soon, we're no different from the goyim. Ari must learn that this," she waved her hand over the beautifully set table, "is who we are, who we were, and who we will be. We cannot ever lose sight of that."

She set her jaw, said nothing more, and promised herself never to lose another battle when they were willing to water down their Jewish faith.

IN EARLY SEPTEMBER 1958, ARI STARTED KINDERGARTEN AT Pampa Elementary School. For Ari, it was the most exciting day of his young life. The teacher, a recent graduate of West Texas State Teachers College, was just about the prettiest woman Ari had ever seen. He was tongue-tied when she bent down to ask him his name and how old he was.

Ruth took his small hand in hers and answered for him, beaming with pride. "This is Ari Rosenbaum, and he will be six years old in November."

Ari knew what to say next. "I can read. Already. My mama taught me. I can also read in Hebrew and Russian and German.

I can also read music. Well, almost." He stood up as straight as he could, wanting to impress this beautiful lady with the kindest eyes he'd ever seen.

She laughed, and it sounded like fairies talking to Ari, and he was in love. His first crush. "Oh my, my, I am impressed, Mr. Ari. Maybe you can help me teach. My name is Miss Ellie, and I might need your help, Mr. Music Man."

With that little suggestion, Ari Rosenbaum's fate was sealed. Music was the way to this woman's heart. And he knew music.

After all the parents had gone, Miss Ellie's kindergarten classroom buzzed with the usual chaos of five-year-olds on a sweltering September morning. The rest of the class consisted of some of the boys from his neighborhood, including Tommy, who Ari was elated to see, and other children he didn't know. Most of the children all seemed to know each other, and he wondered how. He decided to stay as quiet as possible and listen to everything Miss Ellie said.

When Miss Ellie clapped her hands, calling for attention, Ari was ramrod straight, ready to do exactly as she said.

"All right, class, let's start our day with a song!"

As the children gathered on the alphabet rug, Miss Ellie noticed Ari hanging in the back of the group of children.

"Come on over, Mr. Music Man," she said, coaxing him to the front of the room. "Don't be shy."

Ari shuffled forward, clutching his hands together in a balled fist. He had never stood in front of so many children. But he saw Tommy smiling at him, and then Miss Ellie began to lead the class in "Twinkle, Twinkle, Little Star."

A cacophony of off-key voices filled the room, but one sound stood out. Clear and pure, a perfect pitch rose above the rest. Miss Ellie's eyes widened as she realized it was coming from Ari, the youngest child in her class. The rest of the pupils stopped after the first stanza, but Ari, his eyes shut, kept on through the five remaining stanzas. The other children were enraptured.

As the song ended, Miss Ellie knelt beside him. "That was beautiful, Ari. You really are gifted, aren't you?"

The boy nodded solemnly. "I play piano."

"Oh? And what do you play?"

"Bach. Mozart. Beethoven." He rattled off the names as if he was listing cartoon characters.

Miss Ellie blinked, her mind reeling. She'd never encountered anything like this. Here, in the middle of nowhere, where the closest thing to classical music was old hymns on scratchy radios, sat a child who spoke of long-dead composers as if they were old friends.

"Would you like to show us?" she asked, gesturing to the ancient upright piano gathering dust in the corner.

Ari nodded and walked to the instrument with purpose. As his small fingers touched the keys, the classroom disappeared. Miss Ellie found herself transported to grand concert halls her grandmother, who was from Chicago, had told her about as a girl. The music swelled, filling every corner of the room, silencing even the most rambunctious children.

When Ari finished, the silence hung heavy for a moment before Miss Ellie found her voice.

"My word," she whispered, more to herself than anyone else. "What do we do with you?"

EVERY PARENT THINKS THEIR CHILD IS GIFTED, AND AT FIRST, Ruth and Jacob just thought it was parental pride. But there was the way Ari would sing "Eshet Chayil" at Shabbat with such perfection. Then he begged for a piano, a guitar, a banjo, a xylophone. All of that led them to finally believe that their son had a genetic gift.

Playing music became such a drive for Ari that Ruth turned her sewing room into his music room. For his sixth birthday, Ari asked for a record player so he could listen to classical records. Tanya agreed and signed up for a mail subscription of classical recordings by orchestras from all over the world. One record would come each week.

Diligently, Ari would play the records repeatedly, lifting off the needle and replaying a section, then playing it on his piano or guitar, and then listening again. To say he was obsessed with music was an understatement.

His grandmother soon decided he needed outside tutelage, since none of the teachers in the Panhandle had the skill to guide his level of talent. She put out feelers among the Jewish community in Amarillo for recommendations for the best private music teacher in the state.

Soon, a name was mentioned, more than once: Adelai Susskind, from Austria, a former violinist with the Dallas Symphony. The man took some cajoling to come out to the middle of nowhere to assess her grandson—including an offer of one hundred dollars a day, a lovely place to stay with a driver, and all the meals he wanted.

The delicate notes of Chopin's Étude in A minor, better known as the "Winter Wind," filled the living room of the Rosenbaum home. Ari's tiny fingers danced across the keys of the upright piano, his feet barely reaching the pedals.

Mr. Susskind leaned forward, his brow furrowed in disbelief. He'd been skeptical when Ari's grandmother had called, claiming her six-year-old grandson needed advanced instruction. Now, watching the boy tackle one of the most technically challenging pieces in the piano repertoire, he found himself at a loss for words.

Tanya sat at the dining room table, a knowing smile playing out on her stern face. As she went over the books from her company, she entered numbers in the adding machine, a rhythmic counterpoint to the cascading arpeggios pouring from the piano.

When Ari reached a particularly difficult passage, Mr. Susskind held his breath. But the boy's hands moved with uncanny precision, never faltering.

"Impossible," Mr. Susskind muttered, getting up from the chair next to the piano and coming into the dining room, shaking his head. "I've had adult students struggle with this piece for months."

Tanya chuckled. "I told you, Mr. Susskind. Our Ari is special."

"Mrs. Rosenbaum, with all due respect, this piece is far beyond what I'd normally assign to even my most gifted young students. How is this possible?"

Tanya fixed him with a steady gaze. "Mr. Susskind, that boy has been playing since before he could walk. I've watched him sit at this piano for hours, day after day. He hears a piece once and it's like … it's like it becomes part of him."

As if to emphasize her point, Ari launched into the final section of the étude, his small frame swaying with the music's intensity. The room vibrated with the power of the piece, belying the size of the pianist producing it.

Mr. Susskind's objections died on his lips as he watched, transfixed. When the final notes faded, Ari turned on the bench, his dark eyes serious. "Was that okay, Mr. Susskind? Maybe, I rushed the middle section a little. I'm sorry."

Mr. Susskind cleared his throat, trying to regain his composure. "That was remarkable, Ari. Truly remarkable. Perhaps we should discuss your goals for our lessons. I have a feeling we'll be covering some rather advanced material."

Tanya smiled and closed her eyes, listening to the excited chatter of her grandson and the still-stunned responses of Mr. Susskind.

She had known from the moment she had first seen Ari's

tiny hands reach for the piano keys that he was destined for greatness. Now, it appeared, the rest of the world was starting to catch up.

Tanya finally knew what she could spend part of her fortune on—Ari and his future.

7

ARCHER

Nancy Mueller was not happy, not at all. Pastor Griswold's sermon that morning was, in her opinion, anti-Jewish and just plain anti-human. She'd never, in all of her Christian life and all of her time in the churches she'd been in as a choir director and musical consultant, heard a man of God preach with such animosity toward another group of humans. She lamented the passing of Pastor Campbell, who'd kept the younger man in line, making sure his overly conservative viewpoints didn't cross over into blatant hatred. Without the older pastor's wisdom and kindness, the First Baptist Church was not recognizable.

As conflicted as she was, she couldn't talk to Joe Bob about it just yet. When they walked out of church, he was quiet but livid, like a provoked rattlesnake. She knew better than to try to talk to him when he had that look. When they got back to the ranch, he took his favorite horse out of the barn and said he was going to ride the fences and check for lost calves. She knew better.

The time for that had already come and gone, and there was only a minuscule chance that any calves were still out on the ranch. Her husband just needed to ride off some steam.

When Seraphina pulled up in her ancient Chevy truck, Nancy was relieved. Seraphina was the perfect person to talk to about the sermon. Even though she attended the Methodist church, Seraphina didn't necessarily adhere to one church and one doctrine. She was a woman of the plains, finding God in the great outdoor vistas and wide-open spaces. Best of all, she was not one to mince her words.

"My goodness, you are a sight for sore eyes," Nancy said as she climbed up the porch stairs, carrying a tray of Archer's favorite sheet cake and a bottle of homemade lemonade.

"Well, it sure is nice to be seen." Seraphina set the cake and lemonade down on the porch table with a chuckle. "Where are your boys? I came to see you, of course, but I wanna hug my godchild." She scanned the yard and beyond the barn for Archer. The boy adored his godmother, not only because she brought vanilla sheet cake with chocolate buttercream icing every time she came, but also because she talked to the boy for hours, listening to all his made-up stories about every animal on the ranch and all the forces of nature. Archer had the most active imagination of any child. And Seraphina, bless her, fostered his mind as well as his little belly.

"He's in the barn, making up songs and singing to the new calves, to calm them. They were separated from their mothers during roundup."

When Seraphina turned to walk back down the stairs, Nancy stopped her. "Wait, my friend, I need to talk to you."

"What's up Nancy? Is it Joe Bob?"

"No, no, nothing like that ... well ... he's upset too, along with me, but he's off on his horse, checking for calves and broken fences. I just need someone to talk through why I'm so mad. This morning at church—"

"I'll stop you right there. That odious man, that Griswold guy, he's a creep and a woman-hater. I've always had a bad feeling about him, starting from all that hoo-hah over Archer's christening. You should just come over with us to the Methodists. We like everyone, we ain't judgy, and the choir needs some work, and you certainly could help us out in that department."

Abandoning the Baptist church, the choir, and all the work Nancy had put in as musical director was not something she could do, not yet. "Let me tell you what happened. I was really put off with his sermon this morning, blaming the Jews for Jesus's death. I mean, Jesus was a Jew, a rabbi, a leader of his own people, beloved by so many. It wasn't the Jewish people who sacrificed him; it was power and the love of power that had him put to death, not an entire religion. It really left a bad taste in my mouth. And Joe Bob's too—you know how he feels about Pastor Griswold."

"So what's Joe Bob's take on it?"

"Oh, you know him—he's gone all quiet and is off mulling it over. Plus, I didn't want to talk about it in front of Archer. He loves going to church, mostly just for the music."

"I hear you. That boy, he loves to sing. I've never heard a purer voice. But listen, Griswold is not going to get better unless your congregation calls him out on it, en masse. He's the kind of man who enjoys his own backward opinions on the world. Have you or Joe Bob tried talking to him? I mean you are very upstanding members." Seraphina looked earnestly at her friend.

Nancy could affect change if she wanted, she just needed to trust herself more. "I've tried more than once to let him know that our church should welcome everyone, no matter the color of their skin or their beliefs. But that incident with the Rodriguez family was beyond the pale."

"I remember you mentioning that. Wasn't that the family who was in the area picking cotton?"

"Yes. They only wanted to come to church and worship, like all the rest of us. But Pastor Griswold was so horrible to them, they left and never returned. When I confronted him about it, he just said it was for the best since they were migratory and wouldn't contribute to the church long term. And now, after today, Joe Bob—well, he's a man of few words, but I've got a feeling he just might stop going to church if there is another sermon like the one this morning."

"You two know what is best for you. But if you want my advice, I'd say listen to your soul, what it's telling you, and then do that. Now, I really want to see my godchild; he'll be excited I made him a cake." Seraphina headed to the barn, leaving Nancy to think long and hard about her position, her choir, and her love for the members of her church. Nancy made a promise to talk to Joe Bob later on that evening, once Archer went to bed.

Seraphina walked out to the barn. It was a perfect spring day in the Panhandle—the wildflowers were bursting in the fields, and the sky was a brilliant blue. As she got close, she heard Archer's crystal-clear voice and found him inside a stall with two frantic calves, obviously separated from their mothers. Archer had his hands on both of their necks and was singing an old cowboy song she knew well:

> *Oh, bury me not on the lone prairie*
> *These words came low and mournfully*
> *From the pallid lips of a youth who lay*
> *On the bloody ground at the close of day.*

Then Archer stroked their heads as he took the liberty of adding another verse in which the two calves were safe and sound in the barn awaiting their mothers. Seraphina watched, mesmerized, the two calves calmed down and nudged the boy with their soft noses. This boy, with his slight frame, his piano-playing hands, lovely voice, and his soft dark curls, owned her heart.

"Archer," she said gently. "I made you a cake. C'mon up to the house, and you can help me set the table."

"In a minute, Auntie Seraphina. I wanna calm them, they are so sad. We need to find their mamas." Archer looked down on his two babies, stroking them some more and picked up the song again.

"Okay, sweet boy, come up to the house soon. We can talk to your daddy to see if we can go out to the herd after lunch and maybe look for the distraught mama cows later." She knew, however, that reuniting calves with their mothers would be well-nigh impossible. Joe Bob had over fifteen hundred head of cattle from the spring roundup. She knew because she had been there for branding day, something Archer was not allowed to see, considering how sensitive he was about all animals. His mama kept him inside that day and worked with him on learning the guitar. He was already proficient on piano, ukulele, upright bass, and fiddle. It was uncanny how musical he was at such a young age.

Seraphina left Archer in the barn and returned to the house, where she helped Nancy make the final preparations for their Sunday lunch. As they worked together with the seamless efficiency of longtime friends who had been cooking together for years, she asked, "Nancy, do you think it's okay for Archer to worry so much about the calves in the barn? I mean, it's rare that they will ever be reunited."

"Oh, Seraphina, you know, Joe Bob has a way of pulling that off. He figures out which mother cows are upset and looking for their young'uns and cuts them from the herd and rounds them up in the back pasture. Then, he'll bring the calves back there, and they'll sort it out with their mamas. Even though it's extra work, Joe Bob swears it makes for happier cows and better-tasting meat. But if you ask me, the real reason he goes to all that trouble is Archer. That is the only part of roundup we let him see. You've seen it for yourself; it always brings a tear to my eyes." Nancy smiled, well aware that even though Seraphina was pure Texas, as hard as they come on the outside, she had a heart as big as Texas too.

"Well, when Archer gets older, are you gonna tell him where all the cows go when they leave? That ain't gonna be a beautiful reunion in the back pasture."

Nancy fiddled with the temperature of the oven before putting the biscuits in. "No, Seraphina, we won't until we absolutely have to. He's too kind, too sensitive, too much of a thinker. And I can't help but think that he's not cut out for ranching. So, while he's here, growing up in the hardscrabble of this ranch, we'll let him care for his animals and make music and read and just be the sweet boy he is."

Seraphina willed Archer to come inside. She knew, more than anyone, how hard it was to be different in a man's world. Soon, Archer would be starting kindergarten and be around all the children in their community. Hard people with hard sons, who played rough, who couldn't wait to start playing football. Boys who fought, then made up, only to fight again. Her godson was not a fighter, not at all. Nor was he a football player. She was going to have to guide Nancy and Joe Bob in letting him play some sport so he would fit in, even just a little bit, with the other boys. Definitely not football, but maybe baseball or basketball. These youngsters would be his peers all the way through high school, and she could think of nothing worse than him being teased and set apart for being such a loving, sensitive boy.

After lunch, Seraphina, Joe Bob, and Nancy listened to Archer play the grand piano in the living room. It was cooling off, and the windows were open, letting in the prairie air. Seraphina decided to talk to Joe Bob about her godson. "Joe

Bob, you know Archer's going to start school soon, and eventually he'll need to play some kind of sport, like, I don't know, baseball or basketball. Something to help him fit in."

Nancy interjected before her husband could respond, "He'll fit in just fine. I've been teaching him at home, and he can read already, mostly on a second-grade level. I'm worried he'll be bored in kindergarten."

Joe Bob, however, sensed that Seraphina was on to something. Archer's main friends were the animals at the ranch and the ranch hands. He spent too much time with his mother, learning music and reading books. Pretty soon, his son would need to be with other boys and learn what it was like to shoot the breeze, hang out, and play sports. "I hear you, Nancy. But being bored with kindergarten can't be that bad for him. Archer's a scrawny little thing; there's not much to him. Oh sure, he can ride a horse, almost better than any of us, and he's good with a rope. But what he really needs is to be with other boys of his own age. He spends too much time alone, talking and singing to animals. I'm more afraid that no one will want to be his friend."

Nancy was surprised that her normally taciturn husband had so much to say about their son. Maybe he was right. Archer was different than the ranch hands' sons, not just in appearance, but in his personality. He was contemplative, thoughtful and shy. Maybe he needed to come out of his shell a bit. She looked around her living room with its built-in bookshelves lined with books and reference materials. She'd converted the two lower shelves for Archer's books, and they were already full. Besides reading, he was already well on his way musically, having shown a creative gift for making up his own songs. Just yesterday he'd grabbed his fiddle and played a melody he called "Chirpin' Robin," his version of the hit song "Rockin' Robin." And dang if it didn't sound like a conversation between two robins. But she knew her best friend and her husband were right: Archer needed to learn more of what it meant to be a boy.

THE CANYON ELEMENTARY PART OF THE CANYON COMPREHENsive School had only four classrooms and two outdoor classrooms. On the first day of school in September, Nancy led Archer into one of the inside rooms, which had kindergarten on one side and first grade on the other, divided by a makeshift wall of bookshelves and boxes. The room was filled with young, excited children, greeting each other like old friends, which many of them already were. Nancy spotted Hank Verity, of the Verity ranch and the First Baptist Church, standing with his mother, tentatively holding her hand. The boy was large for his age, but was almost too reticent to make friends. Nancy leaned down to Archer. "Look, Archer. There's Hank from Sunday School, so there is one person you know." Archer smiled up at her, but gripped her hand firmly, not ready to walk over to anyone.

The week before, Nancy had met with Mr. King, the school's principal, and the school's new kindergarten teacher, Cathy Erickson, to explain her son's advanced education at the young age of five and a half. When the principal introduced her to Miss Erickson, the teacher shook Nancy's hand. "Mrs. Mueller, how nice to meet you. I've heard all about you from a teacher at the college, who said you were the best music teacher in town."

Nancy asked them both if they could find a way to work with Archer to keep him engaged and not bored. Perhaps he could be a helper and even join the first- or second-grade classes during reading periods. In return, Nancy promised to come in a few times a month to teach a music lesson to the elementary classes. The principal was delighted by that offer, as was Miss Erickson, who said, "I'm just tickled to death. I can't wait. I can learn along with the students; I am terrible at music."

The red-haired freckle-faced teacher looked down at Archer, who was staring blatantly at his new teacher, taking her in as if she were a lost bird. "You must be the famous Archer, the one who can sing scared calves to sleep."

If he was surprised, he didn't show it. Instead, he beamed up at his teacher and said, "I can do that. Yes. But I can also sing to their mamas. And the horses and the goats. All the animals when they are frightened. It makes them calm."

"Well, that is going to be most helpful for me because most of the boys and girls in your class will be a bit scared today to leave their own mamas for the whole day. So, if anyone needs a song, I can ask you, can't I?"

Nancy was pleased that Miss Erickson knew exactly how to capture her baby's heart. When Archer dropped his mother's hand and went over to check out the books, she said. "Thank you so much. He will be such a help to you, I just know it."

"Just so you know, I talked to Miss Renfrow, the second-grade teacher, whom you taught at the college, by the way, and she said sending Archer to her starting next week would be just fine. In the meantime, I thought I might ask you something. This year we are accepting children into the class with some physical disabilities. We have a new family, the Croffords, who have a son with cerebral palsy who will be in kindergarten. I thought that I might ask Archer to maybe be his helper when he needs it—you know, reaching for things, preparing his supplies, just physically. Since you said Archer was so sensitive to the animals on your ranch, I thought he'd be the perfect boy to help Wesley. What do you think?"

Nancy loved the idea and spotted the boy and his mother, standing in a corner. Wesley slumped onto heavy crutches and had on a boot with a thicker sole than the other. His mother had a protective hand on his shoulder as she scanned the room with trepidation. Nancy summoned Archer and walked over to them. "Hello there. You must be Mrs. Crofford. I'm Nancy Mueller, and this is my son Archer." She leaned down to be eye level with the young boy with white-blond hair flipping in his face. "You must be Wesley. I'm going to be teaching music this year. Do you like to sing?"

The boy's face lit up and he was beside himself and answered her immediately, although she could barely understand him.

Archer followed Wesley perfectly. "Me too! I just love the song 'Sixteen Tons.' " The two boys started to sing Tennessee Ernie Ford's hit and burst into laughter.

Nellie Crofford looked like she might cry and said to Nancy, "Oh, my lord, your son, he understood him. Thank goodness! I can't believe it. Thank you. Thank you." The two women watched their sons as they sang some other popular songs from the radio.

When they took a breather, Archer said, "Mama, when you come, Wes wants you to teach us how to sing 'Sixteen Tons,' okay? Please. I know you don't like popular music, but this is such a good one, isn't it?"

"I think that is the perfect song to start with!"

As their sons continued their serenade, Nancy and Nellie walked out of the classroom together, the seeds of a lifelong friendship planted through their sons.

Later that afternoon, Nancy picked up Archer and took him to the drugstore on Main Street for a root beer float. As they sat at the counter, she inquired about his day. "So, was the teacher as nice as she seemed?"

"Oh, yeah, she's great! I really, really liked her and all the other boys and girls." He slurped his float. "But Wes, he was the funniest. Most of the kids couldn't understand him at first, but I helped them. I told them he spoke a secret language, like when the cows bellow and only their calf understands. Once I told them what he said, they all started to get it. He's super funny and loves all the rock-and-roll songs you tell me I shouldn't listen to. Then, Rodney Curtis asked if he could come out to ranch and see the cows and their babies. I said sure! Is that okay, if Rodney comes? I told him I'd show him how to ride a horse like a cowboy, you know, since he lives in town and has never even seen a horse. Imagine, never having seen a horse, Mama!"

Nancy listened to Archer's bubbly, happy recap of his day as she sipped her float with Dr Pepper, which she liked much more than root beer. His huge grin told her all she needed to know.

PART III

THE TEENAGE YEARS

1966–1969

LETTER FROM KAROLINA
NOVEMBER 1966

My darling babies:

Today is your fourteenth birthday! I can barely believe it. You are now the age I was when my teachers at the music conservatory in Prague told my mother I was ready to start performing in public. I wonder, are you playing music for other people? Are you following your hearts?

But, of course, I have no idea what you're doing. I just pray that at this time in your life, music will give you opportunities so that you will not have to spend your time on things that do not give you happiness. I just hope your focus is on whatever makes your hearts beat. Selfishly, I hope it is music.

Every night my prayer is that at some time our paths will cross, but if not, this wonderful lawyer who receives my letters will experience it for me. He will know what makes your hearts beat.

I hope part of that beat is, at least, a single note of music.

I love you.

Your mother,

Karolina

8

DANIEL AND DR. TOM

Daniel filed the latest letter from Karolina away with all the others in the file marked "Boy Twins." As he did every year upon hearing from her, he wished he could write back and fill her in on their lives. She would be thrilled to learn that her twins were musical prodigies. Archer was already composing his own works, not to mention his otherworldly ability to play so many instruments. As for Ari, what a gift the boy had. He recently performed at the Junior Philharmonic in Dallas. Daniel and Elaine had enjoyed their weekend seeing him playing the violin, then moving over to the stand-up bass for an inspiring rendition of Ravel's *Bolero* that earned a standing ovation. Both boys were also loved and supported by their families, and Daniel still felt honored to be included in their lives, as Archer's godfather and as a lawyer and dear friend to the Rosenbaums.

Knowing Joe Bob and Nancy had told Archer he was adopted around the time he was seven, Daniel fully expected the boy would ask him at some point about his birth parents. Of course, because it was a closed adoption, he wouldn't be able to reveal any information to Archer, but he'd prepared an answer just in case: "Sorry, son, but the records are sealed and cannot be opened unless the law changes." So far, Archer hadn't asked, and Daniel was pleased to see how happy, well-adjusted, and loving he was with his parents, never seeming to be affected by knowing he was adopted. All good signs, but Daniel wondered just the same.

By contrast, the Rosenbaums—especially Tanya—were all adamant that Ari never learn he was adopted. Daniel thought back to the boy's bar mitzvah the year before. He and Elaine had brought their three boys so they could all experience the beauty, words, and music of such a moving ceremony at the synagogue in Amarillo. The party afterward was surprisingly fun with Ari performing the Beatles' first number-one song, "I Want to Hold Your Hand" on the piano. People couldn't believe such a popular song could sound so lovely. Such was the power of music and the boy's musical ability. Ari was now a Jewish man, seen so in the eyes of his community. He fit in perfectly, Daniel could see that.

Daniel tidied up his office before heading for home. Dr. Tom had just returned from another international trip and would be joining his family for dinner. As close as he was to Tom, the one thing they never discussed was anything about the twin boys. There were times when Daniel was tempted to break the confidentiality rule with his friend, but he managed to keep his delight in the twins hidden away. He hoped that Tom would be refreshed from his latest vacation and have entertaining stories to tell.

WHEN DANIEL OPENED HIS FRONT DOOR, DR. TOM HAD A HUGE grin on his face, under a navy straw campaign hat. He was so thin Daniel could see a new hole cut into the well-worn leather belt holding up his hiking trousers under a dusty jacket and yellowed shirt. Obviously, he had just returned from a hike at Palo Duro Canyon, and Daniel was a bit jealous—he hadn't hiked the canyon with Tom in months. If he was honest with himself, between having three young sons at home, a jammed law career, and his community-organizing activities, Daniel barely had any time to himself. But he could not complain. His life was full. Tom, still a bachelor, had expanded his focus to saving the lives of mothers and babies all over the world as well as here in the Panhandle. When he wasn't delivering babies or hiking in the canyon, he was off on his foreign travels, often going to dusty or frigid destinations lacking modern conveniences with food that did not sound appealing at all to Daniel. But his latest trip didn't meet that brief.

"Come in, Tom! I want to hear all about New York and Karolina and your time together. Elaine is making a huge dinner—you look famished."

The doctor handed his friend a bottle of Canadian whiskey. "I promise you'll like the taste of this stuff—the Canadians drink like us."

Daniel was relieved it wasn't a bottle with a worm or a boar's hair in it or made with licorice. Daniel's family were all in the kitchen, the boys doing their homework at the table, and Elaine was on the phone, probably organizing for a National Organization for Women's chapter in the Panhandle. Since their youngest son had started kindergarten, she was focusing on gaining equal rights for the women of Texas, and he could not be prouder of her efforts. Many people in the Panhandle were adamantly opposed to women working at all, let alone asking for decent wages as specified in the federal Equal Pay Act of 1963. Daniel was puzzled by why so many of his neighbors and even his colleagues at the law firm were so vehemently opposed to women in the workplace. Hadn't women been working as teachers and nurses forever? What was wrong with women being allowed to get bank accounts, mortgages, or trust funds in their own names? Or, even more so, why couldn't they take out small business loans and start their own companies?

Daniel and Elaine had both been horrified that the Civil Rights Act of 1964 didn't address equal rights for women in the workplace. For too long, women had put up with discrimination. Elaine and Seraphina were active in trying to unite the women of the Panhandle to keep lobbying Congress to try and pass equality for all in the workplace. The new National Organization for Women would be a good start, and Daniel would help them in any way he knew how.

Elaine dropped the receiver against her shoulder to give Tom a quick hug. "My goodness, Tom! You look like you could use a home-cooked meal. Dinner will be ready in about thirty minutes."

Daniel took her hint. "Let's go to my study. We can try the whiskey, and you can tell me about the trip."

He poured out two big shots of the Canadian whiskey and went over to his record player and put on Leonard Bernstein leading the New York Philharmonic in playing Gustav Mahler's Symphony No. 7. They sat on the broken-in brown Chesterfield sofa and clinked their glasses.

"Ah, before I forget ... " Tom reached into his pocket and brought out the program for Karolina's concert featuring a new work by Elie Siegmeister written in response to the war in Vietnam. Daniel read aloud from the program:

> *The Face of War* is a song cycle from 1966 by Siegmeister with a text by African-American writer Langston Hughes. The composer believed that an artist "must be rooted to a time and place," and his social and political concerns led Siegmeister to support civil rights and oppose the war in Vietnam.

"I bet that was quite the show. Was it well-attended, I hope?"

"It was completely full, every ticket sold. All the proceeds went to the fund to help returning soldiers injured over there. Not much moves me to tears, but when Ted Hughes's anti-war poem 'Peace' was sung by Esther Hinds, I almost wept." The doctor took a long drink of his whiskey.

Daniel knew just how anti-war Tom was. Over the years of their friendship, they had talked long and often deep into the night about the horrors Tom had seen in World War II, then the Korean Conflict, and now Vietnam. Dr. Tom was opposed to anything that sent young men to their deaths and firmly believed that what war does to a land and its people can never be justified. At heart, he was a man of peace. Now with so many soldiers dying in Vietnam, the anti-war demonstrations in Washington were putting the United States on edge. Daniel decided to change the subject, "So, Niagara Falls. Is it as amazing as everyone says?"

Tom smiled. "Even more so! Its beauty is almost overwhelming. My God, the gorge itself is just a miracle. Karolina and I explored all around the area. Then we went to Toronto, where she had another concert. After that we spent about a week exploring the Algonquin Provincial Park in Ontario. What a stunning place. Bears are everywhere, and the trees are just as majestic as you can imagine. I was quite surprised with that part of Canada. But best of all, did you know that Canada's national medical system takes such good care of their mothers after birth? I was lucky to get a tour of a maternity ward from one of Karolina's patrons up there. To top it all off, summer in Canada is wonderful, just right. Although I doubt very much I'd like to visit in the winter." Despite being an avid skier and mountaineer, Tom, like many Texans, did not like to be cold.

Daniel chuckled. Winter weather north of anywhere from Texas was just not bearable. "So, how was the esteemed Karolina?"

"Oh, she is so wonderful. And my goodness, she is still such a treat to hear! She is now one of the top-ranked pianists in the world and in such high demand she can pick and choose her performances. Her schedule is booked solid through the fall, and she has landed a long residency in Rome this winter. I'm hoping to visit her there over Christmas so I can see some of the sights with her. You and Elaine will have to come the next time she plays here in the States. Speaking of which, how are Elaine and your boys?"

Just then, Daniel's oldest son knocked on the door. "Mom says dinner is ready!"

Over dinner, the two men exchanged more pleasantries, and Elaine told the doctor about her fervor for women's rights, a cause the doctor could get behind. Tom let his mind drift. Elaine's passion reminded him so much of his beloved wife, Rita. She had been a firecracker and would probably be leading the charge for women's equality. He could see her marching on Washington, running a pediatric surgery clinic, and just being alive. Sometimes he would indulge himself in envisioning Rita being alive and their possible life together, not as a measure of torture, but as a measure of peace for himself. It not only gave him a sense of closure but also a sense of their abiding love. Of course, he knew, it had all ended tragically with the drunk driver who drove over her as she walked to attend her medical rotation. Their life together stolen in an instant. This secret visioning he did, with her in the world still with him, allowed him to see things through her eyes. And his beloved Rita would be right alongside the women right's movement; he just knew it.

After dinner, Daniel and Tom returned to the study. Their conversation organically went to the origin of their friendship —the placement of babies into good homes. Even though times were changing, too many young women still were left to deal with unwanted pregnancies, while fathers still were never held to account. Attitudes had not changed toward unwed mothers, especially in Texas. They were still forced to bear the shame and isolation of giving birth, not to mention the sadness of giving up their child.

"I thought my numbers would go down with the birth control pill being available," Tom said. "But doctors around here still treat it with some sort of conservative stigma I just can't comprehend and refuse to prescribe it, except to married women. The pill is a life-changer for women. Of course, the ones that have it, well, their lives are now their own. I just wish all women had access to it. That way, they can get on with their lives however they see fit." Here he took a long sip of his whiskey as if to quell his thoughts. "The pill is not the devil's work as that idiot preacher Griswold writes about in all his editorials to the local papers. Ugh, that man is insufferable." Dr. Tom was of course, referring to the First Baptist pastor over in Canyon, who had been making a name for himself by speaking out against civil rights, the women's movement, the pill, and of course the "hell-fire" books that needed to be banned, including *To Kill a Mockingbird*, which was, in Tom's opinion, one of the greatest books ever written and should be required reading for all.

Daniel chimed in. "Don't forget his opposition to George Orwell's *1984*. What on earth is he talking about? That's what I want to know. I mean, it's obvious to anyone who knows anything about literature, that it's not promoting communism but preaching against any authoritarianism. We need books like that right now in the U.S. Tensions are so high between Blacks and whites and even between Chicano workers. Between those who are anti-war and those who aren't. I feel sometimes a powder keg is about to go off."

"Yes, with the shootings from the tower at the University of Texas in August, it just shows the mindset of our nation, our youth. We are, it seems, suffering from an extreme case of trauma. Since President Kennedy was shot, our collective grief as a nation is still festering. But we cannot succumb to the violence, to the rhetoric of those who would divide us, and we must find a way through." Tom, with his experience and age, was still hopeful.

The two men refilled their glasses and sat back to listen to Bernstein's Mahler, each of them mulling over life in 1966 in the United States. To both of them, it felt surreal and out of control. Hope was what they would have to focus on.

9

ARI

BEFORE HE STARTED EIGHTH GRADE IN SEPTEMBER 1966, ARI caught his first glimpse of what he wanted to do for the rest of his life: conducting an orchestra. It started with a televised special from the renowned Ravinia Festival outside of Chicago. The soprano Roberta Peters had appeared with the Chicago Symphony Orchestra conducted by Josef Krips, and the wunderkind Seiji Ozawa then conducted a performance of Tchaikovsky's *Capriccio Italien* that turned it into a living, breathing thing. Ozawa was one of the youngest conductors in the world and had been appointed to lead the Ravinia Festival by Leonard Bernstein. Ari was impressed.

When school started a few weeks later, Ari and all of his eighth-grade music buddies were still raving about the Ravinia special. His friends were most impressed by the Ramsey Lewis Trio, and Ari agreed that Lewis was an amazing jazz pianist. But he was still enthralled by the orchestra. Yeah, yeah, the orchestra was good, they said, but Ramsey Lewis was all they wanted to talk about. Well, except for Janey Hamilton, who loved Nancy Wilson's performance. Ari wasn't surprised—Janey was the star singer of the high school's jazz ensemble, so of course, she would prefer the singer.

At lunch, Ari tried again to convince her that it was the great Seiji Ozawa who stole the show. "You know I am right, Janey."

Janey smiled and nodded. "Okay, yes, he is a genius. But you can't say that Nancy Wilson doesn't have the most perfect pitch in the business."

Janey's blond hair caught the sun through the cafeteria window, and Ari was mesmerized by how gorgeous it was, like a shaft of gold. Janey was not only the prettiest girl in school— she was also the nicest. She never stopped inviting him to parties, dances, and meetups. For nearly eighty years, the Hamiltons operated the mercantile shop in Pampa. Ari's parents were friends with Janey's parents, and his grandmother had done business with Janey's grandfather. Despite the closeness of the families, Ari knew he could never ask her out on a date, because she was not Jewish. He was not sure how her family would react, but he knew his Bubbe would blow a gasket if he dated a Gentile. Besides, Janey had caught the eye of the eighth-grade football players, and even Ari's oldest friend, Tommy, had a crush on her. Ari resigned himself to being close friends with Janey, but he still admired her in secret.

The next April, Ari and his mother watched another memorable special, this one featuring Leonard Bernstein himself conducting one of his *Young People's Concerts* with three young soloists. A cellist was featured in Tchaikovsky's *Variations on a Rococo Theme*, a soprano sang Mimi's aria from *La Bohème* and "My Man's Gone Now" from *Porgy and Bess*, and a pianist took on Brahms's Piano Concerto No. 2 in B-flat major. Ari, however, was spellbound by Bernstein.

After the show ended, Ari turned to his mother sitting on the couch. She had a blissful look on her face; she too was relishing the concert she'd just seen on television. "That was just about one of the most beautiful things I've heard in my life," she muttered, gazing dreamily at the blank screen.

Ari nodded. "It was, wasn't it? Mama, I know I want to do. I want to conduct an orchestra. I can hear them, you know—all the instruments, how they should play together. I think Bernstein and Seiji Ozawa have that too. Mama? Mama? Look at me." He positioned himself at his mother's feet. "Mama, I want to do that."

Ruth looked into her son's eyes. Where did he get this drive, this gift, this magic for music? It was God-given, of that, she was sure. She thought of her family, Polish Jews all of them, farmers and blacksmiths, men who could work steel and metal along the railways of Colorado and eventually Texas. In her family, everyone she knew of had been gifted with beautiful voices. Some of her relatives were cantors in Jewish congregations along the railway towns, some played the fiddle and sang Yiddish songs from home. Ruth herself had trained as an opera singer as her minor at the University of Texas, just to satisfy her own musical calling while she studied library science. Opera singers didn't make any money, but librarians always had work, or so her father had told her, but the love of music never left her. But her musical soul was nothing like Ari's. Even though he wasn't her biological child, she and Tanya both had shaped Ari's musical inclinations. As he progressed, they both knew that he needed more than Mr. Susskind, his private tutor from Dallas; he needed to be with other gifted students who lived and breathed music just as he did.

Before she could answer, Ari continued, "Mama, Mr. McCarthy told me about a music camp in Michigan that has a summer program where I can study conducting. There's nowhere in Texas with anything like that. Would you help me write a letter to them to get us some information about their orchestra camp? I can go next summer. It's what I want to do. Please, you must help me convince Bubbe that this really is the best thing for me."

Ruth smiled at her son's boundless enthusiasm. "Okay, Ari. Let's write to that camp. Then I will do what I can, my son. But you must remember how Bubbe is about observing Shabbat. If you were to go away for several weeks in the summer, she will be concerned about how you will be able to honor Shabbat."

"What if I don't want to honor it the way she does? I mean, Mama, she makes us do it, even though we don't really believe like she does. I know what happened to her family with the pogroms and the sacrifices she makes to send support back to Uncle Yacov in Israel, but I am tired of being so different. I mean, I can't even play in the marching band because the football games are on Friday nights. I love the marching band, and those kids have so much fun. But no, I have to come home and eat dinner with you all. It was hard enough to get her to let me do orchestra performances on Saturdays. Please, Mama, please talk to her. I really want to do this."

Ruth would do everything she could to see if this camp would work for her son. She would also talk to Jacob. He had a way with his mother, to make her see sense. Of course, they would never waver from being Jewish, but couldn't they find a way to be adaptable so Ari could pursue his gift? She planned to make this happen, but she would need Jacob's help.

WHEN ARI HAD LUNCH WITH TOMMY AND JANEY AT SCHOOL, HE couldn't stop talking about becoming the next Leonard Bernstein.

Janey laughed. "Bernstein better look out, Ari! You are going to be so famous as a conductor, you might be on a Wheaties box."

Tommy snorted at that. "Ha, ha, ha. You're ridiculous, Janey!"

Ari had to admit that no skinny flop-haired Jewish boy from the Panhandle would ever be on a cereal box. That was for the best athletes in the world, not musicians or conductors. "Maybe one day I'll lead an orchestra, but with the exception of Bernstein and maybe Ozawa, no one really knows who conductors are."

"They are the most important part of any orchestra; they *are* the orchestra! Everyone knows that." Janey said this with such certainty that Ari had to smile. Even though most of their classmates had no idea what a conductor even did, Janey did. He loved that about her. Her family had season tickets to the Dallas Symphony, and their seats were just behind his grandmother's.

Suddenly, Ari remembered what their music teacher, Mr. McCarthy, had told him. "Hey Janey, have you ever heard of Interlochen music camp?"

She shook her head and trained her blue eyes on him. He gulped before continuing. "It's a summer camp in Michigan for the arts. They have an orchestra program and even a vocal one too. I'm hoping to go to the conducting program next summer. Maybe you might want to come and do voice?"

"That sounds amazing, but you know we go to Colorado most summers, and I always attend a girls' camp there. We sing and dance and even do gymnastics. I love it so much, and I wouldn't want to miss that."

"Well maybe you could do both? My mom has written to Interlochen to get a brochure. I'll show it to you when we get it."

"Maybe Ari, maybe. I've gotta run. I have an algebra tutorial."

As she left the table, Ari could smell her lemon-scented shampoo linger in the air. He noticed the entire table of football players table watching her walk out, and one of them whistled at her.

Janey, of course, shot him down quicker than lightning. "Oh, go on, Albert, you big lump. You couldn't call the cows home even if you tried."

That sent the whole table laughing at the immense offensive lineman. Ari hid a grin with a swig of his milk, hoping against hope that his grandmother would let go of her strict Jewish ways and let him go to Interlochen.

THE GOLDEN SUN DIPPED BELOW THE HORIZON, PAINTING THE vast Texas Panhandle sky in hues of orange and purple. Friday night, inside the Rosenbaum home, the Shabbat candles flickered, casting dancing shadows across the dining room. As usual, the aroma of freshly baked challah mingled enticingly with the rich scent of brisket, a testament to Ruth's culinary prowess.

Ari, his unruly dark curls flopping in his face, fidgeted in his chair. Under his fringe, his eyes darted between Bubbe and their surprise distinguished guest, Rabbi Goldstein from Dallas. The rabbi's presence added an air of formality to the dinner, and Ari sensed the weight of unspoken tension in the room. His grandmother had called in the big guns, obviously in response to his request to go to Interlochen.

"So, Ari," Rabbi Goldstein began, his voice gentle but authoritative, "I heard you play the piano and the violin at the celebration of Yom Kippur at the Rosensteins' home in Amarillo, two years ago, I believe. You're quite the musician."

A spark of enthusiasm lit up Ari's face. "Yes, sir. I've been playing the piano since I was about four, when I could reach the keys from the piano bench, and learned the violin shortly after. I also play the stand-up bass, the trumpet, the oboe, and the drums. Oh, and the flute, but I think I am best on the piano.

What I really want to do now is study conducting. I've been talking to my music teacher about conducting, and he's going to let me try that out next year when I start high school. He also told me be about the Interlochen summer music camp in Michigan that has a program for conducting."

"And you wish to go, but you would be gone for several weeks, yes?"

Before Ari could answer, Tanya interjected, her face stern. "It's out of the question. He won't be able to keep Shabbat or eat kosher. It's not right for a Jewish boy."

Ari's shoulders slumped, but Ruth placed a comforting hand on his arm. "Mama," she said, "times are changing. I've contacted the camp, and they will figure out a way to keep kosher and ensure the Jewish children honor Shabbat. Ari should have this opportunity."

Ari's father, nodded in agreement. "The boy has talent. If he does want to be a conductor, there aren't many avenues for him here in Texas. Interlochen could open many doors for him."

Rabbi Goldstein raised his hand to still the brewing argument. "Ari, do you understand why your grandmother is concerned?"

Ari hesitated, then spoke softly. "Because she wants me to stay connected to our faith and traditions."

The rabbi nodded his approval. "Observing Shabbat and keeping kosher aren't just rules, Ari. They're a link to our past, a way to honor the struggles and sacrifices of those who came before us. Your grandmother," he gestured to Tanya, whose eyes glistened with unshed tears, "she lived through times when practicing our faith could mean death. Her family had to flee from the pogroms, and the rest of her family were lost in the camps. For her, these traditions are a lifeline."

A heavy silence fell over the table. Ari looked at his grandmother and perhaps for the first time noticed the weight of history etched in the lines of her face.

"But," the rabbi continued, "our faith also teaches us to use the gifts God has given us. Music, Ari, can be a form of prayer, a way to touch the divine. So if there is music to be played and a lesson to be learned on Shabbat, may you offer it all to God."

Ari straightened in his chair, a glimmer of hope in his eyes. "Bubbe," he said, turning to his grandmother. "I promise I won't forget who I am or where I come from. I'll take my kippah, my siddur. I'll say the Shema every night. And when I play, I'll carry the songs of our people in my heart."

Tanya's stern expression softened as her eyes met Ari's. "You're a good boy, Ari. But what if they camp can't help you keep kosher?"

"I've been reading up on it," Ari said eagerly. "I can stick to fruits, vegetables, and packaged kosher foods. And I'll fast if I have to."

Ruth leaned forward. "I am sure if our family made a donation for other kids like Ari who need to keep the faith, the camp would make that work."

Rabbi Goldstein smiled. "It seems young Ari and his parents have given this much thought. Sometimes, Tanya, preserving our faith means adapting to new circumstances while holding onto the essence of who we are."

Tanya looked around the table at the hopeful faces of her family, and then back to her grandson. With a deep sigh, she reached out and patted Ari's hand. "All right, my prince. Who am I to stop you? You may go, but I'd like you to work with your music teacher first to see if you do, indeed, want to conduct. If you do and Mr. McCarthy approves, you can apply to the camp next year. If you go, you'll write to me every week, and you'll tell me everything you're eating and how you observe Shabbat. Deal?"

Ari's face split into a wide grin. "Deal, Bubbe! Thank you!" He jumped up, rushing around the table to embrace her.

What Ari didn't know was that even though Tanya had been

balking at him going to Interlochen, she had already been making inquiries about him possibly studying music at Tel Aviv University. The ten-year-old institution had recently incorporated the prestigious Samuel Rubin Israel Academy of Music, which had one of the most rigorous and competitive conducting programs in the world. In fact, Borger Pipeline and Steelworks had submitted the paperwork to start an endowment at the music school in the Rosenbaum family name. Her dream was for Ari to eventually go to Tel Aviv University, not only to attend the conducting program but also to explore his Jewish faith more deeply. And having the rabbi's blessing made her feel better about him going to Interlochen.

As the family resumed their Shabbat meal, the candles seemed to burn a little brighter, illuminating a path forward that honored both their traditions and Ari's dreams.

10

ARCHER

Spring roundup was going on all over the Panhandle, and the Mueller ranch hands discovered many heads from the nearby Verity and Walker-Ross Ranches. That wasn't unusual; the three ranches shared non-fenced boundary lines for decades. Trucks with huge trailers were parked up near the back stocks, ready to load up the cattle belonging to each ranch.

Archer and his friend Hank Verity rode their horses back to the barn behind the stray cows they'd found that morning. Archer paused on the back of his horse, Dandelion, to take in the whole scene, which was a form of controlled mayhem with the cowboys whistling and whooping, the baying and mooing of the cattle, dust fluttering up everywhere. Archer listened under the sounds and heard the grinding of the wheels of the trailers as cattle were loaded up inside, metal clanking against the sound of the hooves, cows issuing distinct moos as they reunited with their calves. To him, it was a movie soundtrack played by an entire orchestra, perhaps entitled *Spring Roundup*

'67 With Wildflowers. What would it sound like? Would he add more strings than bass? How could he make dust with music? This was how his mind worked, how it had always worked.

Hank yelled, "Watch out Archer, you're gonna get stampeded —quit listening to the god-damn sounds and pay attention!"

Archer smiled and turned Dandelion slightly to the left as a cow rushed over to her calf, slipping just past the side of the distracted teenager.

"That was close! But damn, Archer, you can ride a horse!" Hank bellowed as he rode past Archer, toward his father and their ranch hands who were cutting cows from the rounded-up stragglers.

ARCHER HAD BEEN LOBBYING HIS FATHER FOR YEARS TO GET A color TV, but it was his mother who'd used her money from teaching the year before to buy their new GE Porta-Color television—or the "monstrosity" as his father called it. Joe Bob had relented to placing the TV on the counter in the kitchen, and Archer would sometimes catch him watching *Bonanza*. Father and son would laugh together because it was kind of ridiculous —a rancher watching a TV show about ranching. On weekday evenings, Joe Bob commandeered the television to watch the nightly news. He was radically opposed to the U.S. presence in Vietnam, just as President Kennedy had been. So the television remained.

The first show Archer and his mother had watched together was *Color Me Barbra*, a CBS special featuring Barbra Streisand singing her entire album of the same name. It was the TV event of March 1966, and Archer and Nancy loved it. Archer drank a cold bottle of Coca-Cola, and his mother sipped instant decaffeinated coffee. The two didn't say a word, each captivated by Streisand's performance. His mother's face was transfixed as

Streisand sang her version of "Any Place I Hang My Hat Is Home." For Archer, it was the star's version of Chopin's "Minute Waltz" with her funny lyrics. What a piece of music! Chopin had dedicated the waltz to one of his students, with whom he was madly in love. It made Archer think you could write music for any feeling or emotion. He firmly believed that music came from experience, of which he seemingly had none. He knew that the composition of music was almost mystical, formed by different instruments playing in congruence.

When the show ended, he stared wistfully at the television, wishing *Color Me Barbra* could go on and on. "Mama, do you think maybe someday I could write a piece of music like that Chopin waltz?" he asked. "You know he dedicated it to a student who he fell in love with, charmed by her beauty and vision and intellect. I need to meet a girl like that; I need to have experiences, Mama. I think I need to do something, go somewhere different than here. You know I love the open country and the canyon and the animals, but I need to see the world. I need to hear more music."

From then on, Nancy and Archer watched every program with musical guests or performances. One of their favorites was Leonard Bernstein's *Young People Concerts,* and they hadn't missed any of them.

On the night of the spring roundup, Nancy reminded Archer over dinner that another *Young People's Concert* was scheduled for that evening. After Archer helped his mother with the dishes, they tuned into the program, which featured a young cellist, soprano, and pianist joining the New York Philharmonic conducted by Bernstein.

After the show ended, Nancy had to wait for her son to process what they'd just seen and heard. "Well, son, what did you think?"

Archer finally opened his eyes and said dreamily, "Mama, that was extraordinary. I really want to go to New York to see

Bernstein and hear all kinds of music. Can't we go see Aunt Irene this summer?"

Nancy had heard this before. Archer was constantly asking his mother to let him travel to places beyond Dallas or Houston for music and arts and experiences. New York City was the destination he asked for most often. Irene was Nancy's mother's youngest sister, who'd married a corporate oilman and moved to New York. Irene had extended an open invitation to Nancy and her family to visit whenever they wanted. "Archer, look at me, son."

He trained his liquid brown eyes on hers, and she thought she might lose her breath once again at his fragile beauty. "I'll talk with your father about it. I know he'd like to hear some jazz, and you and I both want to go to Carnegie Hall and Lincoln Center. But we might have to wait another year or two so we can save up for a trip like that."

He jumped up from the barstool he was sitting on. "Oh, Mama, really, really? That would make me soooo happy!" He let loose with a roundup-worthy whoop. "Dad can get Roberto to run the ranch. It will be fine. When we go, can we stay for a month or two? I want to visit Juilliard too and the other music schools, maybe the Brooklyn Academy of Music. I'd love to study music in New York someday."

Her son's joy filled the room. Nancy decided to talk to Joe Bob about getting their son out of the Panhandle and giving him some of the experiences he longed for. "I will talk to your father. It might not be this summer, but I'll see what we can do. Now, go practice your piano. And don't forget, you still need to write a 'Minute Waltz' for me!"

11

ARCHER

ARCHER WAS DREADING ANOTHER BASKETBALL GAME. HIS FRIENDS and teammates were pumped up about it, but he did not care. He said nothing all day, thinking more about Chopin's Nocturne in E-flat major, the piece he was supposed to be practicing for the high school spring recital.

Once the game started, the squeak of sneakers on polished wood echoed through the crowded gymnasium. Archer, who was super lanky compared with his more developed friends, darted down the court, pushing his floppy dark hair, his eyes frantically searching for an open teammate. The smell of sweat and floor wax filled his nostrils, a scent he'd never quite gotten used to.

"Mueller! Over here!" shouted Jimmy Tanner, the team's center, waving his arms wildly.

Archer hesitated, then lobbed the ball in Jimmy's direction. It sailed over Jimmy's outstretched fingers, nearly landing out of bounds before another teammate snatched it from the air.

Coach Gillespie's gravelly voice boomed from the sidelines. "Come on, Mueller! Get your head in the game!"

Archer nodded, but his mind was still replaying the nocturne. His fingers twitched, longing for the cool touch of ivory keys instead of the rough texture of the basketball.

The crowd's cheers grew louder when the opposing team scored again. Archer's teammates shot him pointed looks. They were down by two points with less than a minute left on the clock.

"Time out!" Coach Gillespie bellowed, gesturing for the team to huddle around him.

As Archer jogged over, he caught sight of his parents in the stands. Joe Bob was on his feet, red-faced and shouting encouragement. His mother sat quietly; her worried eyes fixed on Archer.

"All right, boys," Coach Gillespie said, his voice low and intense. "We've got one last play. Mueller, you're our point guard. We need you to take the shot."

Archer's stomach churned. "But Coach, I—"

"No buts, son. You've got this. Now get out there and win this game!"

The whistle blew, and Archer found himself back on the court, the ball in his hands. The crowd's shouts faded to a dull hum as he dribbled, searching for an opening. Ten seconds left. Five.

He jumped, the ball leaving his fingertips. Time seemed to slow as it arced through the air, falling short of the basket. In a desperate lunge, Archer leaped after it, arm outstretched, as he fell headlong into the windowed door behind the goal.

A sickening crack filled the air as his hand smashed through the windowpane. Pain exploded through his fingers, and he crumpled to the ground, cradling his bloodied hand.

The gymnasium erupted into chaos. Coach Gillespie was at his side in an instant, carefully examining the wound. "It's deep," he muttered, quickly wrapping Archer's hand in a towel. "We need to get him to the hospital."

As they rushed him off the court, Archer caught snippets of conversation from his parents, who had hurried down from the stands.

"Will he be able to play in the next game?" his father asked anxiously.

His mother's voice was sharper, more concerned. "Joe Bob, for heaven's sake! What about his piano recital?"

Hours later, Archer sat on a hospital bed, his bandaged hand resting on his lap. The doctor, a kindly man with graying hair, addressed his parents. "The tendon in his middle finger was severely damaged," he explained gently. "We can perform surgery, but I'm afraid Archer won't be able to play basketball or the piano at a high level again."

The words hit Archer like a physical blow. Basketball, he could live without. But the piano? Music was his passion. Tears welled up in his eyes as he imagined a future without the comfort of Chopin or the challenge of Beethoven.

His father's face fell. "No more basketball? But he was just starting to improve!"

"Joe Bob," Nancy said, her voice thick with emotion. She turned to Archer, placing a comforting hand on his shoulder. "I'm so sorry, sweetheart. I know how much your music means to you."

Archer nodded, unable to speak. As his parents continued to talk with the doctor, he stared out the window. His dream of playing before packed concert halls and receiving standing ovations was slipping away like sand through his fingers.

Yet, as he watched the sky turn a brilliant orange, a small part of him felt a flicker of relief. No more pretending to care about basketball. No more disappointing his teammates or his father. Perhaps, he thought, this was an ending, but it could also be a beginning. Of what, he wasn't sure yet.

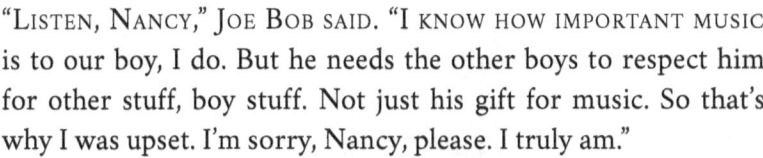

"Listen, Nancy," Joe Bob said. "I know how important music is to our boy, I do. But he needs the other boys to respect him for other stuff, boy stuff. Not just his gift for music. So that's why I was upset. I'm sorry, Nancy, please. I truly am."

From the living room, Archer overheard his father apologizing in the kitchen, for what Archer didn't know. But he was apologizing anyway.

"Ok, thank you, I hear you. But it's like you don't see him at all. Basketball isn't his focus—it never was. He did that to please you. And now, well, we need to refocus our attentions for him; he won't be going to college on a music scholarship, but there are other avenues for him." She paused to take a swig of the whiskey Joe Bob had poured for her. It had been a stressful day for them all. Nancy wasn't much of a drinker, but she needed a shot after a hard day.

Archer heard his mother's tone change, and he knew she had a new idea forming. "Let's finally do it. Let's plan a trip to New York to see Aunt Irene and Uncle John. We could all use a change of scenery, and it would be wonderful to experience the city. You need to get some more perspective on things too. I bet there are people in New York who loved Kennedy like you did, who hate the Vietnam War. People who don't believe in the separation of the races, but in equality, like you do. It will do you good to focus on something else other than the ranch. Plus, Archer needs to see what New York has to offer. He's meant for bigger things, and you know it."

Joe Bob looked surprised, and took a deep drink from his own glass as he mulled over her idea. "I think you are right—we need to get away. After Archer's accident and us leaving church, I think we all need a reset button. I'd love to go hear Muhammad Ali speak out against the war and the damned draft. Maybe he'll be in the city."

"Oh, Joe Bob, we weren't the first and we won't be the last to leave the church. It's not like we left God; we just decided that the Methodists were our speed. Plus, they needed a good choir director." Nancy went over to her husband and hugged him.

Their family leaving the First Baptist Church had been the talk of the town. Many people agreed with their reasons, but remained behind with the odious Pastor Griswold. Joe Bob tended to keep his views to himself, preferring to put them into practice rather than simply talking about them. Their ranch manager was Roberto, a vaquero from Mexico who'd come up twenty-five years ago and never went back. Roberto's whole family lived in Canyon now, and the Mueller ranch employed more Mexican Americans than any other ranch in the area. And in 1960, when many in the county had refused to vote for John F. Kennedy because he was Catholic, Joe Bob had been proud to vote for him. Archer would never forget his father weeping in November 1963 when the president was assassinated. Joe Bob was respected enough to have different views and was man enough that no one said anything to him about being different.

Archer wished his father could realize just how alike they were. Archer was different from his classmates, except for his best friends Hank and Wes. He cared nothing for sports, especially football. All he thought about was music. Like his father, his thoughts were not akin to those of his contemporaries.

Archer had to focus; his hand needed to heal. His mother was devastated he wouldn't be able to play the piano like he used to, but Archer would still be able to play something. Wouldn't he? That's what mattered. The doctor said he'd get some use of his hand back, but the prolonged use of his injured finger, once it healed, would cause him pain. He hoped he could still piano, even in small sessions, and maybe even try the drums.

A couple of weeks after his injury, Hank plopped down next to Archer at the cafeteria and dove into his packed lunch.

Between mouthfuls, he said. "Want to hike the canyon on Sunday morning? I hear the Goodnight bison herd has had some calves, and I wanna try and photograph them for the school paper."

Hank was an excellent photographer, and one of their favorite things to do together was catch sunrises at Palo Duro Canyon. It was there that Archer started to hear the music of nature. The wind was an oboe; the call of the eagle, a violin. Yes, he needed to go back and bring his notebook so he could jot down all the music he heard and turn it into a score in his heart. Plus, he wondered what the baying of a bison calf sounded like. Maybe that would be a low bass drum with a trumpet lifting. "I'd love that. I've been going stir-crazy lately, and I'm tired of my mom watching me like a hawk. How many calves, do you know?"

"I'm not sure, but if we get there early, we might catch them drinking at the Third Falls at South Cita Canyon. But we gotta leave super early. You okay with that?"

Hank was obsessed with light, Archer was obsessed with sound, and both of them were obsessed with the canyon. "Sure. And now that I'm allowed to drive to school, I'll pick you up a little after four." When he turned fifteen, Archer's dad gave him his old Ford F150, and he quickly became the designated driver for Hank and Wes, not to mention helping to maneuver Wes's wheelchair and Hank's cameras and tripods. He didn't mind at all, because the driver always picked the radio station.

"Great. And let's see if Wes wants to come with us. I'll get my mom to make some donuts for us." Hank grinned, knowing full well how much Archer loved his mother's donuts.

Archer smiled. "Yum! I'll get my mom to whip us up some pigs in a blanket, and I'll bring some coffee."

Sunday morning couldn't come soon enough; Archer wanted to hear the sound of those calves.

Their trip to the canyon that Sunday paid off in more ways

than any of them expected. They did see the bison calves, and Hank's photos were featured on the front page of the next edition of the school paper.

For Archer, the canyon reminded him about the way he thought about music, how all-encompassing it was to him. Like a composer, yes, exactly like a composer. His injury did nothing to inhibit him from making a score out of everything he heard. In fact, it was all amplified for him on that trip. On the way home, he realized that that would be his focus now. Maybe in New York he could meet with a composer, someone like Steve Reich, the visionary genius who'd revolutionized what composing could be. What if Archer wrote to him before their trip? Maybe the man would meet with him.

Yes, that was his answer.

Composing.

12

ARI

Ari's first summer at Interlochen had gone so well that his grandmother and his parents agreed to let him return the next year and then for his third time in the summer of 1969. Ari did not miss the Texas heat; in fact, he wasn't missing anything about Texas. Everything about the camp was perfect—the weather, the food, the people, and, of course, the music. Interlochen was a heaven on earth for musical kids. Ari considered it a real gift to be there. But he did not say that in his letter home. Instead, he wrote:

> Dear Bubbe,
>
> Your donation to the camp for us to have kosher food is, as they say, a "godsend." There are many more Jewish campers this summer as compared to my first summer. Many are from New York, a few from Milwaukee, and more from Chicago.
>
> I have so many invitations to visit friends in the fall. I'd love to see New York and visit my friend Noah Templos. His

father went to the Samuel Rubin Israel Academy of Music in Tel Aviv and is now the first chair cello for the New York Philharmonic. Noah's dad has invited all of us to come see them perform. If we can make a trip of it, we have a place to stay with Noah's family. Something to consider!

Love,

Ari

Never had Ari made such a fast and strong friendship as he had with Noah. Both young men spoke multiple languages, but music was their unifying force. Noah didn't mind Ari's slight Texas twang, even when they spoke in Yiddish.

Many of the other campers considered Ari to be different, and not just because he spoke with a Texas twang. It quickly became apparent that Ari was musically their superior, which led to some jealousy, to say the least. The summer before, it had taken only a couple of weeks before he was selected to conduct their camp orchestra, beating out several older candidates. When he returned for his second camp, the director had appointed him as the conductor without holding any formal tryouts.

Ari was by no means a show-off; in fact, he was the opposite. He tried to play down the fact that he could play almost every orchestra instrument. And this year, as he'd done the previous summer, Ari had worked as a conductor with each section: the strings, the woodwinds, the brass, and percussion. But this summer, he would be conducting the performance of the high school orchestra at Les Préludes, the final concert on the last evening of camp.

Noah's parents and Ari's family were all coming for Les Préludes. Ari was trying his best to be laser-focused; he wanted everything to be perfect. If Noah's father could put in a good word for him with the Rubin Academy, that could improve his chances of being admitted. That would not only make Bubbe happy, but it would be a dream to study at one of the best music schools in the world.

At the middle of the second week of the camp, students were scattered around the Interlochen Bowl, the campus's historic outdoor performance venue, holding instruments or sheet music. Snippets of Bach and Mozart carried through the air, along with the gentle susurration of waves from Green Lake. Clusters of teenagers practiced harmonies, while others sat under the trees, rehearsing solos or duets.

As the conductor, Ari stood on the stage of the Bowl and waved his baton, gesturing energetically to campers of all ages to take their seats so they could rehearse. His wavy dark hair flopped into his eyes over and over, and every time he brushed it back, some of the musicians assumed he was signaling to them to start the first number. The disjointed burst of the opening startled Ari, who frantically waved them.

Noah laid his cello on the floor and approached Ari. "Here, take this," he said, handing him a bandana to tie back his curls.

Ari smiled. "Thank you, Noah." Once he'd fastened the bright red cloth to his head, all one could see was his intense gaze indicating his focus. Once everyone was seated, he raised his baton. As the orchestra started, Ari's hands shaped the music, despite the fact that his mind wasn't fully on Brahms. No, it was on Annalisa Goldfarb, the beautiful first-chair violinist.

Lisa's shiny black hair perfectly brushed her shoulders as she moved with the grace of a ballet dancer with her bow, as if music was weaving itself into her being. Whenever she played a particularly difficult run, her lips would curve into a small smile and she would look up to her conductor, her gold-flecked brown eyes sparkling.

Ari was distracted, to say the least. He caught Noah's eye, and his friend smirked. Noah knew the truth before Ari did.

Ari berated himself to focus on the percussion section

beating a drum roll on the air, trying to get Milton Ayers from Detroit to return to the beat. At the same time, he was doing his best to not steal another look into those gold-flecked eyes. *Ari, you're here for music, this music. Do not let a girl lead you astray.*

No matter how hard he tried, no matter what mistakes he allowed, Lisa's presence was distracting, overwhelming, and captivating. Ari tried. Harder. The sound of the orchestra rose and fell, but in his mind, the beauty of Brahms was colored by Lisa's image. A girl who, unknowingly, had become his muse.

As the rehearsal continued, his precision had dulled, and his baton occasionally faltered in midair. Ari made mistakes—subtle ones. But mistakes nonetheless. This summer at Interlochen was supposed to be about his musical future, but Lisa was threatening to derail his carefully laid plans.

Unbeknownst to Ari, Lisa Goldfarb was equally entranced. It was impossible not to notice the young conductor from Texas. He was a genius—everyone said so. Lisa thought he was magnetic. As the orchestra launched into the Brahms symphony, she pretended to concentrate on her violin, but her heart was more than aware of Ari's intense brown eyes and long arms. Lately, she'd sensed something different in his movements —uncharacteristic hesitations and moments where his usual meticulousness wavered. Was he under pressure? Or was he, like her, all too aware of something else? She knew Ari was a prodigy; someone destined for great things; but, seeing him falter, even just slightly, made Lisa realize he might not be as composed as he should be. Strangely, it was this vulnerability that endeared him to her more.

She occasionally glanced up and locked eyes with Ari. She couldn't read his stare—was she messing up? Lisa could feel a blush crawling up her cheeks as she struggled to regain her confidence and equilibrium. Was he watching her, or was he just focused on the music?

Lisa was not someone who ever wanted to stand out. She preferred to let the violin speak for her. But her instrument could not deflect Ari's attention from her.

After the rehearsal ended, Lisa went to the cafeteria to write a letter home to her father. She filled him in on her musical progress, but she also wanted to assure him that she was saying her prayers and keeping kosher—after all, he was a rabbi. She'd overheard one of the counselors saying that someone had provided an endowment for the camp to order food from the kosher bakery in Grand Rapids, and the kosher meals the cafeteria now served was one of the reasons her father had agreed to let her return. Lisa was grateful for the kosher snack tray, especially the apple cake, which became her daily late-afternoon treat.

After she finished her letter, she found herself musing over Ari and his glances, not entirely sure what she made of his attentions. Part of her felt flattered, but another part of her was cautious. Interlochen was supposed to be about music, about becoming better musicians, and a distraction like Ari and his smoldering eyes would complicate things.

NOAH CONFRONTED HIM AFTER REHEARSAL, NOT TO CHIDE HIM over a poor performance, but to tell him to just talk to the girl. "C'mon, you can do it. There is nothing to be shy about. You are both musical, both Jewish, both driven, and you both obviously love being here. You have loads in common. Just say hello or you play well, or something. If you don't, we are gonna blow that last recital for our parents, and all of us will blame you."

Noah was joking, Ari was sure. Nonetheless, his words hit home. Ari just had to buck up and talk to her. He spent the rest of the afternoon walking around Green Lake and couldn't stop thinking about her eyes. When he made it back to his starting point on the campus, Ari was thirsty, so headed to the cafeteria. There, as if by some miracle of the gods, was Lisa, eating apple cake from his grandmother's kosher snack tray. Ari took a deep breath as he whispered, "Thank you, Bubbe, for being so devout," then walked to Lisa's table, his footsteps seeming to pound on the wooden floor. She was reading a book and didn't seem to notice.

"Hey, Lisa," Ari said, his voice cracking. "Um, do you like the apple cake?"

She nodded, shyly. "Yeah. And this one is actually better than my grandmother's, but don't tell her I said so." Her smile was magnificent.

"Well, I guess you have me or, rather, my grandmother to thank for it."

She looked puzzled. "Did she bake it and send it all the way from Texas?"

Wow! She knows I'm from Texas, he thought before replying. "No, no. She paid for all the kosher food to be here this summer. It was the only way she'd let me come—well, that and attending Shabbat services with the visiting rabbi." He was relieved that his voice sounded like his own again.

Lisa seemed shocked. "You won't believe this, but the only reason my father let me come back this year was because of the kosher food. He's a rabbi, and there was no way he was going to let me almost starve again."

She smiled again, and Ari's heart raced. *Thank you, thank you, thank you, Bubbe,* he said again in his heart. "When you meet my grandmother at Les Préludes, you can tell her. She loves to be proven right. After my first summer here, I told her Noah and me would be the only Jews the next year, but I was again proven wrong. She was right, at least about the kosher food."

Lisa motioned for him to sit down. "Well, I will tell her

thank you for sure, and I am sure my dad will too. Would you like some cake?" She broke off a piece and handed it to him.

He caught a whiff of her shampoo, which was like minty strawberries. "Mmmm, thank you." He swallowed. "You, well, I just wanted to say ... you're incredible on the violin. The way you play—it's ... it's amazing."

"Thank you, Ari. I think you're pretty incredible yourself. Everyone's been talking about what an amazing conductor you are."

Ari shifted in his seat, awkwardly scratching the back of his neck. "Thanks, but ... I don't know. I feel like I haven't been as focused lately. I keep getting ... distracted."

Lisa raised an eyebrow, as if to ask what could possibly distract a prodigy like him.

That's when Ari hesitated. He was dangerously close to revealing the truth about the source of that distraction. He cleared his throat and smiled. "Anyway, I was wondering if ... well, maybe you'd like to—I don't know—go over some of the music together? I'd love to hear more of what you're working on with the strings."

For a second, Lisa looked at him, weighing something in her mind. Then she nodded, her eyes lit, the gold more pronounced. "Sure, that sounds great. Maybe tomorrow after rehearsal?"

Ari grinned, but then opted to play it cool. "Yeah, tomorrow. After rehearsal. Yeah, that sounds perfect."

THE NEXT DAY, ARI COULDN'T FIGURE OUT WHAT HE WOULD SAY to Lisa. The orchestra sounded good, better than good. It was a blessing to be here with so many kids that loved music like him. Going over the overture again, he caught himself once again making small mistakes and missing cues. It was antici-pation. Nothing more. He knew his talent and ability were being tested by Lisa. *Focus, only twenty minutes more,* he told himself.

When rehearsal finally ended, Ari gathered up his score sheets, barely saying goodbye to the other musicians. He caught Lisa's eye from across the room. A small wave of nerves rippled through him. After so many rehearsals watching her from afar, he was about to have her all to himself—no orchestra, no distractions, just the two of them.

They walked together to the practice cabins, which were a bit tucked away from the main campus, and found a bench surrounded by the tall pines. Lisa took out her violin.

Ari had no idea where to start or how to act—he was still rattled by her and not at all himself.

"So," Lisa broke the silence. "Which piece do you want to go over?"

Ari clears his throat, gathering himself. "Actually, I was thinking ... maybe something different. Something spontaneous?"

Lisa quirked her eyebrow at him again. "Spontaneous, huh? What did you have in mind?"

He stared down at her violin, then glanced back up to meet her eyes. "Play something for me. Anything. Whatever you feel like."

For a moment, she stared at him, as if trying to figure him out. Then she shrugged and smiled. "Alright, but don't laugh if it's something weird." She lifted her violin to her shoulder, closed her eyes for a moment, and then played. It was not anything from the repertoire they had been rehearsing—it was soft, slow, and melancholic. Her fingers moved delicately across the strings, her bow gliding with a smooth elegance. The melody was haunting, filled with a quiet longing.

Ari was mesmerized by the way the notes seemed to flow straight from her heart. For those few minutes, the world narrowed to Lisa and her music. Ari forgot everything else and lost himself in the music and the sight of her playing with such beauty and intensity.

When Lisa stopped, her cheeks were flushed and there was a glint of vulnerability in her eyes. "So, what do you think, maestro?" she asked softly, a slight nervousness in her.

Ari swallowed twice, trying to find his voice. "That was … incredible. You're incredible. I don't recognize the piece. Who is it?"

"It's from *Barefoot in the Park*. The composer is just a genius, and it's one of my favorite films. Even though it's about a couple of newlyweds in New York, it reminds me of growing up in Chicago." She smiled shyly, as if sharing something personal was an overstep. "Sorry, I mean … you know that right? I'm from Chicago. It must be strange, you being from Texas and me a city girl from Chicago. We're so different."

"Not at all. We are both Jewish, we both love music, and we both want to be the best at what we do. I see us as almost the same."

Lisa laughed out loud as she thought just the opposite. This beautiful young man was from an oil-rich family in Texas who spoke Hebrew with the funniest accent she'd ever heard. She was from the heavily Jewish West Rogers Park neighborhood in Chicago where her father was rabbi. But when she looked up at him to respond, her face softened. Maybe he was right, they were both so committed to their music and their faith. Lisa just stared at Ari, stunned again by his natural beauty.

After a moment of silence, Ari took the risk, even though his heart was pounding and his mouth was dry. "Lisa," he started, his voice a little shaky, "I know I've been distracted lately. And I think … I think it's because of you."

She blinked, taken aback, and said nothing.

Ari pressed on, the words spilling out faster now. "You're all I've been able to think about the last few weeks. During rehearsals, during the concerts, it's like I … I just can't focus.

You've completely thrown me off my game, but in the best way possible. I've never met anyone like you."

The air between them was still. Lisa's expression was unreadable, and Ari felt a rush of panic—did he just ruin everything?

But then Lisa slowly smiled, her eyes softening. "You noticed *me?*" she asked, her voice gentle but amused.

Ari rubbed the back of his neck. "How could I not?"

"I thought maybe … you were just focused on the music. I didn't know I could distract someone like you."

Ari shook his head, his curls hiding his eyes briefly until he shoved them back. You're all I've been able to think about. It's impossible to focus when you're there, playing like that. It's like the music's coming from you, not the violin."

Lisa's heart swelled, but she managed to whisper, "I've noticed you too, Ari Rosenbaum. You're kind of hard to miss."

They sat in silence, both feeling as if everything had been said between them.

Eventually, Lisa stood up and put her violin back in its case.

Ari rose. "What happens now, Lisa?"

"Now, you kiss me, Ari Rosenbaum. You kiss me."

The late summer sun cast a shadow through the Bowl on the evening of Les Préludes. With the falling light, the Star of David on Lisa's delicate neck shimmered as she rosined her bow. She glanced surreptitiously toward Ari, nestled back in the green-room doorway, his fingers absently touching the mezuzah he'd hung there at the beginning of camp. Their eyes met. Lisa smiled quickly, thinking of their weeks of shared Shabbat dinners, stolen glances during services with the visiting rabbi, and quiet conversations by the lake about music, faith, dreams—plus kissing. So much kissing. The two could barely hide their feelings any longer. The whole camp buzzed with gossip about their romance. Not only were they two of the best musicians at camp, but they were also leaders—Ari because of his musical genius and Lisa because of her incredibly kind heart.

In the audience, Rabbi David Goldfarb sat beside his wife, Rosa, his shiny black kippah distinctive among the crowd. Next to them, Ari's parents fidgeted with their programs, while his grandmother sat regally in her reserved seat, her elegant dress a reminder of her wealth. Few of the campers were privy to the fact that it was her generosity behind the kosher meals and the peaceful Shabbat services.

When Ari walked out to the conductor's podium, the crowd applauded, and Lisa's heart fluttered. His white button-down Oxford shirt gleamed under the stage lights. She thought of the first time they spoke and how shy he was. But only at first. His timidity, although endearing, had vanished. He was, without a doubt, one of the most confident boys she'd known and the most beautiful. His floppy hair was still in his eyes, despite him trying to slick it back with Brylcream. As he raised his baton, she smiled, delighted that the young conductor some called a young Bernstein was hers.

The first movement of Brahms's Symphony no. 4 in E minor flowed out like prayer, with the strings and brass weaving together in perfect harmony. They'd been practicing it all summer, and at the last rehearsal Lisa thought it finally sounded alive, visceral. Her violin sang under her bow; she felt Ari's direction like a tangible force, guiding every note.

During intermission, Tanya Rosenbaum turned to Rabbi Goldfarb and said, "Please let me introduce myself. I'm Tanya Rosenbaum. I noticed your daughter's name in the program, and presume you are Rabbi Goldfarb of Temple Sholom in Chicago?"

The rabbi's face lit up. "Yes, I am. You must be related to that marvelous young conductor!"

Tanya smiled proudly. "Ari Rosenbaum is my grandson. And if I recall, your temple has a connection to Kibbutz Masada."

Rosa jumped in. "That is our temple's sister kibbutz in Israel! How do you know of it?"

"A close relative teaches at Tel Aviv University, and he has mentioned that the kibbutz is connected to the music department."

"Indeed! The kibbutz has close ties with the Samuel Rubin Music Academy. Our Lisa has been dreaming of going there after high school."

"Please, tell us of your relative at the university," Rosa said. "Perhaps we have met him."

The three of them proceeded to chat amiably about Israel, the university's music program, and the kibbutz until the ushers asked them to take their seats.

Jacob and Ruth exchanged worried glances. They were both concerned about Tanya pushing Ari to go overseas to study music. Israel was a long way from Texas, and considering the rising conflicts between Israel and its neighbors, Ari's parents had every right to be worried. Tanya had been a huge supporter of the Six-Day War in 1967, sparking many discussions over their dinner table about the idea of sending Ari to such a volatile part of the world to study music. Although Tanya insisted there would eventually be a resolution to the ongoing conflict, Ruth and Jacob were uneasy about letting their only child go to Israel. Ari's parents were grateful he'd been at Interlochen for the last three summers and had missed out on all of the debates at home.

The second half of the program featured the piece that inspired the name of the concert: Franz Liszt's symphonic poem "Les Préludes." Ari conducted his orchestra as if he was living every note of the music, sweating, and moving like a lion attacking its prey. It was something to behold. He was truly lost in his own genius. The crowd sat silent with wonder. Lisa's violin wove through the symphony like a golden thread, her notes speaking of something deeper than mere melody. Both families watched their children create something beautiful together.

After the final notes faded and Ari received a standing ovation, the families gathered in the reception hall. Rabbi Goldfarb observed Ari and Lisa standing close together. "You know," he said quietly to Jacob and Ruth, "our Kibbutz Masada isn't just any kibbutz. It's become a haven for young musicians. Protected, nurturing. A place where one can study both the Torah and Tchaikovsky." He paused as his daughter and Ari shared a quiet laugh. "And its security is unparalleled."

Tanya placed her hand on her son's shoulder. "Sometimes our children must follow both their hearts and their heritage. And sometimes that involves great change. And now our Ari, with his desire to be with his people in Israel and be amongst some of the greatest musical teachers in the world, will be one to forge a new path for the Rosenbaums."

Ruth started to disagree with her mother-in-law, but then she looked over at her son. His hands were interlaced with Lisa's, their eyes locked together, and she knew, right then, her son's heart was captured. If this young woman was going to Israel, then there was no power in the universe that would stop him from joining her. Ruth turned to the rabbi. "Tell me more about this kibbutz, the one your temple is associated with."

Ari and Lisa stood by the lake later, their reflection rippling in the dark water as the sliver of the late summer moon twinkled in the night sky. Lisa rested her head on Ari's chest and entwined her fingers in his unruly curls. He touched the Star of David around his own neck—a mirror to hers—and they both knew that this summer's end was just their beginning.

13

ARCHER

The sirens of Amsterdam Avenue drifted up to Aunt Irene's pre-war apartment like distant trumpets, and Archer closed his eyes, letting the city's chaos arrange itself into melody. His fingers tapped against the windowsill—not the same as they did on the Steinway in Aunt Irene's music room, but the music in his head was the same. Archer had been working on his new melody at the piano for thirty minutes or so, which was about as long as his maimed hand would let him. The melody in his head played out some more, and he itched to add some snares to it and perhaps some horns. Six stories below, the summer evening continued to hum with possibility, different from the sounds of Palo Duro Canyon and the wind in Texas, but music just the same.

"Honey, your hand," Nancy interrupted him as she walked into the living room and saw Archer rubbing his damaged hand. The severed tendon had healed as well as it could, but they both knew he would never execute Rachmaninoff's third piano concerto as a first-rate pianist again. What his mother didn't know, not yet, was that he'd been filling notebooks with his own compositions, turning the wind through Palo Duro Canyon, the rippling of the wind across cotton fields, and the rhythmic clip of cattle hooves into symphonic movements. At the moment, he'd been coupling the sounds of Texas with New York taxis honking and steam rising from the subways into a sonata of his own.

Archer was still buzzing over the surprise his mother had arranged from him during their visit to Juilliard that morning.

He had to admit, he had been a bit down before they arrived. The letter he had sent to composer Steve Reich in care of Juilliard's Composition Department had been answered by a secretary who said that Mr. Reich would be out of the country during Archer's visit. She had, however, included a phone number to call to arrange a visit. When he and Nancy arrived at the school and got the grand tour, his mother had a surprise for him at their last stop, the Composition Department.

"Archer," she said, just as he thought their tour was ending. "Our tour isn't quite over. You have a meeting."

"A meeting? With who?"

Just then a distinguished gentleman with a brushy mustache emerged from an office. "Excuse me, young man. Are you Archer Mueller?"

Archer eyed his mother, who had a Cheshire Cat grin. "Um, yes, I am."

"I'm pleased to meet you, Archer. I am Andrew Thomas, the new head of the Composition Department. I hear that you might be coming to Juilliard and are a composer in the making. Let's talk in my office."

Archer was flabbergasted. The new head of the department was taking the time to talk with him, a mere high school student from Texas?

Nancy waved him on. "Go ahead, honey. I'll wait in the lobby."

He mouthed, "I love you, Mama," as he followed Mr. Thomas and proceeded to have his first-ever conversation with a real composer. That surprise had followed a magical event at Carnegie Hall the night before. Ravi Shankar's Festival From India had swallowed him whole. Shankar's sitar wove patterns Archer never imagined possible, each note bending time itself. Archer heard something familiar in the Indian classical master's improvisations—the same endless horizon he knew from home but transformed into sound. During intermission, he'd ducked into a bathroom stall and scribbled furiously in his pocket notebook: "Progressive time signatures for prairie wind section— 7/8 shifting to 5/4?" The whole performance made Archer realized that the music of all movement, of all landscapes, could be made manifest, and it was his true calling to make it happen.

That evening over another of Aunt Irene's splendid dinners, they each shared the highlight of their day. Archer and his mother had visited Juilliard that morning, and Archer couldn't stop talking about how wonderful the school was and his conversation with Andrew Thomas.

Joe Bob smiled as he listened to his son, pleased at how animated he was. He himself had had an interesting day with Uncle John. Back home in Texas, the only person he could talk to about his anti-war views was Daniel James, but in New York, he quickly realized he had a like-minded friend in Irene's husband. The two of them had gone to an anti-war meeting earlier that day, and he couldn't stop thinking about everything he'd heard there.

Nancy's own revelation had come that afternoon, when she and Irene had attended a women's march. "You should have seen these women, Archer! Burning their bras right there on the boardwalk. Made me remember that summer I wanted to wear pants to church, and Mama nearly fainted. I so wish Seraphina was here with me." She caught her breath and winked at Archer. "Sometimes you have to leave home to remember who you really are."

"Speaking of remembering," Irene interjected, "we need to finish up so we can catch a cab for the play."

ARCHER'S HEART KICKED HARD AGAINST HIS RIBS, THOUGH HE couldn't say why. The musical *1776* was the talk of Broadway, and Aunt Irene had gotten them the best tickets. The city kept doing this to him—throwing doors open before he even knew they were there to be opened.

Later, in the dark of the theater, Archer's attention wandered whenever the usher with the russet-colored curly hair and impossible cheekbones passed by. She moved like music herself, each gesture as precise as a conductor's. During intermission, while Irene and Nancy went to the ladies' room, she had caught Archer turning his playbill into staff paper and jotting down musical notes to the sonata he was hearing in his head.

"Composing?" she asked.

Archer nearly dropped his pencil. He looked up and noticed her name tag said "Barbara." He asked shyly, "Like Streisand?"

"I wish! I'm named after an aunt who ran away from the family years ago. My father always had an affinity for her independent spirit." Her voice was the most melodic one he'd ever heard.

They chatted briefly about the play, and when Barbara pointed out the rhythmic patterns in the dialogue, Archer was startled; he'd never met anyone who heard the world the way he did. So he had to ask, "Do you hear music, too?"

"Yes. I hear it mostly in words like poetry or lyrics." The

lights dimmed briefly, signaling the end of intermission. "I better get back to work."

Archer wanted desperately to continue the conversation with this intellectual beauty. "Can I get your address so I might write to you?"

She laughed heartily. "Most guys just ask for my number! What do you want, to be like a pen pal?"

"Something like that ... I don't live here in the city."

"You don't say!" she teased him, as she eyed his pressed Wrangler jeans and shined-up black snakeskin church boots.

"No, ma'am. I'm from Texas, a place you might think of as another planet, but a stunning one at that. I'm planning on coming back to the city to study music, but I'd love the opportunity to get to know you before I come back." Archer gave her his most open Texas grin.

Barbara smiled back. "I have never met anyone like you before. So ... yes. Yes, you may."

She reached for his pencil and playbill and wrote her address, next to his script of music inspired by Sherman Edwards's genius.

Archer carefully folded the playbill and placed it in his jacket pocket.

After the play, as he and his family walked up the aisle, he saw Barbara again.

"Write me soon!" she gave him a last brilliant smile.

Archer smiled shyly and patted the jacket pocket that held his new treasure.

ON THEIR LAST NIGHT IN NEW YORK CITY, THE MUELLERS ALONG with Irene and John sat at Big Wilt's Smalls Paradise in Harlem, a classic jazz joint owned by basketball star Wilt Chamberlain.

All of them were mesmerized by a quartet playing what the bassist called "freedom jazz."

Joe Bob nodded along, his foot tapping out the complex syncopations. Nancy watched her son, scribbling in his note-book, as if re-creating the scene in music.

"Dad?" Archer asked during a break. "I need to ask you something. I've talked to Aunt Irene a lot since we've been here, and she and I think it would be a good idea if I came here for college. I want to study composition at Juilliard." He pulled out his notebook, the pages dense with notation. "I've been hearing symphonies in my head since I was little. Not just playing them —but writing them. The ranch, the storms, the cattle drives … I want to turn it all into music people have never heard before."

The silence that followed felt like a Texas noon as Joe Bob reached for the notebook. His callused rancher's hands turned the pages slowly. "These marks here," he said finally, pointing to a passage marked "Prairie Dawn," "they're like that roll a horse gets into on a long ride, ain't they? When everything just flows?"

Nancy slid her hand into the crook of her husband's arm, and Archer saw tears in her eyes. "New York's got a way of showing you who you really are," she says softly. "All of us."

The jazz ensemble picked up again. Archer felt the damaged tendon in his hand throb slightly, but it didn't matter now. There were so many ways to make music, and he'd found his.

He took his notebook back from his father, turned to a fresh page, and wrote at the top: "Variations on an American Family —For Orchestra and City Sounds, 1969."

PART IV

THE COLLEGE YEARS

1971–1975

LETTER FROM KAROLINA
NOVEMBER 1971

To my babies who are no longer babies as you reach your nine-teenth birthday:

One of the delights of my life has been to write you a letter each year on your birthday and remember that you are both here and doing what you are doing because I brought you into this world.

I say this in all of my letters, but I pray that you, like me, have music. Music is my soul, my love, my heart that overflows with every note I play.

I've traveled the world, performing in many cultures, and learned that we must treasure the beauty and richness of not just the varied musical instruments, but also of vocal music throughout the world. For me, I always hear and play my piano. For me, it is the orchestra and its performance that presents the ultimate musical experience. People and instruments from all walks of life coming together to perform is peace in its rarest form.

But I can also hear the notes of nature. I hope, my children, that you too, sit out under the trees wherever you are and listen to the birds, all the while hearing music of the spheres.

I close by praying that in some way music in some form is part of your life. Even if I never know for sure, I will keep praying.

Know that I have never stopped loving you and hope that someday, by some miracle, we will meet again.

All my love,

Your mother

14

DANIEL AND DR. TOM
AMARILLO, TEXAS

IT HAD BEEN A SCORCHING TEXAS SPRING DAY, AND EVEN THE AIR-conditioning blasting inside the Petroleum Club's bar barely put a dent in it. Daniel could feel the sweat seeping through the back of his starched shirt as he nursed a whiskey and wondered what was keeping Dr. Tom. To pass the time, he watched Walter Cronkite on the old black-and-white TV perched above the bar. That evening's news focused on a new offensive by the North Vietnamese army and more continued anti-war protests in major American cites. Daniel was grateful to be in Amarillo, secretly relieved that all the violence and protesting was left to others.

As he watched the day's tally of the dead in Vietnam, he sent a silent prayer to God to express his gratitude that the young men he loved had not been sent to Vietnam. Danny Junior was in his sophomore year at Texas Tech University, which meant he was exempt from the draft, and Will and Mike were still in high school. His godson, Archer Mueller, was at the Juilliard

School in New York, studying composing. And Ari Rosenbaum was in Israel, studying conducting at Tel Aviv University and living in kibbutz. But all too many boys from the Texas Panhandle were joining up and dying in a jungle far away from home. Daniel was adamant that the United States had no business carrying on a war in Southeast Asia and needed to get out. Who cared what the world thought? Too many young men were dead on both sides.

Daniel was all too aware that he had a family to protect and a career to maintain. His opinions, well, he had to keep them to himself, except when he saw Joe Bob Mueller and Dr. Tom. All three of them opposed the Vietnam War and the ugly politics it invoked. Daniel could share his views with each of them, but they all had to be quiet in public.

He needed a reprieve from the horrifying news of the world and was looking forward to hearing all about Tom's latest adventure with Karolina, this time in the Soviet Union.

Once again, Tom had joined her on tour, this time visiting Leningrad, Poland, and Czechoslovakia. With help from Karolina and her manager, Dr. Tom had petitioned repeatedly for a visa to be able to go behind the Iron Curtain with her. The Soviet Union finally approved his visa after his third petition, a few weeks before his scheduled departure.

Daniel was just about to call the hospital to check on Tom when the doctor walked in, as thin as ever but with his hair a bit grayer and his face unshaven, which was quite out of character with his usually fastidious grooming habits. Daniel thought he resembled an intrepid explorer rather than a meticulous, thoughtful obstetrician.

Tom embraced him heartily. "Daniel, my friend, I have missed you! I'm sorry for not corresponding for the last two months, but traveling in the Eastern Bloc countries, well, it doesn't allow for much communication."

Daniel returned the hug. "Well, we have been a bit worried,

but I knew you would come back eventually. You said you were not ready to retire, not just yet."

Dr. Tom was well into his sixties now, but still fit and well. Daniel could probably take a page out of his friend's book and hike more and maybe get out of the office too. As always, he was only slightly jealous of his single friend and mentor's life. "Well, as you know, this country is trying to wear me out. I still love what I do, but I am seriously considering going back to charity work in another country to round out my career. I feel like, well, the USA hasn't really made a good name for herself out there in the world with this horrible action in Vietnam. I have much to tell you about the Soviet Union and Poland and Czechoslovakia." The barkeep came over and Tom pointed toward Daniel's whiskey. "I'll have what he's having, and bring another one for my friend."

They took their drinks and moved to a table under a fan. Tom regaled Daniel with stories about the stunning beauty of Leningrad, the stark realities of life in the Polish countryside, and the poor quality of life for the working classes of Czechoslovakia. The two men talked honestly about what Communism looked like in the countries where it was thriving.

Daniel asked, "Is it really necessary to try and stop Communism from gaining ground in Vietnam? Is that why our troops are there, killing and dying in ever-growing numbers?"

As always, Dr. Tom had the most loving, humane response. "My eyes saw what they saw beyond the Iron Curtain—the decaying remnants of once thriving empire that is now starving their people for gain at the top. There is no redistribution of wealth, as most citizens live in utter squalor. Their health care is a joke, and many are dying of neglect from their own governments. If anything, we should be trying to help the real people, rather than waging war. Despite all of that, the people who I saw, talked to, broke bread with, are intelligent, highly educated folks who just want a better life. And so many of them know more about music than I will ever know."

Daniel listened, enthralled, and hoped that once his young sons were out of the house, he and Elaine would be able to start traveling and seeing the world.

"So, enough about me, Daniel. How are Elaine and the boys?"

"Well, the biggest news, besides the fact that women can now be ministers in the Methodist Church, is that Danny Junior has decided on pre-law and has his heart set on going to law school at the University of Texas in Austin. I'm delighted, but Elaine is not—she would be perfectly happy to have him stay at Texas Tech and go to law school there. She loves that he comes home on most weekends, even though she complains about doing his laundry."

Tom chuckled. "And what about Will and Mike?"

"Well, Will thinks he wants to go into sports medicine at Tech. He was a student assistant for the football and basketball teams, so we'll see how that goes. And Mike is on the junior varsity basketball team and is planning to go out for track, since he's the athlete of the family. Which reminds me—Elaine wanted me to ask if you received the invitation."

"I did! I will not miss that. Any chance I can talk Will into going the pre-med route?"

"You have a green light from me to start that conversation. He's always worshipped the ground you walk on, so that might not be such a hard sell."

Daniel wished he could give Tom an update about the twins, who were both thriving in their music studies. Daniel thought back to when Archer came to him to ask for his help in persuading his father that he should go to Juilliard. The day Daniel drove out to the family's ranch, Joe Bob surprised him. The Muellers had just recently returned from a month in New York City, and Joe Bob had decided to not stand in his son's way, since his son's musical talent was just too great to ignore. Plus, as Joe Bob put it, "Archer doesn't have the stomach for ranching. He only has ears for song."

"Oh, before I forget," Tom interrupted Daniel's thoughts as he rummaged around his battered leather doctor's bag and pulled out a letter. "This is for your files. I know it's a bit early, but Karolina wanted you to have it." The doctor looked away, sipping his whiskey, his body language indicating that he wanted the conversation to change direction.

Daniel took the letter and slid it into his briefcase. "So, what kind of charity are you thinking of working for when you finally retire?"

"It's an arm of UNICEF, called Save the Mothers. I'll be in and out of Kenya, Botswana, and South Africa to start with. Karolina is helping as well; with all of the traveling she's done over the year, she knows how disproportionate maternal care is. But that means I'll probably be moving to London, probably by early fall. It's an easier place to be based out of for traveling to Africa, and Karolina has a flat there. But, I promise, I swear, I'll come back every year or so for one of our overnight hikes."

Daniel was not surprised by Tom's decision. He'd known for a while Dr. Tom was serious about Karolina and some kind of missionary work. It made sense. But Daniel was sad to know his friend would not be a part of his daily life anymore "Well, I'll hold you to it!" He held out his glass to say cheers, then continued. "You know, I want to travel more too. Once we get Mike off to college, I feel the urge—no, the calling—to help others as you do. Obviously, I don't have the medical skills, but I'm still strong and perhaps my legal knowledge can help my fellow man. So here is to our friendship and to our service."

The two men clinked their glasses together and talked of peace and service and their friendship.

15

ARCHER

After meeting Barbara Salinger during that memorable performance of *1776*, Archer had written her as soon as he got back home. A little over a week later, her reply arrived, and he was impressed—it was the work of a true wordsmith. Archer wrote her back and quickly received another magical letter from Barbara. They wrote every week through his junior and senior years, and when Archer received the news that he had been accepted at Juilliard, his parents allowed him to call Barbara. That started a string of monthly calls. With each passing exchange, they fell more in love. Not only was she the most beautiful girl he'd ever seen, but she was also the smartest.

In late August 1971, when he arrived at Grand Central Station, he was exhausted, overwhelmed, and thirsty. But he wasn't too tired to find a pay phone to make two calls: one to Aunt Irene, who told him to meet Uncle John at the station's landmark Oyster Bar, and the other to Barbara to let her know he'd arrived. He then found his uncle and celebrated with oysters and champagne.

When his uncle's chauffeur-driven black Lincoln Town Car pulled up in front of the walk-up on the Lower East Side, Archer's heart skipped a few beats. There was Barbara, waiting for him on the stoop. Girls back in Texas would never have been that forward, but Barbara was not only a New Yorker but a Brooklynite—bold, confident, and completely indifferent to what others thought. Aunt Irene had taken to her immediately, and they became fast friends. All they talked of was the feminist movement and the rights of women in the workplace and in the culture. Archer knew both his mother and Aunt Seraphina would be proud.

The two of them fell into a perfect rhythm with a unique respect for one another. Barbara wanted to be a playwright and was in her sophomore year studying theater at Barnard, with an eye on getting her MFA in playwriting at Columbia. She continued to work as an usher two nights a week at an off-Broadway theater. She'd gotten Archer a job as a ticket taker at a friend's community theater in Greenwich Village. Whenever Archer wandered to the subway stop after work, the remnants of Bob Dylan's folk scene were his soundtrack.

Archer was spellbound by Barbara and Manhattan. When they weren't at school or working, the two of them wandered all over Manhattan—listening to jazz, eating at funky delis, seeing avant-garde performances, and listening to experimental music. They always sought out the weirdest theater, the craziest music productions, and the quietest parts of the parks.

Going to Juilliard had been the right decision for Archer. Never had he been more challenged or felt more alive. Studying music, in all its variables, at one of the best schools in the country, had been the best choice he could have made. His advisor, Dr. Hoffman, who would guide him through his time at the school, had told him on his very first day that the composition program would be the making of him. At first, Archer thought the old man had it in for him, an injured pianist from Texas who had grown up on a ranch. But the two of them developed a mutual respect over their shared love of Antonin Dvořák. His *New World Symphony* was the score Archer wished he could have written. To say it was his touchstone would be an understatement.

Dr. Hoffman asked much of Archer, but perhaps his strangest request was young Archer learn the entire biography of every composer before he studied or played their music. Archer, who never left home without a spiral notebook and a pen, wrote down quotes about his favorite conductors and ideas he then would have about music. Among his discoveries was that Dvořák had been influenced by music he heard in the United States when he became the director of the National Conservatory of Music of America from 1892 to 1895. One of his favorite quotes was from Dvořák:

> I am convinced that the future music of this country must be founded on what are called black melodies. These can be the foundation of a serious and original school of composition, to be developed in the United States. These beautiful and varied themes are the product of the soil. They are the folk songs of America and your composers must turn to them.

Archer then jotted down what he knew about that quote:

> When Dvořák came to America in the 1890s he taught at a music school and he told the students, "Do not compose like me. Do not be like me. Instead listen, listen to the sounds around you. Listen to the sounds and the music of the peoples all around you, of native Americans, of African Americans, of other immigrant groups and

from that moment on, if you do this all the time, you will find your voice." … Active listening … Dvořák wrote of the wide-open spaces of America, such as the prairies of Iowa. This is what I hear when I think of the canyon at home, what I hear when I think of the baying of the calves for their mother. I hear the wide-open space of air between the skyscrapers of New York. But will I hear the sound of my symphony, of all the people I see on the streets, of the children I hear at the theater? Of the sounds I hear from home?

In April, he and Barbara decided the time had come for Archer to meet her family. So here he was, for the first time, crossing the East River to Brooklyn. When his fourth bus stopped at his destination, he looked up to see Coney Island's giant Ferris wheel dominating the view. He packed up his notebook and put his light jacket on, even though it was April. A chilly wind whipped in from the ocean and right through him as he disembarked. He was immediately bombarded with the smells—hot dogs and popcorn and diesel—and sounds of Coney Island—bells from various booths and rides, the dinging of a carnival game, and erratic *pop-pop-pops*. They made him think of Sergei Prokofiev's *Peter and the Wolf* and how the timpani represented the hunter's shots. What instrument could he use for the sound of the arcade games at Coney Island?

As he got off the bus, Barbara was there to greet him. "There you are, lost in thought, again. You are going to get run over one of these days, my love." She slipped her arm around his waist and led him along the sidewalk. "C'mon you. Mama and Papa are waiting, as are Bubbe and Saba, my cousins, my aunties and uncles. You better be ready for the Jewish third degree." Her glorious smile and those adorable freckles made him fall in love with her all over again.

"I was born ready! Your family has nothing on my Aunt Seraphina's third degree about the evils of the big city, I can promise you that."

They walked east on Surf Avenue toward her family's bakery, and Archer thought maybe a bassoon would capture a bus backfiring. The evening buzzed with life—the distant screams from the Cyclone, the tinny carousel music, the constant murmur of Russian, Hebrew, German, Yiddish, and English blending together like instruments in an urban symphony.

Archer stood at the edge of the Coney Island boardwalk; his eyes closed against the disappearing sun and his fingers twitching as he conducted an invisible orchestra playing his score.

"What do you hear, babe?" Barbara asked. "Tell me so I can hear it too."

He opened his eyes but kept his hands moving. "Everything. The waves are the cellos, deep and constant. The seagulls—that's the woodwinds, scattered and free. But the people, Barbara," he turned to her, his face alight, "the voices of the people, they're like a chorus speaking in tongues, rising and falling. There's so much history in those voices."

Barbara pulled out her own notebook from her bag, scribbling quickly. "That's exactly what I'm trying to capture in my new scene—the cacophony of voices. My grandmother's old walk-up was like that, a Tower of Babel, but somehow everyone understood each other's pain without words."

"Pain?" Archer's hands stilled. "I hear triumph in those voices. Like a major key emerging from minor chords."

She touched his arm, the silver bangles on her left wrist jingling. "That's why I love you, Texas boy. You hear the hope. I sometimes get too caught up in the tragedy." She gestured toward Nathan's Famous, where a cluster of elderly men argued animatedly over hot dogs. "See Mr. Abramowitz there? He lost his entire family in Treblinka. But every day he comes here, argues about baseball, eats a hot dog, and laughs. That's my next scene—finding joy in the aftermath."

Archer pulled her close, humming softly. "Let me write it with you. Not the words—the score. Something that captures both the sorrow and the survival."

"A Coney Island Symphony?" she teased, but her eyes were serious.

"Why not? Dvořák had his *New World Symphony*. This is a new world too, right here." He swept his arm across the vista of roller coasters and beach. "Your world. Teaching me that there's music in stories I never knew existed."

Barbara stood on tiptoe and kissed him, tasting salt air and possibility. "And you're teaching me that every story, even the darkest ones, can have a melody of hope." She pulled back, grinning. "Even if you still can't pronounce 'verklempt' properly."

"Hey now," he drawled, exaggerating his Texas accent. "I'm learning. Yesterday you only corrected my Yiddish twice."

Coney Island's neon lights flickered on, and Archer's fingers started moving again, capturing the moment in invisible notes. Barbara watched him transform her world into music, while in her mind, she was already setting this scene to paper—two artists bridging cultures with love and art, under the fading light of a Brooklyn sky.

As they walked down Mermaid Avenue, Barbara stopped to get a copy of the evening *New York Times* for her father.

"C'mon, you lazy lout!" Barbara pulled him into a quick embrace. "Fair warning—Papa's been pacing all morning, reading about Golda Meir's visit to Romania. He's in quite a state."

Before Archer could respond, the bell above the bakery door

chimed and a woman called out, "Barbara! Bring him in before he freezes!"

The warmth of the bakery enveloped them like a blanket. A transistor radio on the counter played Simon and Garfunkel's "Bridge Over Troubled Water" while four generations of Salingers arranged themselves in what was clearly a carefully orchestrated casual gathering. Behind the counter, Archer counted at least three aunts pretending to arrange pastries while stealing glances at him. Two teenage cousins sat at a corner table, arguing about whether they'd be allowed to go to the peace rally planned for next week.

Barbara's father, Emil, rose from his chair by the register, where he'd been marking passages in *Commentary* magazine. He was a tall man with wire-rimmed glasses and a stern face that broke into an unexpected smile. "So, this is the Texas virtuoso! Tell me, young man, what does your father think about Nixon? All of the hard-hat riots against the peace protesters remind me too much of the Brownshirts in Vienna."

"Abba," Barbara warned, but Emil waved her off.

"No, no, these are important times. When we left Vienna in 1932, we thought we'd seen the worst of nationalism. Now look —Jordan expelling the Palestinians, Nixon increasing bombing in Vietnam, the National Guard killing students at Kent State two years ago." He shook his head.

"Emil," his wife, Ruth, cut in, carrying a steaming pot of coffee. "The boy's just arrived. At least let him try my strudel before you recruit him for the revolution." She turned to Archer. "Barbara tells us you were at the peace moratorium last week. Good for you."

Barbara's grandmother pushed a plate of cookies toward him. "In Vienna, before the Anschluss, we had discussions like this in the cafes every day. Culture, politics, art—all one conversation. Now here, my grandchildren march in protests. Progress, *nu?*" Her accent was thick, almost incomprehensible to his Texas ears. Archer looked closely at her, remembering Barbara's account of her life. She had remained in Austria to run her famous bakery after all her children, sisters, and brothers had fled to America. She'd refused to leave her beloved Vienna even after the annexation of 1938. It was Barbara's father who had returned to Austria using an assumed name of an American banker and forced his mother to see the truth. Armed with fake visas, the two barely escaped out of Marseille on one of the last steamers to hold Jewish refugees. Two days after their departure, the German officials began sending all the remaining Jews of Austria off to a "work camp." Her family's apartment building, the bakery, and their wealth and possessions were seized by the Nazis. At eighty-three, she still talked as if her Vienna still existed and one day she would return.

"Speaking of culture," Barbara's Aunt Kara interjected, "what did you think of Bernstein's *MASS* at the Kennedy Center in Washington? Such controversy! The Catholics picketing, the critics divided."

"Lenny always stirs things up," Emil said fondly. "Remember when he had the Black Panthers at that party? The *Times* was scandalized." He turned to Archer. "You know, young man, this is what we lost in Vienna—this freedom to provoke, to question. Even if some call it radical chic."

As the evening progressed, they moved upstairs to the large apartment where Emil and Ruth lived. As Walter Cronkite murmured the latest casualty reports from Vietnam on the television, Archer found himself seated between Barbara's grandfather, who wanted to compare cattle ranching to the Hungarian agricultural cooperatives of his youth, and a cousin who taught music at Abraham Lincoln High School and had strong opinions about both Arnold Schoenberg and student boycotts.

"You should have seen our student walkout last week to protest the war," the cousin was saying. "We were singing 'Give

Peace a Chance' in the hallways. Some parents complained, but I told them music and protest have always gone together."

Emil looked up from the *Times* Barbara had given him. "Did you hear that Golda Meir's Kibbutz Merhavia is hosting our cousins from Spain? They are considering moving there permanently. I am not sure what to think. Meir is so dismissive of the Palestinians—she will have to answer someday for not recognizing them." He talked more of Israel, and Archer smiled and nodded his head, trying to take it in but knowing he would never understand.

"Abba thinks everything is political," Barbara said with a fond grin. "Even my theater workshop. He came to see my scene about the garment workers' strike and gave me three books about labor movements."

"Everything *is* political," Emil insisted. "Look at Israel right now—Meir talking peace while building settlements. Just like the Americans talking peace while bombing Cambodia. The same old story in new clothes." He sighed. "We thought after Hitler, the world would learn. But here we are in 1972, and what's changed? At least the young people are waking up. Your generation might do better than mine."

Ruth appeared with more coffee and rugelach. "Emil, you're overwhelming the boy. Let him tell us about his music. Although," she smiled at Archer, "in this family, even Mahler gets political analysis."

Archer, who had been quietly absorbing it all, straightened up. "Actually, I am writing a symphony, and I've been thinking about incorporating some of these themes into my work. The clash between tradition and protest, the way different voices can conflict and harmonize."

Emil leaned forward, interested. "Like composer Charles Ives? American chaos becoming American music?"

"More like ... " Archer closed his eyes, hearing the mixture of voices around him, the television's war reports, and the distant rumble of the subway. "Like a dialogue between generations. Between the Old World and the New. Between peace and violence. All in counterpoint."

When he opened his eyes, Emil was nodding slowly. "Good answer, young man. Very good. Now, what do you think about Henry Kissinger? And remember—in this family, we value honest debate."

The family leaned in, ready for another round of discussion that would likely last until midnight, when Emil would finally remember to ask Archer about his intentions toward his daughter, right after they finished analyzing Soviet policy in the Middle East.

THE BRISK SPRING AIR BIT AT THEIR CHEEKS AS THEY WALKED toward the bus stop. Barbara's arm was linked through Archer's, her body close against him. "Well," she said, a laugh bubbling up, "you survived the Salinger family inquisition."

Archer chuckled. "Your father didn't just interview me. He practically conducted a diplomatic summit." He mimicked Emil's accent. " 'So, what is your position on the Nixon doctrine in Southeast Asia? And by the way, what are your intentions regarding my Barbara?' "

"And what did you say to that?" Barbara playfully elbowed him.

"I said, "Sir, I love your daughter, and it is my hope that, I can ask her to—"

"You didn't! You haven't even talked to me about that yet!"

"Wait. Don't interrupt me. What I said was I intend to ask her to live in sin with me."

Barbara laughed. "Seriously, you didn't say that to him!"

"Busted! I told him the truth. That at the moment, I'm too

young to think about a marriage, but that I hoped one day I would consider that."

"Fair enough," Barbara said, sounding pleased. "He liked you. Do you know how I know? He didn't once mention your Texas background as if it were some kind of anthropological curiosity against our cultural Eastern European Jewishness. And Bubbe offering you more strudel? That's basically a marriage proposal in our family."

By the time they reached the bus stop, Coney Island was quiet except for the distant rumble of the elevated train. A few late-night workers and night-shift employees waited with them.

"Your family ..." Archer paused to search for the right words. "They carry so much history. Every conversation feels like it's happening on multiple levels—what's being said, what's being remembered, what's being fought for."

Barbara squeezed his hand. "They are survivors," she said simply. "We know how to keep talking, keep arguing. It's how we remember."

The bus arrived, warm and bright against the dark street. Archer gave her a farewell kiss before boarding. He found a seat in the back and waved goodbye. The bus wound through Brooklyn's nighttime streets—past bodegas with their lights still on, past housing projects, past streets where poverty and possibility seemed to dance together.

Archer stared out the window, enveloped in the quiet hum of the bus. He started to drift off, but then something stirred in his heart. His mind awoke, hearing something he'd never heard before.

It was the underlying rhythm of safety. The quiet confidence of a society that could argue about a war without fear of being disappeared. The privilege of dissent. He heard Emil's passionate arguments about Cambodia, about Israel, about American foreign policy—arguments that would have gotten him killed in Vienna thirty years earlier.

The symphony he'd been struggling with suddenly crystallized.

He would call it *Counterpoint: An American Dialogue.* The first movement would capture the immigrant experience—those jarring, beautiful moments of cultural translation. The second would capture the voices of protest—cacophonous, raging, yet hopeful. And the third movement ... that would be the sound of safety. Not necessarily quiet or peaceful. But fundamentally, essentially safe.

He could hear it now—the low brass representing the underlying stability, the woodwinds the arguments and protests, the strings the personal narratives weaving through. A musical representation of a society robust enough to contain its own contradictions.

Outside, New York continued its endless conversation—stores closing, night workers heading home, the city never truly sleeping. Archer pulled out his notebook and began to sketch the musical notation, his pencil moving almost of its own accord. The bus's gentle motion, steady breathing, the city's background murmurs—all of it was music now. All of it was his composition.

16

ARI

Tʜᴇ ᴀꜰᴛᴇʀɴᴏᴏɴ sᴜɴ ʙᴇᴀᴛ ᴍᴇʀᴄɪʟᴇssʟʏ ᴏɴ Kɪʙʙᴜᴛᴢ Mᴀsᴀᴅᴀ ᴀs Ari Rosenbaum carefully placed another cutting of a date palm tree into the sandy soil before wiping his brow. Around him, other workers moved with practiced efficiency through the grove, the rhythm of their labor like a well-rehearsed orchestra.

Six months ago, he wouldn't have known a viable cutting from a dead one, but David Gross, the retired Israel Defense Forces captain who managed the date operation, had taught him well.

"*Yalla,* Ari!" David called out. "The water truck will be here in twenty minutes. Let's finish this row!"

Ari quickened his pace, his hands moving to an internal metronome. Everything in his world eventually came back to music. Even now, collecting samples for experimental growing program at Tel Aviv University's agricultural school, he found himself counting beats in a date palm symphony:

One, two, three, plant the cutting;
Four, five, six, pack the soil;
Seven, eight, move forward.

His morning's work would end soon, giving way to afternoon rehearsals and evening composition time. But first, there was lunch to prepare for the whole kibbutz—it was his and Lisa's turn in the communal kitchen rotation. The thought of Lisa brought a smile to his face. She'd been up since dawn, working with the goatherds, probably with one of the kibbutz's little girls following in her shadow.

In his pocket, he felt the weight of his mother's latest letter. He didn't need to open it to know its contents. She was probably worried about the Ma'alot attack on May 15, in which the Democratic Front for the Liberation of Palestine killed 25 hostages. But she didn't understand. As far as he was concerned, that would be like worrying that a tornado warning in Lubbock posed an immediate danger to their home in Pampa. How could he explain that his work with the orchestra he was building wasn't just about music? That what he was trying to create here, in this ancient landscape, would combine music with a plea for peace?

He reached into his other pocket, touching his worn notebook. Inside were his growing orchestra notes, and more important, ideas for the piece of music he was searching for—in his mind he'd named it "Harmony of the Land." He was creating an orchestra that brought together different peoples of this land that had grown to love. The perfect composition would combine western classical structure with Middle Eastern modes and traditional Jewish and Arabic themes interwoven with modern orchestral techniques.

Opening the notebook during his water break, he reviewed his latest notes about the composition of his dreams:

Movement 1: "Dawn at Masada"

- Opening: Rachel Mizrahi's violin solo (Holocaust survivor, Warsaw Conservatory graduate) interweaving with Yusuf Mahmoud's ney flute (young Palestinian prodigy)

- Theme represents sun rising over ancient fortress

- Gradually adding Ibrahim Al-Rashid's arghul

- Builds to full orchestra's movement ... but what?

Movement 2: "Waters of Conflict, Waters of Peace"

- Based on traditional water-drawing songs from both cultures

- Features the Cohen sisters' Yemenite vocal traditions

- Counterpoint between Amira Hassan's qanun and Sarah Leibowitz's cello

- Percussion section blending David Katz's military precision with Bedouin rhythms from the boys I met in the village.

Movement 3: "Voices of the Land"

- Weinberg twins' dual violin conversation

- Incorporation of shepherd's flute motifs (Ahmed's contribution)

- Building to full orchestral fusion—here again, what music can I use?

- Final theme combining "Hatikvah" fragments with traditional Arabic peace songs

A distant explosion interrupted his thoughts—another exchange of artillery fire. David looked up, his weathered face showing the practiced calm of a veteran, but Ari noted how his hand instinctively moved toward a weapon he no longer carried.

"Just another day in paradise," David said wryly, but his attempt at humor couldn't mask the tension. Three kibbutz members had been called up for reserve duty just last week. The War of Attrition was living up to its name.

The water truck arrived, and with it came Lisa, her dark hair escaping from beneath her work scarf, violin case strapped to her back even during her agricultural duties. She never went anywhere without it—the violin had been the only possession her grandmother had managed to save when she escaped from Warsaw during World War II.

"You've got a letter," Lisa said, handing Ari an envelope. "From Ibrahim."

Ari opened it eagerly, scanning the carefully written English:

> *Dear Ari,*
>
> *Yesterday's rehearsal here was interrupted by air-raid sirens, but before we had to stop. Then something magical happened. When Rachel and I played the passage from Rachmaninoff's Symphony No. 3—her violin and my arghul speaking to each other across centuries of division—I saw tears in her eyes. Later, she told me it reminded her of playing chamber music with her neighbors in Warsaw, before the world went mad.*
>
> *I think your crazy dream might actually work.*
>
> *But there are complications. My uncle discovered I was practicing with Jewish musicians. There was a fight. I'm still coming to rehearsals, but I have to be more careful now.*
>
> *Nevertheless, I'll see you on Thursday, inshallah.*
>
> *Ibrahim*

Lisa read the letter over his shoulder, her free hand unconsciously moving to the violin case she always carried on her back. "What are we going to do if Ibrahim has to back out?" she asked. "He's your right hand, when you're not able to be in Tel Aviv."

"We'll have to see." Ari had already pulled out his notebook, scribbling frantically. "Listen to this—what if we incorporate it all? The tensions, the fears, but also the hope. In the second movement, when Rachel and Ibrahim play together, we'll have the percussion building underneath—like distant artillery—but their melody rises above it, transforms it ... ugh, I really need a piece of music written for this conflict, for this region. For now, though, we will stay with Rachmaninoff's Symphony No. 3. After all, it he wrote it to express his longing for Russia after he was forced to emigrate. At least we have Noah playing the cello solo in the motto theme opening the first movement, and that establishes a poignant mood of hopelessness. But I still would love to find a work that juxtaposes conflict and peace more directly." Ari's face was lost in thought.

Lisa smiled, recognizing the familiar light in his eyes. This was the Ari she'd fallen in love with, at the Interlochen music camp and again, more deeply, here at the kibbutz, when he'd spent hours describing how Bach's Mass in B Minor could be reimagined with Middle Eastern instrumentation. "Well, we still have Dvořák's *New World Symphony* too. I still like your idea of performing both of them.'

They walked together toward the communal dining hall, passing the kindergarten where the children were singing "Zum Gali Gali"—the old pioneer song now mixed with popular Israeli radio hits. Maya, one of their newest orchestra members, was leading the singing while keeping an eye on the little ones. Her family had arrived from Morocco just three years ago, bringing with them musical traditions that stretched back to medieval Spain.

In the kitchen, they found the head cook already preparing lunch, with help from Noah, Ari's best friend from Interlochen. The radio on the counter was tuned to Kol Israel, mixing news updates about border skirmishes with popular songs. Arik Einstein's "Prague" was playing—its lyrics about distance and longing seeming particularly poignant as Sharon kneaded dough for the evening's challah.

"Letter for you, Lisa," Noah said, nodding toward the

counter. "And Ari, your mother called the office again. She wanted to make sure you're safe."

Ari rolled his eyes and made a mental note to call his mother later. He and Lisa jumped in for their own kitchen duties—Ari chopping vegetables while Lisa prepared hummus—falling into the familiar rhythm of kibbutz life. Around them, children ran in for quick drinks of water, elderly members played backgammon in the corner, volunteers from Sweden and France practiced their Hebrew with patient kibbutzniks.

"I think the kibbutz itself is like your orchestra," Lisa said, adding olive oil to the hummus. "Everyone playing their part, different rhythms coming together." She paused, listening to the mix of languages and sounds around them: Hebrew, Arabic, French, English, Yiddish, Ladino, the clatter of dishes, children's laughter, the distant bleating of goats.

Ari nodded. He pulled out his notebook again, turning to the latest revision of his composition:

Interlude: "Daily Bread"
- *Based on rhythms of kibbutz work songs*
- *Percussion echoing food preparation sounds*
- *Gradual integration of Moroccan work songs (Maya's contribution)*
- *Building to collective harvest theme with a cello solo by Noah*

"We should add something here," he said. "That Yemenite grinding song the Cohen sisters were teaching us, but scored for Western instruments. Then when their voices come in later … could we incorporate it?"

Their planning was interrupted by the sound of approaching aircraft. Everyone in the dining hall paused, heads cocked, listening to identify the engine sound—a skill that had become second nature. After a moment, they relaxed. The planes were Israeli Mirages, not Egyptian MiGs.

"You really think this can work?" Lisa asked softly, not looking up from her hummus preparation. "Not just the music and all the people, but everything it represents?"

Ari was quiet for a moment, thinking of Ibrahim's letter, his mother's worries, the sound of warplanes overhead. Finally, he said, "When the Weinberg twins play together, you can't tell where one violin ends and the other begins. When Rachel and Ibrahim play their duet, it's not a Jewish violin and an Arab clarinet anymore. It's just music. Pure music." He paused, then added, "Maybe that's what peace will sound like, when it finally comes."

The lunch bell rang, and the dining hall began to fill with hungry kibbutzniks fresh from their morning work. Soon they would eat quickly, then head to the kibbutz's bomb shelter that doubled as their rehearsal space. The acoustics weren't ideal, but there was something appropriate about creating music of peace in a room designed for war.

Today's group would be small, since Ibrahim, Rachel, and some of the others were still in Tel Aviv. Ari planned to have Lisa work with the Weinberg twins on their violin part of the Rachmaninoff and Noah with the cellos and violas. Then he'd spend some time with the woodwinds and percussion.

The orchestra was still incomplete, the perfect piece of music not yet found, harmony still imperfect, but like the ancient fortress rising above them, it was being built one stone at a time. Above them, the Israeli jets continued their patrol, drawing contrails across the desert sky like musical staffs waiting to be filled with notes.

THE NEXT WEEK, ARI VISITED PROFESSOR SAMUEL FRIEDMANN'S office at the Academy of Music to present his idea for his final project. The academy was a testament to the young Tel Aviv

University's ambitions. Though the music school had only been established in 1966, it already housed some of Israel's most promising musical talents. Through the window, Ari could see the modernist architecture of the growing university, a stark contrast to the ancient landscapes of the kibbutz.

"So, Rosenbaum," Professor Friedmann said, adjusting his wire-rimmed glasses as he reviewed Ari's project proposal, "You want to form an orchestra made up of people from both sides of our borders?" The professor's Vienna-trained sensibilities were evident in his precise German-accented Hebrew. "That's an ambitious undertaking."

Ari shifted in his chair, acutely aware of the framed photographs behind the professor's desk—images of him conducting the Israel Philharmonic Orchestra, standing along-side Leonard Bernstein, teaching master classes in Europe. "The school's mission statement speaks about building bridges through music, about being a cornerstone of Israel's cultural life," Ari said, his Texas accent still evident despite months of Hebrew immersion. "What better way to fulfill that than by bringing together musicians from all backgrounds?"

Professor Friedmann picked up Ari's preliminary notes, his eyebrows rising as he examined the unusual Instrumentation. "Qanun alongside first violins? Ney flute paired with classical flute? And these modal progressions," he hummed a few bars. "You're drawing from both maqam and Western traditions."

"The academy is uniquely positioned to support this," Ari said. "We have connections to both the Israel Philharmonic and international conservatories. If we could demonstrate that music can transcend—"

A distant explosion interrupted him. Both men paused, but neither commented on it. Such interruptions had become commonplace.

"Your academic record is excellent," the professor observed. "Top marks in conducting, theory, composition. Professor Klein

speaks highly of your work with the student orchestra. But this
... " he tapped the score, "this is more than just a student orchestra, isn't it?"

Ari thought of his ensemble: Rachel with her Holocaust
survivor's hands still creating beauty, Ibrahim defying his family's disapproval to play clarinet in a Jewish orchestra, the Weinberg twins who had found each other again after the war
through their music.

"The school's partnership with the Israel Philharmonic gives
us a unique opportunity," Ari said. "We could show that music
isn't just about performance—it's about building something
new. Something that bridges east and west, ancient and
modern."

Professor Friedmann rose and walked to his window, which
overlooked the campus where students hurried between classes,
some in military uniforms, others in traditional religious dress,
all part of the complex tapestry of Israeli society.

"You know," he said quietly, "when we established this
school, there were those who said it was ridiculous to focus on
classical music in a country fighting for its survival. What use
are Mozart and Beethoven when we need soldiers and farmers?" He turned back to Ari. "But culture, culture is what makes
survival meaningful. It's why we survive." He picked up his pen
and signed the project approval form. "I'm approving this on
two conditions. First, I want regular progress reports. Second,
when you rehearse here, I want to observe." A slight smile
crossed his face. "I must admit, I'm curious to hear what peace
sounds like in B-flat major."

Ari clutched the approval form, his mind already racing with
possibilities. The school's resources—its practice rooms, its
library, its connections—would be invaluable. "Thank you,
Professor. I won't let you down."

"No," Professor Friedmann said, "I don't believe you will.
One more thing. Next week, Zubin Mehta is conducting a

master class. I think he would be very interested in your project. After all, it's not just about music, is it? It's about who we are becoming as a nation, as a people."

Walking out of the building, Ari looked back at the ambitious young music school, its walls still fresh with paint, its halls already filled with music. Like his orchestra, like Israel itself, it was a work in progress—something new being built on very old foundations.

Ari dug around in his bag to retrieve the notebook holding his wish list for the dream score he wanted to find. He added a new entry:

Special thanks to the Samuel Rubin Israel Academy of Music, Tel Aviv University, for their support in bringing together diverse musical traditions in pursuit of harmony, both musical and human.

17

ARCHER

Before he left New York to spend the summer back home, Archer met with his composing professor at Juilliard to discuss his progress on *Counterpoint: An American Dialogue*. His professor told him, "Mueller, you've got perfect pitch and technical brilliance, but you're missing the spiritual dissonance that makes Shostakovich revolutionary. Find me something that breaks the heart and heals it in the same measure."

With that in mind, Archer decided to take the Greyhound bus home instead of the train, in the hopes of stumbling across some kind of inspiration. Seven days of Greyhound purgatory from New York City to Amarillo had left Archer raw, bleary-eyed, cramped, and saddened beyond belief by what he saw of his country. Indescribable poverty. Vietnam vets begging for money, strung-out and emaciated. Homeless families living in alleys. New York City had given him random glimpses as to what was going on, but the scale of the despair pervading middle America was hard to comprehend.

During his three-hour layover at the Memphis bus station, Archer was drawn by a voice that cut through the humid air like a shaft of pure light. The old man was sitting on a milk crate outside the Arcade Cafe, his clothes more patches than original fabric, shoes split at the sides and held together with electrical tape. But when he opened his mouth to sing "Wade in the Water," the world stopped. Archer and Barbara had spent a lot of time in the blues clubs of Harlem and the basement clubs of the Bronx, but nothing that he heard there had ever stopped him in his tracks.

The blues progression was a simple I-IV-V, but the way the old man's voice caught, swooped, and soared as his callused fingers pulled out microtonal shadings existing in the spaces between notes from his battered Gibson made Archer question his years of classical training. When the song ended, the old man launched into another piece, this one about hard times and hope, and Archer heard the same transcendent quality of Bach's Mass in B Minor, that perfect marriage of suffering and grace.

When the song ended, Archer offered him a drink of water. "Got my shoes from the dump behind Sears," the man told Archer. "But my voice?" He'd pointed skyward. "That came straight from God's own choir." The bluesman's voice had carried the same paradox Archer was trying to capture.

ON HIS FIRST DAY BACK, HE AND HANK AND WES MADE THE TREK to Palo Duro Canyon at dawn, as they used to do in high school. One of their favorite trails was easy enough for them to guide Wes's wheelchair along. Once they reached the rim, the first rays of the sun caressed the walls while the Texas wind started to weave its own melody through the rocks.

Here, a thousand feet above the canyon floor, the wind moved differently than it did in the crowded urban spaces of

New York. It whispered through the juniper and mesquite, played across the ancient rock faces, creating something that was almost out of Archer's reach.

"Listen," Archer whispered, more to himself than his companions. His fingers floated as he conducted an invisible orchestra. The wind's low moan through the canyon—that would be the cellos in a sustained G minor pedal tone, with the bass clarinet weaving a chromatic descent beneath. But now he heard something else: the bluesman's solo voice, rising from the strings, bending notes. He decided then and there that he would break every rule he'd learned at Juilliard so that the classical orchestra could sing the blues, incorporating the bluesman's microtonal shadings that existed between the notes of a standard scale.

"You're doing that thing again where you disappear into your head," Hank said, sweeping a booted foot over the loose shale. "If I didn't know you any better, I'd be worried you'll fall off the rim."

"Well, Hank, if he does, you better be ready to catch him since I can't." Wes sipped water from a metal flask and passed it to Archer.

"Shush," Archer said. A new orchestration was forming: the harsh realities transformed by this ancient space, not diminished or denied, but held in perfect tension with the canyon's timeless peace. The poverty and suffering Archer had witnessed on the bus trip home would be voiced in the brass section, with its aggressive tone clusters building to a fortissimo climax. Underneath it all, steady as a heartbeat, would be the canyon's voice in the strings, and now, weaving through it like a revelation, that blues progression he'd heard in Memphis, transformed into a classical motif that would appear in each movement, changing keys and character but always recognizable. The blues line would be his passacaglia, the thread that held it all together.

"First movement," Archer muttered, yanking out his note-book and letting his pencil fly across the staff paper:

First movement: Canyon at Dawn—Adagio misterioso, full orchestra with prominent English horn solo
Second movement: Bus Station Nocturne—Allegro con fuoco, heavy brass and percussion

He paused, hearing again the Memphis bluesman's voice soaring over his guitar.

Third movement: That's where the blues come in. Start with a fugue based on "Wade in the Water" and let it break down into controlled chaos, then build it back up with that blues progression as the foundation. The classical orchestra and the blues voice finding each other, like Bach meeting Robert Johnson at midnight.

The canyon walls held the glowing light like burnished copper, and somewhere in the distance, a coyote called—a perfect minor third that sent a shiver down Archer's spine. Here was the peace that had eluded him through seven states and countless bus stations. Not an escape from the world's pain, but a vast enough space to hold it all, transform it, and perhaps even make sense of it through the mysterious alchemy of music. The Memphis bluesman had shown him how joy could coexist with hardship, how beauty could emerge from struggle. Now the canyon was teaching him how to orchestrate it.

He scribbled "Blues in the Classical Style" at the top of the page. Then he immediately crossed it out, replacing it with the old title, "Counterpoint." But he crossed that one out as well. All of the sudden it hit him: "Symphony No. 1 in G Minor: A Testament to Wind and Stone."

Below it, in smaller letters, he added:

For the man outside the Arcade Cafe in Memphis, who taught me how to hear between the notes.

THAT EVENING, THE KITCHEN SMELLED OF NANCY'S CHICKEN-fried steak and cream gravy with sharp black pepper and sweet corn bread. Archer watched his mother's hands tremble slightly as she ladled more gravy onto his plate. She'd been quiet while he talked, but her hands kept moving—adjusting his napkin, refilling his tea, touching his shoulder as she passed behind his chair.

"The Vietnam vets in Oklahoma City," he continued, pushing a piece of steak through the gravy, "there were so many of them. This one man, he'd been a helicopter pilot. Both legs gone above the knee. His sign said, 'Saigon 1968 Da Nang 1969.' He was sitting there in a wheelchair held together with baling wire and looked about our age." He paused, thinking of Wes, who was exempt from the draft but not from his infirmity, and Hank, who'd gotten his draft notice but whose number had not been drawn.

Joe Bob's face tightened, his fork pausing halfway to his mouth.

"Another vet," Archer went on, "he wasn't begging. He just sat there rocking, staring at nothing. People walked around him like he was invisible. His boots were spit-shined perfect, but his jacket was in tatters."

Nancy made a soft sound, somewhere between a sigh and a prayer, her hand finding Joe Bob's across the table.

"Then there was the family in Little Rock." Archer's voice caught. "Mother, father, three little kids sleeping on their suit-cases at three in the morning. Youngest couldn't have been more than four. They had these little American flag stickers on their bags. Father kept trying to clean the kids' faces with a paper towel from the bathroom. Mother was feeding them crackers from her purse, making a game of it, pretending they were on an adventure. But it was obvious they were without a home. And there was nothing I could do, except witness it. See it for truth."

"Lord, have mercy," Nancy whispered, then bustled to the stove, bringing back a fresh batch of cornbread that no one needed. Archer knew that was her way of holding back tears—keep moving, keep serving, keep loving.

"But Mama, Daddy," He leaned forward, needing them to understand. "That's why what happened in the canyon this morning with Wes and Hank was so important. All that pain I saw, all that suffering—the canyon knew what to do with it. The music I've been hearing, it's like the canyon taught me how to hold it all. The hurt and the hope together."

Joe Bob nodded slowly, methodically cutting his steak. Archer recognized his expression from childhood; it indicated his father processing something deep, taking his time with it. "Like our preacher said Sunday," he finally offered. "Joy cometh in the morning." He reached over and squeezed Nancy's hand. "Your mama and I been praying for you to find your way through this composition; we know how important it is to you."

"Found it in those bus stations," Archer said softly. "Found it in that Memphis bluesman's voice. Found it watching the sun rise over Palo Duro Canyon this morning. It's all the same song, somehow."

Nancy wiped her hands on her apron, then touched Archer's cheek as she used to do when he was small. "Well then," she said, her voice steady again, "you better write it down before it flies away. But first—" She turned to the counter. "Seraphina brought you a sheet cake this morning. She'll be over tomorrow to spend some time with you. She wants to hear about those Take Back the Night marches you and Barbara went to. We don't have anything like that here in the Panhandle."

Archer smiled, remembering when Seraphina and his mother had visited him the year before and joined a march for a woman's right to serve on a jury. He'd taken Seraphina to the bakery to meet Barbara's family, and he never would have thought Seraphina and Barbara's Viennese grandmother would have so much in common—a gun-wielding Christian ranch owner from the Panhandle eating pastries and discussing women's rights with a Jewish business owner who'd escaped the Nazis. The world was changing.

After downing a healthy serving of cake and clearing the dishes, Archer headed to the barn to write to Barbara. At the barn's doorway, he turned to watch his parents through the kitchen window. His father had pulled his mother close, and they were swaying slightly, as if they were dancing to music only they could hear. Maybe, Archer thought, that's what his symphony was really about—not just the pain or the peace, but the love that held them both together. God, he was grateful to have been raised around so much love.

> *My love, Barbara,*
>
> *I'm sitting in our barn right now, where the night is orchestrating its own symphony—one that makes me miss you with an ache that feels like Tchaikovsky's sixth symphony, that passage in the first movement that always makes you cry. Remember how you grabbed my hand at Carnegie Hall when we heard it last fall? God, I miss your hands. I miss the way you brush your hair back when you're concentrating on a line from one of your plays, or how you hum 'Rita May' by Dylan when you're cooking, how you always know when I'm stuck on a piece before I do.*
>
> *My journey home was harder than I could have imagined—I saw things that would break your heart, that broke mine.*
>
> *You were worried about me taking the bus instead of flying, about what seeing the "real America" might do to my music. You were right—it changed everything. I saw poverty that would make*

you weep. I saw the veterans abandoned by the country they served. I saw hunger and hopelessness in children's eyes. But then I saw the canyon this morning, vast and eternal, and I understood something that I think Mahler knew when he wrote the Resurrection Symphony: Peace isn't the absence of pain. It's the space big enough to hold both the suffering and the beauty, the darkness and the light.

But this morning, something extraordinary happened. Remember how stuck I've been on the symphony? How everything I wrote felt either too artificial or too raw? Today, in Palo Duro Canyon with Wes and Hank, I finally heard it—really heard it.

It starts with a G minor pedal tone in the low strings—the canyon's voice at dawn. Then the woodwinds enter one by one, like morning light creeping down the rock faces. But here's what I could never figure out before: how to bring in the darkness without letting it overwhelm the piece. In Memphis, I heard a blues singer who showed me the way—he was singing spirituals with quarter-tone inflections that would scandalize old Berkowitz at Juilliard. I'm going to write those bent notes into the classical framework, Barbara. Break every rule they taught us.

The second movement—this is where I need a true pianist's heart; it's going to be brutal. Tonal clusters in the brass like bus station fluorescent lights, percussion that captures the diesel engines and crying babies and broken men's cardboard signs. But underneath it all, always, there's this passacaglia based on "Wade in the Water" that the Memphis bluesman sang in 7/8 time, but fluid, like the Chopin rubato.

You'd love it here tonight. The new calves are testing their legs, staying close to their mothers. Listen: that low moo from the brown cow? Perfect B-flat, like the opening of Brahms' Fourth. The wind in the eaves is giving me this gorgeous polyrhythm against the breathing of the cattle. I'm writing it all down. Even the barn cats padding through the hay are part of it—their movements will be echoed in the pizzicato strings during the development section.

The final movement, Barbara—this is where it all comes together. I'm starting with a fugue based on the blues progression, but then it modulates through all twelve keys like that Berg piece we studied last semester. The main theme fragments, splits apart like light through a prism. Then the orchestra divides into three distinct voices: the strings carry the canyon's peace in long, sustained harmonies; the brass captures the pain of what I witnessed; and floating above it all, a solo violin plays a melody that somehow reconciles everything. I can hear it so clearly—it's the same melody I hear in my head when I think of Beethoven's Opus 109 piano sonata.

The symphony's all there now, Barbara. Every note, every movement. I can hear it as clearly as I can hear these calves breathing. It begins in darkness—all those bus stations and broken people—but it doesn't end there. It transforms them, lifts them up into something larger, like the way the Texas sky seems to go on forever. The final chord is going to be G major, but with the third omitted, leaving it suspended between joy and sorrow, just like life itself.

God, I wish you were here. I wish I could show you how the stars look like notes on an endless staff, how the crickets are singing in perfect fifths, how even the screen door's creak is musical in this place. I miss the cramped practice room at school, the way you'd bring me coffee during all-night composition sessions, how you can tell by a single wrong note when I'm trying to force the music instead of letting it come naturally.

When you hear it, when the symphony premieres, you'll understand what I can't quite say in words. You'll hear how love persists, how beauty survives, how peace exists not in spite of suffering, but somehow right beside it. You'll hear the canyon and the blues and the pain and the hope, all woven together. And in the violin solo near the end, if you listen carefully, you'll hear my love for you, written into every note.

I'll be home soon—only two more weeks and I will return. And

Barbara? Thank you for believing in the music even when I couldn't hear it myself.

All my love,

Archer

P.S. The cadenza in the third movement? I wrote it in 13/8 time just to drive you crazy. Some things never change.

He folded the letter as he listened to the soft symphony of the barn—the cattle's steady breathing, the wind in the eaves, a mother cow's gentle lowing to her calf. Tomorrow he would begin scoring the music properly, but tonight, in this sacred space of childhood, he simply let himself be still, held in the peace he'd traveled so far to find.

18

ARI

Tʜᴇ ᴇᴠᴇɴɪɴɢ ᴀɪʀ ᴀᴛ Kɪʙʙᴜᴛᴢ Mᴀsᴀᴅᴀ ᴡᴀs ᴛʜɪᴄᴋ ᴡɪᴛʜ anticipation as the first notes of Dvořák's Symphony No. 9: *From the New World* rose into the desert sky. The first half of the People's Orchestra for Peace's inaugural program, featuring Rachmaninoff's Third Symphony, had gone off beautifully. Now, under the warm glow of floodlights rigged up around the communal amphitheater, Ari Rosenbaum stood tall, his baton cutting decisive lines through the darkness as he coaxed his eclectic ensemble through the opening bars. Around him, the musicians sat straight-backed, their eyes fixed on their conductor, a tapestry of ages, ethnicities, and backgrounds sewn together by the power of music. Rachel's violin sang out with a lifetime of sorrow and resilience as Ibrahim's arghul answered with a longing that transcended borders. The Weinberg twins, their movements perfectly synchronized, wove their dual violin melodies like two sides of the same heartbeat. Noah and the other strings provided a backdrop before their time to shine came later. Behind them all, the Cohen sisters' soaring voices lent a hauntingly beautiful counterpoint, their Yemenite rhythms underpinning Dvořák's *New World* theme. Ari was in his element, swaying with the music, as if his baton was a wizard's wand. The entire orchestra was a murmuration of sound. It was spectacular.

Ari's great-uncle Yacov and his partner, Hiram, applauded enthusiastically, delighted by their nephew's performance. In the row in front of them, Professor Friedmann sat transfixed, his fingers tapping along unconsciously. When he had approved Ari's final project to form this orchestra, he had never expected that it would come to such a magnificent fruition. Next to Professor Friedmann was Zubin Mehta, the celebrated conductor of the Israel Philharmonic, and beside him was Noah's father Aaron Templos, the first-chair violinist of the New York. All three of them leaned forward, their eyes never leaving the makeshift stage, riveted by Ari.

As the first movement ended, the applause that rose from the audience was thunderous. Even the children, who had been allowed to stay up past their bedtime, were cheering and clapping with unbridled enthusiasm.

"Remarkable," Mehta murmured. "Absolutely remarkable."

Friedmann nodded, a smile playing at the corners of his mouth. "Just wait. You haven't heard anything yet."

His prediction proved true in ways that even surprised him. Applause boomed out at the end of the second and third movements, then as the strains of the fiery finale faded, the audience jumped up in an exultant standing ovation.

In that moment, the very air seemed to hum with possibility that towered over politics, religion, and the bullet-scarred borders dividing this ancient land. Here, in this makeshift concert venue under the desert stars, music had forged a new kind of harmony.

When the tumult subsided, Friedmann motioned for Ari to

join him and his esteemed guests. The young conductor approached, his brow glistening with sweat, but his eyes alight with triumph.

"Ari, my boy," Friedmann said, clasping the young man's shoulder. "I must admit, you've exceeded my expectations. And that," he gestured toward the stage, "is no small feat."

Aaron Templos stepped forward, glowing with admiration. "I've played *New World* more times than I can count, but I've never heard it quite like this. The balance, the emotion—it's as if these musicians are speaking a language I'm only just learning to understand."

Then Zubin Mehta, one of Ari's heroes, fixed Ari with an intense stare. "You've done something remarkable here, young man. Something that goes far beyond mere music."

Friedmann nodded. "Which is why I'd like to propose a collaboration of the Rubin Academy of Music, the Israel Philharmonic, and your ensemble, Ari, to present a concert in Tel Aviv to showcase the unity and diversity of Israeli culture. What do you say, Ari?"

Ari's eyes widened, his heart racing. This was more than he could have ever hoped for—a chance to take his vision beyond the kibbutz and beyond the school. To show the world that harmony was possible, even in the midst of conflict. "I ... I don't know what to say," he stammered, his voice thick with emotion. "That would be more than I ever imagined."

Mehta watched Ari and shook his head as if stumped by a problem. He couldn't comprehend such a young, innocent man leading a group of musicians to make such a unique sound.

Templos clapped him on the back, his own eyes suspiciously bright. "Then say yes, my friend. Say yes, and let's show the world what peace can sound like."

Ari knew his dream was no longer just his own. It had become something bigger, something that could transcend the very divisions that had torn this land apart. With a deep breath, he gave his answer.

"Yes. Yes, of course. Let's do it."

Ari turned around only to be yanked off the ground in a huge bear hug. "Ari, my boy!" Yacov shouted. "You did it! You did it!"

Hiram clucked at Yacov to tone it down, then shook Ari's hand. "What a lovely performance, Ari. Congratulations."

"I just wish your Bubbe could have been here to see it," Yacov said, refusing to release his nephew.

Ari hugged him back before disentangled himself. "I do, too, Uncle Yacov. She, if anyone, would have appreciated it. But she's going to love my big news."

Yacov raised on eyebrow. "Oh? What is that?"

"Wait a minute. Lisa! Lisa! Come here!" Ari waved his arms to catch her attention.

Lisa said her goodbyes and joined them. "What's up, Ari?" She snuggled up against him and smiled at Yacov and Hiram.

"You have to hear my big news! Zubin Mehta and Professor Friedmann just made me an offer to have the People's Orchestra partner with the Rubin Academy and the Israel Philharmonic."

Lisa shrieked and planted a kiss on Ari's cheek.

Yacov bounced up and down with joy. "My dear boy! What a wonderful opportunity! And I hope that means you won't have to go back to the States."

Ari smiled conspiratorially. "I just might be working on my doctorate here! What do you say, Ms. Goldfarb?"

"I say that's your best idea yet! Now, if you'll excuse me, I need to check on how the kitchen is doing with the reception."

～

"LISA! THERE YOU ARE!" ARI SAID, STILL BOUNCING WITH excitement when he found Lisa sitting on the bench outside the dining hall. "I've been looking for you everywhere! I was just interviewed by a reporter from the *Haaretz*, and he—" Ari stopped short when he saw her tears. "What's wrong, darling?"

Lisa held a letter in her trembling hands. The evening breeze carried the scent of orange blossoms from the nearby grove, but she barely noticed it through her tears.

She held up the letter. "Papa wants me to come home. He says Israel is too dangerous now, especially for me."

Ari knelt beside her, taking her hands in his. "Your father has worried since the moment you set foot back here a year ago. You did what he wanted—you finished your studies in Chicago. You came back of your own accord to work with the children here on the kibbutz and be in our orchestra. He can't tell you what to do now." Ari's expression shifted from concern to something else—determination, mixed with tenderness. "Ah, it's not just the danger, is it? He is worried about you being alone here with no husband or father to care for you. I know he is Orthodox, but it's 1974. Shouldn't he be more with the times?"

Lisa's eyes teared up again. "You know I love him; I can't dishonor him. But I don't want to leave. I love living here in Israel and being with you. And I wanted to pursue my MFA here. I can't go back." Lisa looked out over the desert and took in the crystal-clear sky, the half-moon, and the mist coming off the nearby mountains.

"Then, perhaps," Ari softly, "it's time I give you a reason to stay."

Lisa's breath caught as Ari repositioned himself onto one knee, still holding her hands. "Lisa, you know I've loved you since the moment you walked into that first rehearsal at Interlochen. Your music, your spirit, your heart—they've become part of my soul. Prime Minister Rabin is making real changes here. We could live in Tel Aviv, and I can continue to work with the orchestra, you could study for a master's and be first chair in the orchestra." He squeezed her hands gently. "Lisa, will you marry me?"

She stared at him, tears flowing freely now, but for an entirely different reason. The letter slipped from her lap, forgotten.

"Yes," she whispered. "Yes, Ari I'll marry you. In fact, that is now your best idea of the night!"

A FEW DAYS LATER, THEY CELEBRATED THEIR ENGAGEMENT WITH A hike through Ari's favorite place in Israel—the stunning Makhtesh Ramon crater in Israel's Negev desert. The place had echoes of Palo Duro Canyon back in Texas. He loved bringing Lisa here because it felt like he was sharing something akin to his home and his childhood with her. The vast rocky landscape stretched out before them, sculpted by millions of years of erosion into dramatic ridges, cliffs, and crevices. As they descended into the heart of the canyon, Ari couldn't help but feel inspired by the raw natural beauty surrounding them. And that led him to daydream about how his People's Orchestra would soon be collaborating with Zubin Mehta and the Israel Philharmonic. What would that look like?

As they rounded a bend and came upon a serene oasis with a small spring-fed pool reflecting the towering cliffs above, Ari suddenly felt a surge of inspiration. The tranquility of the scene, combined with the monumental scale of the canyon, sparked an idea in his mind. Perhaps the solution lay in finding a piece that balanced moments of stillness and contemplation with bursts of power and grandeur—mirroring the complex emotional land-scape of the Middle East. He couldn't help but think of all his hikes in Palo Duro Canyon, how the place held such immense peace for him, but it had also been the location of the decisive battle of the Red River War, in which Colonel Ranald

Mackenzie and the Fourth Cavalry slaughtered an entire herd of Comanche horses. Ari was coming to believe that rivers of blood could coexist with the peace of the wind. Juxtaposition. That is what he wanted to find someday in a symphony, perhaps one that could showcase the new partnership.

Lisa broke up his thoughts. "Ari, you know I am not romantic at all, but this is supposed to be a celebration hike for us, and you are lost in thought again." She was smiling at him, but Ari knew she was right.

Ari reached in his pocket and pulled out a small box. "Sorry. Let's make it completely official. Will you wear this ring as a sign of our engagement?" Inside the box was a thick gold band inlaid with a large blue-green Eilat stone, the stone of Israel, of the Jews, of King Solomon, of the Eilat Mountains, of their home.

Lisa slid the ring onto her finger. "It fits! This is perfect. I love you, Ari Rosenbaum."

19

ARCHER

By the time he returned to New York for his final year at Juilliard, Archer had completed his symphony and given it to the professor who was already putting together the orchestra to play it at Juilliard's graduation performance at Carnegie Hall. The night before the performance, Archer had never been happier. He was in the city he loved and walking on the Riegelmann Boardwalk at Coney Island with Barbara. The salt-tinged breeze off the Atlantic ruffled her long hair as they strolled through the evening crowds. They found a place where the crowds thinned, leaving them a quiet stretch of weathered planks to themselves.

He turned to Barbara. "Sweetheart, I have something to ask you." He dropped to one knee and clasped her hands. "Barbara Salinger, would you be my wife?"

Barbara turned her lightly freckled face to him with a radiant smile, "Archer, I'll marry you, of course, but I need you to know that Bubbe, as much as she loves you, is not happy about me marrying a non-Jew. My family loves you, but it's just the Jewish thing, and the fact that you don't know your real parents, that you are adopted. For her, bloodline is important."

"Your grandmother doesn't understand," Archer said, squeezing Barbara's hand. "Our love isn't about religion or race —it's about two creative young people finding each other." He paused, then added carefully, "Although, I can understand why finding out about my own background might be important to her. I mean what if my birthparents were Jewish?" He said this to appease her because there weren't many Jewish people in the Panhandle. But for some reason, Archer had always doubted that his birth mother was from his hometown of Canyon. But he didn't say this to Barbara.

Barbara sighed, her thumb tracing the calluses on his fingers. "Bubbe told me the other night she thinks the only way for our people to survive is to stay together, that if I marry outside the faith, I'm betraying everything she endured to be one of the last of our line."

Archer pulled her close, feeling the tension in her body. "Then we'll prove her wrong. It's like my symphony—holding contradictions in balance, finding the peace that exists alongside the pain. Just like us."

"I know." Barbara rested her head on his shoulder. "It's beautiful, Archie. But sometimes beauty isn't enough when there's so much history and tradition at stake. Bubbe lost everything in Vienna—her neighborhood, her business, most of her family, all her friends. All gone. I can understood her hesitation."

The lovers walked in silence for a few moments, the distant laughter of children on the Ferris wheel and the crash of waves the only sounds. Archer thought of Palo Duro Canyon, how it had taught him to stop trying to resolve the dissonance and instead let it exist in harmony. Could he do the same here, with the weight of Barbara's family history pressing in?

"When I heard that bluesman in Memphis," he said slowly,

"he took the suffering in his life and transformed it into something holy. Not by escaping it, but by singing it—by making it part of a greater whole. That's what I want our love to be. Not just surviving, but thriving, in the face of everything."

Barbara lifted her head, eyes shining. "I know, it's in the symphony, I like to think it's our love that is golden thread that weaves it all together—the darkness and the light, the pain and the peace. And maybe," she hesitated, then continued more firmly, "maybe finding out about your own roots could help, too. For both of us."

Archer pulled her into a fierce embrace, feeling the familiar comfort of her body, the way her heart beat against his. In that moment, he heard the entire third movement, a rapturous fugue that would build to a transcendent resolution—yearning minor themes resolving to a joyous, open-fifth chord. Not an ending, but a beginning; he couldn't wait to hear it all played with the orchestra.

"Okay. I will start looking into my own past. For you, for us, for the music. In the meantime, we need to go shopping for a ring. I didn't dare pick one out without your approval."

Barbara laughed. "Oh, Archie, you know me too well!"

20

DANIEL AND ARCHER

Daniel watched as Archer paced the length of his law office, his footsteps muffled by the thick Persian carpet Nancy and Joe Bob Mueller insisted on giving him last Christmas as gift for negotiating the sale of their cattle to a slaughterhouse in New Mexico.

At twenty-two, Archer had grown into everything his parents hoped he'd be—kindhearted and strong like Joe Bob, but with a grace that spoke to the musical talent Nancy fostered in him from such a young age. His success at Juilliard was the icing on the cake. Archer had already achieved so much beyond the wildest dreams of his parents and even his godfather. And now here he was on the cusp of his musical career and getting married to the charming Barbara.

"Well, Archer! This is the first time in years that I've seen you in consecutive months. Elaine, Mike, and I really enjoyed joining your parents for the premiere of your symphony. I always knew you had an ear for music, but that was amazing.

The whole time, I kept thinking how familiar it was and how much it sounded like the canyon, even in New York City."

Archer smiled. "I was really glad you were there. You, if anyone, would notice that. I'm not sure most of the audience at the concert even noticed those parts."

"I bet they recognized your nods to New York City, at the least. The pairing was simply genius, Archer. Now, what can I do for you, son?"

"Uncle Dan," Archer began, stopping at the window that overlooking the flat desert landscape west of Amarillo. "I need your help in finding my birth parents."

Daniel's chair creaked as he leaned back, making sure not to topple over with the request. He'd always wondered when Archer would ask this question. After all, his parents had told him from the time he was around seven that he was adopted. The afternoon sun caught the dust motes dancing between them, and for a moment, he was transported back to that day in 1952 when two identical baby boys were next to one another in the hospital as their mother slept after a long delivery, leaving Daniel with the task of delivering the boys to separate families.

"Sit down, Archer," Daniel said softly. "Tell me what's brought this on. Your whole life, this has never been an issue. You've never seemed troubled by the adoption before."

Archer dropped into the client chair, running a hand through his dark hair. "It's Barbara's grandmother. She's the last of her line, and she barely got out of Vienna before everyone she knew and loved was murdered or sent to the camps to die by the Nazis. I admire her, greatly, as does Barbara. And ... well ... I don't know my bloodline, and Barbara's grandmother is hesitant. She wants to know if maybe I could be Jewish." He spread his hands helplessly. "Barbara says it doesn't matter to her, but I can see how much her grandmother's hesitation bothers her."

Daniel nodded, keeping his expression neutral even as his

mind raced. Somewhere in Israel, Archer's twin brother, Ari Rosenbaum, was leading an orchestra, practicing for a huge performance. Ari, unlike Archer, had never been aware that he was adopted. This was Tanya Rosenbaum's decision, and Daniel knew how important the Jewish lineage was to her. And now Barbara's grandmother was raising the same issue about Archer. Daniel was not one to question either grandmother. But he could not simply tell Archer about his birth parents or his twin brother. Daniel took a moment to acknowledge that this would have been amusing if it weren't so fraught with complexity.

Daniel chose his words carefully. "Your adoption was sealed for a reason, to protect you, your parents, and your birth parents. That is what everyone wanted at that time. Your parents have always been open with you about being adopted. That's more than many children get."

"I know, and I love them; they truly are my parents. This isn't about that. I am an adult now. Surely there must be some way to learn at least something about my biological family's history?" Archer's eyes, so like the those of the brother he didn't know, pleaded for help.

Daniel stood up and took over pacing the carpet. Behind him, he could hear Archer shift in his chair. "I'll tell you what," he said finally, turning to Archer. "Let me make some inquiries. I can't promise anything—you understand that—but I'll see what can be done within the bounds of the law."

Archer's face brightened. "Really? That would mean everything to me, to Barbara, to us, to her grandmother. Thank you, Uncle Dan. Thank you." The young man stood and hugged his godfather and pounced like a puppy out of the office.

Daniel returned to his chair and sat alone in his darkening office, the weight of unspoken truths heavy on his shoulders. He would have to call Judge Harrison, of course—the old man had always had a soft spot for unusual cases and would share his wise perspective. At some point, he would need to talk to

Karolina. He thought about how happy his old friend Tom must be, ensconced in his life with Karolina in London, the perfect home base for his mission work with mothers in impoverished countries. Dr. Tom's postcard a couple of months before had been from Yemen, of all places.

The last time Daniel had actually seen Tom was about a year ago in Dallas, when he and Elaine went to see Karolina perform with the Dallas Symphony. Tom had never been happier. Daniel had been concerned about meeting Karolina for the first time since the twins had been born. As curious as he was to see her after all these years, he wasn't sure what to expect and worried that meeting her in front of Tom would be awkward. It turned out that they didn't meet with Karolina at all. They drove to Dallas, saw the performance, and then retired to their hotel so they could get an early start the next morning to make the drive to Lubbock for Texas Tech's Parents Weekend with Will and Mike.

But to honor Archer's request, Daniel wouldn't be able to avoid contacting Karolina much longer.

Oh, this was a complicated situation, indeed. But Archer was right: He was a man now, and maybe he did have a right to know about his birth parents.

Daniel pulled out his Rolodex, a thumb hovering over Tom's number in London. Sometimes, Daniel thought, the truth, once started, could never be contained again. But then he called Judge Harrison instead.

"You know, Daniel," Judge Harrison said, rising from his desk to retrieve a thick law book, "adoption law has come a long way since I first put on this robe. For centuries, adoptions were parent-focused. They occurred when a child lost their parents, lived in poverty, was born out of wedlock, or when more labor was required around the home."

Daniel nodded, remembering his law school lectures. "Massachusetts, 1851. The first modern adoption law."

"Exactly right." The judge settled back, a gleam of approval in his eyes. "That was the turning point—recognizing adoption as a legal operation based on child welfare, rather than adult interests." He paused, tamping his pipe. "And now here we are, watching another shift in the trend toward openness."

"Judge, what I really need to know is whether Dr. Brewer or I can legally share information with the parties involved."

The judge's face softened. "You're worried about Tom's position in all this? Don't be. The trend toward openness hasn't just affected adoptees and birth parents—it's changed how we view the role of facilitators like yourself and Tom." He pulled out a drawer and extracted several files. "Look here. Just in the past few years, I've handled dozens of requests from adopted children and adoptive parents to open their records. You know what I've learned?"

Daniel leaned forward. "What's that?"

"With proper consent documents, these situations almost always resolve themselves smoothly. The key is preparation, Daniel. Draw up mutual-consent documents for each party involved—birth parents, adoptive parents, the adoptees. Make it clear exactly what information they're agreeing to release, whether it's from the court papers or Tom's medical files."

"And that protects Tom legally?"

"Absolutely." The judge closed the drawer with a decisive thud. "It's not just legal protection—it's good practice. Gets everyone's expectations aligned, prevents misunderstandings. Have you talked to Tom about this yet?"

Daniel shook his head. "I wanted to clear the legal ground first."

"Smart. You know, Daniel, I've been on this bench long

enough to see how these stories usually play out. The ones that go smoothly? They're the ones where someone like you takes the time to do it right. Draw up those consent documents. Get everyone's signature. Then neither you nor Tom needs to worry about overstepping.

"Speaking of Tom, tell him he is missed. He did more for the families of the Panhandle than he knows. He handled my niece's adoption. He took such care in finding the right match. He has done the work of the Lord, if you ask me. He has nothing to worry about if some of these children start to ask questions. He always did the right thing, in my opinion."

Daniel felt some of the tension leave his shoulders. "I appreciate this, Judge. More than you know."

"Just doing my job." The judge leaned back in his chair. "And Daniel? When you draw up those documents, make sure they're comprehensive. Include provisions for medical history, identifying information, family background—everything. Better to have permissions you don't need than need permissions you don't have."

As Daniel gathered his briefcase to leave, the judge added, "You know, sometimes I think back to that Massachusetts law of 1851. They got something fundamentally right—putting the welfare of the child first. Even when that child is twenty-two and about to get married."

Walking back through the courthouse corridors, Daniel was already drafting the consent documents in his mind. He'd need separate ones for Joe Bob and Nancy, for Karolina, and both boys, just in case. The complexity was daunting, but the judge was right—doing this properly from the start would protect everyone involved. Especially Dr. Tom, whom Daniel wanted to protect the most.

He checked his watch. If he hurried, he could have the first drafts written before Tom returned to the Panhandle in a couple of weeks. The sooner Daniel got this framework in place, the sooner he could help Archer.

But what was he to do about Ari? He'd forgotten to ask the judge about telling Archer he had a twin. Maybe he could leave that to Karolina? He thought of all her letters to her babies and knew instinctively she would welcome this turn of events. But did he need to tell her that even though one of her sons wanted to know about his birth parents, the other was still in the dark. How would he handle this? But then he heard the judge's advice again: Solve all the problems ahead of time, make all the concessions. Daniel would draw up all the consents, for all the Rosenbaums as well, just in case.

Who knew? Maybe he would end up facilitating Ari and Archer finally knowing of each other's existence.

PART V

THE PEOPLE'S CONCERT FOR PEACE

1975–1976

LETTER FROM KAROLINA
NOVEMBER 1975

My dear children,

Today you are twenty-three years old. I am sometimes taken back with the swift passage of time. So much has happened to me, and so much has changed. I wonder, what has happened in your lives? Are you well? Are you happy? Are you fulfilling your dreams? Are you playing music?

For so long, traveling the world has been my focus, to play the piano for all who want to hear. I started so young. I was fifteen, alone on stages all over the world, with only my mother to accompany me. What I have seen and experienced has shaken me to my core and built me up again. The world is a tragic and joyful place all in one. But something rattled me a few years ago that made me want to stop my itch to perform anywhere under any and all conditions. Ever since then, I've only agreed to play in the concert halls of peaceful European countries. I was afraid of strife and protest.

But something my closest friend Tom said to me the other day has ignited in me again the idea to travel to a faraway place and play my piano for those who want to hear it. I will be performing soon in Tel Aviv for a symphony honoring Yitzhak Rabin's signing of the Sinai Agreement. Tom told me that Israel and Palestine have for too long been pawns on the chessboard of the rest of the world. Now, with Rabin, there is a chance for both countries to live peacefully as neighbors.

I want to celebrate this, so I will travel again. And this time I will be with young people your age—another reason I said yes. Maybe by playing with young adults your age I can catch your energy; I can be a part of the world you are trying to change. I can be with you.

Happy birthday, my loves. You are forever in my heart.

Love,

Your mother

21

ARI

THE AFTERNOON SUN SLANTED THROUGH THE VENETIAN BLINDS, casting shadows across Professor Friedmann's cluttered desk. Sheet music spilled from every surface; a metronome ticked softly in the corner. Ari and the professor were discussing, once again, what symphony would be appropriate for a special performance that had just been commissioned to celebrate Prime Minister Rabin's most recent achievement, the Sinai Interim Agreement between Israel and Egypt.

Zubin Mehta had had been approached by Rabin himself, who asked him to put together a performance to commemorate the hopes for peace in the Middle East. Mehta immediately thought that Ari's People's Orchestra for Peace would be perfect for the occasion with some support from the Israel Philharmonic. After talking with Professor Friedmann and Ari, they agreed to scout around for a new symphonic work that would fit the bill and then bring the finalists to Mehta.

So far, the right work had not yet appeared. "I've been searching everywhere," Ari said.

Lisa watched him repeat that gesture she knew so well—running his fingers through his disheveled dark hair, which was the longest and shaggiest it had ever been. And with the beard he had grown, Lisa thought he looked like a true hippie, *her* hippie. She bit back a smile but couldn't suppress a tiny sigh of happiness.

"I've been through every archive, every collection I can find. But nothing feels unique to us, to our orchestra, to our time, to our desire for peace. Nothing is enough." He paced the small office, careful not to disturb the towering stacks of scores that seemed to defy gravity.

"You make a fair point. Perhaps we need to look at some of the great symphonic works, see if we can find one that aligns with Rabin's message." The professor stood to scan his bookshelves. "Beethoven's Ninth, with its 'Ode to Joy'—that celebrates the universal brotherhood of man. But the lyrics are in German, and we'd need to translate them."

Ari considered it for a moment. "It's too European-centric. We need something that truly bridges East and West, that can resonate with Israelis and Palestinians alike."

"Yes, you're absolutely right." Friedmann paused, tapped his finger against his lips. "I know you've already done it, but what about presenting Dvořák's *New World Symphony* again? Perhaps we could adapt it in some way and incorporate some traditional Israeli themes."

Ari had had his heart set on something new and unique, but he loved his professor's enthusiasm. "It does have that sense of discovery, of finding common ground in unexpected places. That would fit. Let's give it a try and see how we can make this work."

Friedmann smiled. "Excellent. With your talented musicians and my, ah, extensive musical knowledge, I'm sure we can craft something truly special for Rabin's big day." He paused mid-stride, his eyes lighting up. "Wait, I may have just the thing!" He hurried back to his desk, shuffling through the papers and folders until he produced a battered manila envelope. Pulling out the contents, he reverently laid a stack of handwritten sheet music on the table.

"Remember Aaron Templos, who came to your first performance at the kibbutz?" Friedmann asked.

Ari nodded. "He's my friend Noah's father."

"Well, a month or so ago, he sent me this, an original symphony from a young Juilliard composer. It was performed at the end-of-year concert, and Aaron tells me the performance was spellbinding."

Ari's brow furrowed as he examined the music. "An unknown symphony?"

Friedmann nodded emphatically. "Aaron swears it's a dazzling blend of Native American modalities and Western orchestral grandeur, with nods to American blues and Negro spirituals, similar to *New World*. I've read through it a few times, imagining how it might sound with a full orchestra. And now, with what we're trying to achieve for Rabin's peace agreement … " His eyes gleamed with excitement. "This could be it, Ari. The perfect piece to unite hearts and minds."

Ari's fingers traced the title of the music, Symphony No. 1 in G Minor, *A Testament to Wind and Stone,* by Archer Mueller. He read the notes, his mind racing, a magnificent smile slowly spreading across his face. "Oh, my God, Professor! This is a work of genius. I can see all the elements of the struggles of the Jews and the Palestinians here, plus the nod to the origin of a land, creation and destruction, and peace and war. Let's not waste another moment. Let's get the orchestra together and start working on it."

"I'll take it to Zubin to see what he thinks." Professor Fried-mann patted Ari's back, his own expression overflowing with pride and anticipation. "My boy, this could be it. Something that will make history."

A WEEK OR SO LATER, AFTER ZUBIN MEHTA HAD GIVEN HIS BLESS-ing to Archer Mueller's symphony, Professor Friedmann called the young composer to get his permission to perform his work. The young composer was thrilled, and they were finishing up the agreement.

The evening breeze carried the scent of jasmine through the open windows of the Academy's rehearsal room, where scattered sheets of Archer Mueller's symphony lay across the Steinway like fallen leaves. Ari sat at the piano, one hand trailing over the keys, while Lisa sat cross-legged on the floor surrounded by orchestration notes. Professor Friedmann occupied his usual spot in a worn leather armchair, his wire-rimmed glasses reflecting the last rays of sunlight.

"The wind section in the third movement," Ari said, playing a phrase with one hand, "it's like he captured the sound of wind through canyon walls. But this piano part," he shook his head, dark curls falling across his forehead. "It's unlike anything I've ever seen. It's not just accompaniment—it's like a voice crying out from the stone itself."

Lisa gathered her notes closer. "The way it weaves between the other parts—it's almost like a separate conversation happening alongside the main dialogue. But who can play it? It needs someone who understands both classical structure and—I don't know—something else," she gestured vaguely, searching for words.

"Wilderness," Professor Friedmann offered. "Someone who can make a piano sound like both nature and human struggle." He cleaned his glasses thoughtfully. "It's perfect for the Rabin celebration, though. This symphony—it speaks to both peace and persistence. The way the themes resolve in the final movement—"

"But we *still* need to find a pianist with a sophisticated sensibility," Ari interrupted, running a hand through his hair in frustration. "The Israel Philharmonic's pianists are excellent, but this needs someone special. Someone who can capture both the technical complexity and the soul of it."

Professor Friedmann replaced his glasses, a slight smile playing at the corners of his mouth. "Perhaps we need to think bigger. What about Karolina Strapovic?"

The name hung in the air like a whispered prayer.

Lisa sat up straighter. "Karolina Strapovic? She is the most famous pianist in the world. Why would she come to Israel for us? And she has stopped traveling as much."

"Yes, but she's mostly in Europe these days, living in London," the professor said. "And Zubin knows her well enough to speak to her regularly. All it would take is one phone call from him."

"But would she do it?" Lisa asked, getting to her feet. "This is a celebration for Rabin and the Sinai Agreement. It's political as much as musical."

"That's precisely why she might be interested," Friedmann replied. "Remember her performance of Bach's Goldberg Variations as as protest in Prague a few years ago? She understands the power of music as both art and statement." He picked up one of the bottles of wine he kept for their "study" sessions. Through the window, they could see the lights of the university's security fence—a reminder of why celebrations of peace carried such weight here.

"To the Sinai Agreement," Friedmann said, opening the wine and pouring three glasses. "It's more than just a disengagement of forces." He paused, handling the bottle with careful reverence. "To give up those passes, those oil fields—many think Rabin is mad. But he sees the bigger picture."

"The buffer zones," Ari nodded, accepting his glass. "The early warning stations. It's like the symphony's structure—separate elements creating space for peace."

Lisa looked up from her notebook where she'd been sketching rehearsal schedules. "That's why the timing of the third movement is so crucial."

"Which brings us to our own logistical challenges," Friedmann said, settling into his chair. "Combining the People's Orchestra with the Israel Philharmonic; It's not unlike negotiating our own peace agreement."

Ari set down his glass. "The Israel Philharmonic players— some of them look down on community orchestras. They forget that half of our musicians are Russian conservatory graduates or players from the famous Vienna Philharmonic Symphony."

"And the other half?" Lisa asked, though she knew the answer.

"Arabs who practiced between shifts in the fields along with Holocaust survivors who kept music alive in the camps, former young Arab soldiers who carry instruments instead of their rifles. Men of the countryside who have never stopped playing for their God." Ari's voice carried quiet pride. "Different backgrounds, different training, but when we play—"

"That's precisely why this performance matters," Friedmann interrupted. "We'll need to work with Zubin on how to structure our combined orchestras. We can't throw the orchestras together immediately—like the agreement, we need a staged approach."

Lisa consulted her notes. "I've been thinking about that. We'll have to rehearse in sections first. The strings in the central section, but flanked by the wind players, Ari. They're stronger, especially in that crucial third movement. Then split the brass sections."

"We'll need to contact Karolina immediately. Until she signs on, we can't set a date for the performance," Ari added.

"And through it all, this extraordinary piano part," Lisa murmured, touching the score. "Like a voice of hope running through the complexity of withdrawal agreements and buffer zones."

"That's why we need Karolina Strapovic," Friedmann said firmly. "She'll understand." He glanced at his watch. "The orchestra hall should be quiet by now. I'll call Zubin. Don't finish off the bottle until I get back!"

Once the professor left to go to his office, Ari could hear Lisa's pencil scratching out rehearsal schedules. The symphony score lay open before him, its complex annotations like a roadmap to peace—or at least to the possibility of it. Ari couldn't help but think the young composer who wrote this must have known something of the Israeli conflict.

Within a few minutes, Friedmann returned with good news. "Zubin loves the idea, and he'll call Karolina tonight."

"If all goes well, we'll have a couple of months at least," Ari said, "to negotiate our own agreement between orchestras."

"L'chaim," Friedmann raised his glass. "To peace through diplomacy!"

"And through music," Lisa added softly.

Through the open window, a nightbird called—a single clear note hanging in the darkness over the Negev, where new boundaries were being drawn in the ancient sand.

22

ARCHER

The late afternoon sun slanted through the bay windows of the tiny apartment in Chelsea, casting long shadows across the thick faux Persian rug from Pier One. Archer sat at the baby grand Steinway piano, absently touching keys without pressing them. The piano, a gift from Archer's irrepressible Aunt Seraphina, occupied most of the living room. Barbara perched on one of the two folding chairs at the folding table that served double duty for guest seating and dining, her eyes bright with excitement. In her hand was a gilded invitation for a symphony performance in Israel.

"I still can't believe Karolina Strapovic agreed to do it," Barbara said, shaking her head. "Didn't you say she hasn't performed outside mainland Europe and the UK in what, three years?"

Archer's fingers finally pressed down, producing a soft chord. "More like seven or so, since she was caught up in one of the Prague Spring uprisings during her performance in 1968.

Her concert in Prague was interrupted with Soviet tanks in the streets. It scared her so badly she barely leaves London now. Professor Friedmann told me that she was moved by the concept of bringing together the People's Orchestra in Tel Aviv and the Israel Philharmonic. And to think they'll be playing my very own symphony. Apparently, Karolina Strapovic called it 'music as diplomacy.'"

Barbara smiled. "And to think it's all to celebrate the Sinai Agreement—finally peace in the Middle East."

"It all sounds so pretentious when you say it out loud."

"It sounds perfect and well deserved," Barbara corrected him. "This is a true triumph, sweetheart. My whole family is thrilled, just thrilled. You know my uncle's cousins in Tel Aviv, who survived Mathausen and Dachau, worship Rabin. They say he is a true hero of Israel." She slid from the chair arm to sit beside him on the piano bench. "My parents are so excited that they'll get to go and bring Bubbe. Besides your parents, who else is going to come with us to Tel Aviv?"

"Aunt Seraphina, of course, as well as Uncle Daniel and Aunt Elaine." Archer's hands stilled on the keys, thinking about what to say to Barbara, knowing she was waiting to hear whether he had any updates on finding his birth parents. "I'm hoping by the time we go to Tel Aviv, Uncle Daniel will have made some progress with the adoption records." He looked over at her, expectantly. All he wanted was for her to know how much he wanted to be with her and would do anything to make sure she was happy.

Barbara caressed his arm gently. "Thank you again for looking into that. And I know how hard the waiting has been for you."

"I love my parents—they're my parents in every way that matters. The adoption, it's just a fact, like having brown eyes or being right-handed." He turned to face her. "But I also want to know, medically speaking, in case there was anything I should be aware of. If anyone can work this out, it's Uncle Daniel."

"So have you heard anything new?" Barbara asked, cautiously.

"Nothing that we don't already know. The records were sealed. It was a closed adoption. He's still looking into it." He shrugged, then smiled. "But speaking of family histories, how is your grandmother handling the news about us going to Israel?"

Barbara laughed, but there was a touch of relief in it. "Much better now that there is peace. I don't think she would have wanted us over there during all the fighting. I've reached out to my uncle's cousins, so we will have someone to show us around." She paused, as if summoning up the right thing to say. "You know, Arch, I love you, I don't care if you are a Gentile or not, but when you told my grandmother you would convert if she wanted, well, that meant the world to me."

"I will do anything you want me to in order to make your family happy with our being together." Archer squeezed her hand.

"They are thrilled, and so am I. All I want is to be with you. I don't need a big wedding; all that really matters is making Bubbe happy."

"And I know your grandmother is thrilled that we are all going to Israel. Even if it's to watch your Gentile boyfriend's symphony be performed." His eyes twinkled as he said it. "I just want you. All the rest is dessert, if I get you." He got up and pulled her into a hug.

"Stop!" Barbara swatted his arm, laughing. "Bubbe's even more excited that we might get to meet Rabin. He's the sign of hope Israel needs."

"He is," Archer agreed, turning back to the piano where he found the main theme of his symphony and played it softly. "Music, peace, love—they're all connected. That's what my symphony was about, really. The wind that carries the music.

The stone that builds the foundations. The hardness, the fragility, and the strength of the human spirit." He trailed off, lost in the melody for a moment.

Barbara leaned her head against his shoulder, listening. "Play it again," she whispered. "The part in the canyon, when the wind speaks of love."

The melody shifted, becoming something warmer, deeper, filled with questioning phrases that resolved into certainty. Outside, the New York traffic provided a distant counterpoint, while in their tiny apartment, Archer's melody spoke of hope, of bridges being built, of love crossing every boundary.

23

DANIEL

The late Texas sun was too warm today. Daniel turned on his desk fan, and thought about telling his secretary to buy a new one. He wondered if it would be as hot in Israel as it was in Texas. Tanya Rosenbaum sat perfectly straight in her chair, her silver-streaked hair gleaming, her hands folded neatly in her lap. She thought she was here to sign some papers with Daniel for the business. Daniel hated misleading her, but he wanted her away from her family for the surprise he was about to deal to her.

But before they began, Tanya filled Daniel in on Ari's latest accomplishment. "You should hear him talk, Daniel," she said, pride warming her voice. "The way he's brought his orchestra together … and now they will team up with the Israel Philharmonic to perform for Rabin himself to celebrate the Sinai Agreement." She shook her head in wonder. "Who would have thought my grandson would be conducting in Tel Aviv for the prime minister?"

"The Sinai Agreement is historic," Daniel agreed.

Tanya smiled. "Ari says the mood in Israel is hopeful. Cautious, but hopeful. Anyway, the concert will be sometime early next year; they haven't set a date yet. But we're making plans to go. Why don't you and Elaine consider joining us? You've been such a big support for our family, and Ari has always looked up to you."

"That is a wonderful idea, Tanya. Of course, I'll have to talk it over with Elaine. And Ari himself? He must be over the moon about the concert!"

"He's flourishing. He and Lisa have started their graduate studies. They've moved into a small flat near the Rubin Academy. I would have preferred that they waited until they married, but as Ari reminds me, this is the seventies and young people have different ideas about relationships. At least they are starting to make plans for their wedding next spring. There's been some talk about them getting married in Chicago. I think Lisa's parents are hoping for that. But I'll be perfectly happy if they marry in Israel."

"Tanya." Daniel's gentle interruption made her stop, her smile fading at his tone. "There's something I need to tell you. Something important."

She set down her teacup with a slight tremor. "What is it? Surely those bastards at Zapata aren't balking at our deal?"

He wished this was about her pipeline extensions with Zapata Oil. But no, this was a much more delicate subject. "No. All of that is fine; you just need to sign the contracts. This is something else entirely. It's ... well, it's about Ari's adoption." He watched her face pale slightly. "There's something I need to tell you. Something, well, that might cause an issue. Ari was not an only child; there was a twin brother who was also adopted. That boy, well, he is asking questions about his birth parents."

The silence that followed was heavy as desert air before a

storm. When Tanya spoke, her voice was barely a whisper. "A twin?"

"Yes. And, well, he has a legal right to know about his birth parents, if all parties agree."

Tanya stood abruptly and went to the window. Below, pickup trucks and sedans crept down Main Street, their drivers unaware of the earthquake happening in the lawyer's office above them.

"Ari must never know about it," she said, her voice hard. But then she swallowed, losing some of her resolve. "Never."

"Tanya, I am so sorry, but I didn't want this to blindside you. You and I have had the best working relationship I could imagine. I respect you and think highly of you. I'd never consciously do anything that might upset you. But this is something I think you need to know."

She turned back to Daniel, her eyes bright with unshed tears. "Ari has always felt, well, incomplete, somehow. Even in Israel, where he's so happy, where he's found his calling and his true love. He tells me sometimes that something's missing. That he feels a gap he can't explain." She pressed her fingers to her lips. "I always wondered if he always somehow sensed he was adopted."

"Maybe it's more specific than that. He had a twin. And some of the latest scientific research is looking into the inexplicable bonds that twins often have."

Tanya returned to her chair, gathering herself. "These birth parents," she said carefully, not meeting Daniel's eyes. "Are they ... are either of them Jewish?"

Daniel considered his response, thinking of Karolina and her annual letters. "That's something I'm trying to verify," he said carefully. "Would it matter to you? To Ari?"

She sighed. "It might matter to the family. But to Ari? He is Jewish, through and through. To us, and to him." She shook her head slowly. "Maybe what matters more is the truth. Even if I'm not ready to admit that yet. Let me think, Daniel, let me think on it. I need to do what is best for my boy."

"Take some time," Daniel said softly. "Think about it. This isn't something we have to decide today. And if you decide to proceed, I'd like to meet with Jacob and Ruth to explain this to them."

Tanya nodded, but her eyes were distant, already calculating the cost of secrets kept and secrets revealed, of gaps that might finally be filled, of a grandson who might soon learn he was only half of a whole.

A FEW DAYS LATER, AS HE AND ELAINE WERE ENJOYING A QUIET dinner, the phone rang. As much as he wanted to ignore it, Daniel worried that it might be something connected to work. So he was relieved when Nancy Mueller said hello back.

"Daniel, we've just had some exciting news, and I wanted you to be the first to know."

"I'm all ears, Nancy."

"It's Archer. Remember his symphony that debuted at Juilliard?"

"How could I forget it? That was a marvelous performance, and Elaine and I are still talking about how wonderful it was."

"Well, his symphony is going to receive its world premiere at a very special event. It's some kind of a concert for peace early next year, in Tel Aviv, Israel. Can you believe it!"

Daniel almost dropped the phone. "That's ... that's amazing, Nancy."

"Yes, and you won't believe this: The concert is honoring the prime minister of Israel."

All Daniel could say was, "Really?" There was no way he could explain why he was so shocked to Nancy Mueller, of all people.

"So I wanted to ask you: Once we have the details, would you and Elaine consider joining us? Seraphina is going, so I thought it would be fitting that Archer's godfather be included too."

"I think it's safe to say we wouldn't miss this for the world."

"Well, let Elaine know. I'm having lunch with her next week, and I hope I have more details by then so we can figure it all out. Bye, Daniel."

When Daniel sank back into his chair at the table, Elaine asked, "Who was that?"

"Um, Nancy. She's asked us to go to Israel—seems young Archer's symphony is going to be performed for the prime minister."

"Oh my goodness! That is fantastic! Tell me all the details."

Before he answered, he couldn't help but think to himself: *Oh my love, if only I could!*

24

ARI

THE CANDLES CAST LONG SHADOWS ACROSS YACOV AND HIRAM'S dining table, their flames steady in the evening air that drifted through the open windows of the old stone flat in Jerusalem. Outside, the ancient city was settling into its weekly pause, the muezzin's call having faded minutes before, leaving only the whispered echo of prayers from the Western Wall. Lisa smiled as she observed Ari watching both of their families, all at the table, his face at peace. Tanya, Jacob, and Ruth were staying with Uncle Yacov for some sightseeing before the big day of the People's Concert for Peace. Lisa's parents were staying in Tel Aviv and had joined them for dinner.

Yacov and his life partner, Hiram Schluesser, had always been so kind to the young couple. They had even hosted an engagement party for them the year before. Lisa was overcome with emotion as she watched the interplay of light across the faces gathered around the table, each visage a study in the complex choreography of family, politics, and devout faith.

Hiram, with his professor's careful precision, had arranged the table as meticulously as he might catalog the architectural treasures of his beloved city. Yacov sat at the other end of the table, his shoulders still bearing the tension of weeks spent surveying the Suez Canal's rebirth after the years of war with Egypt.

There was something in Ari's eyes, Lisa noticed, a barely contained excitement simmering beneath his composed exterior. It was the upcoming concert, she knew. It was all he had talked about the past few months, all they both had been preparing for. But now with his family here, talk was of the reason for the concert and the man it was to celebrate, Yitzhak Rabin.

Tanya Rosenbaum's presence commanded attention without effort. After all, she was a woman who'd navigated oil company boardrooms and supervised pipeline installations in the oil fields with equal authority. Yet here, in her brother's home, she softened as she watched her own family.

"You should have seen him," Yacov said, breaking the contemplative silence that had fallen after the blessing. "Rabin, standing there in Geneva, showing the world that Israel could be both strong and wise." His voice carried the weight of personal investment. "After Golda stepped down, we needed someone who understood both the soldier's and the diplomat's path."

Hiram's eyes met Yacov's as a silent current of shared conviction passing between them. "The transition hasn't been simple," he added, his academic's precision tempering Yacov's enthusiasm. "After the Yom Kippur War, Golda's resignation opened wounds we're still trying to heal. But Rabin," he paused, selecting his words with characteristic care, "Rabin brings something different. He's a son of Israel who speaks the language of international diplomacy."

"Different?" Tanya's question carried the sharp edge of

CEO's pragmatism. "In America, we hear mixed reports. Some call him a hero; others say he's compromising too much."

Ari leaned forward. "Bubbe, you should've felt the energy in the streets when the interim agreement was announced. It was like," he glanced at Lisa, drawing strength from her presence, "like the whole city could breathe again."

"The canal," Yacov interjected. He had been one of the lead engineers on the reopening of the Suez Canal in June 1975, and his professional reserve momentarily cracked. "You can't imagine what it means, seeing Egyptian and Israeli engineers working side by side. A year ago, I was calculating blast patterns to clear war debris. Now, since the canal reopened, we're planning more shipping lanes."

Ruth spoke softly. "In America, in our synagogues and living rooms we ask how we can trust Egypt after 1973. After everything."

"Trust?" Yacov's question hung in the air like the smoke from the candles. "Perhaps it's not about trust yet. Rabin understands this. He was chief of staff of the Israeli Defense Forces in '67 and led us to victory. Now he leads us toward something harder than war—the first steps toward peace."

The conversation paused as the housekeeper brought out the main course. In that moment of domestic routine, Lisa noticed how the weight of history seemed to press down on them all: Yacov's hands, callused from rebuilding what war had broken; Tanya's shrewd assessment of each opinion offered; Jacob and Ruth's careful navigation of their place in this unfolding story; and even her own parents' cautious optimism at this new direction for their beloved Israel.

"Three kilometers of withdrawal in the passes," Yacov continued, his engineer's precision bleeding into the discussion. "Electronic monitoring stations. American technical support. Each detail negotiated, argued over, finally agreed upon. This is how peace is built—not in grand gestures, but in the careful measurement of every step."

The Shabbat candles burned on, as Lisa realized that her soon-to-be Texan family members were probably a little over-whelmed with such political talk, so she asked Ari, "My love, tell everyone about how we were able to get Karolina Strapovic for the concert. That was a miracle."

Tanya's eyebrows lifted slightly—the minute gesture of someone who had spent decades evaluating the true worth of things. "I have wondered about that," she said. "Karolina Strapovic is beyond the greatest living pianist. Some say she is one of the greatest of all time. Why come here for a people's orchestra to celebrate a man she has never met?"

"Well, we were fortunate that Zubin Mehta knew Miss Strapovic so well. When she agreed to play," Ari said, his voice dropping to a reverently hushed tone, "the entire project shift-ed." He studied the play of candlelight on his wine glass. "You have to understand what it meant—Karolina Strapovic, who commands waiting lists at Carnegie Hall and who hasn't played outside of mainland Europe in years—"

"The last time she premiered a new work," Lisa added, "was in Prague, during the Prague Spring, and the riots there scared her from committing to anything technical or new again, and she barely ever leaves London."

"She didn't just agree," Ari offered quietly. "She waived her fees and even canceled an entire season with the London Phil-harmonic and came to Israel to rehearse with us."

"After we sent her the score for Archer Mueller's symphony," Ari continued, his hands moving in remembered wonder, "she told Zubin that she sat for almost an hour without speaking. Just reading. The kind of stillness that feels like standing in the eye of a storm. Then she said something to him in Czech."

"What did she say?" Ruth leaned forward.

"She said," Ari's voice caught slightly, " 'Finally, someone writes music that remembers what music is for.'" His fingers traced invisible patterns on the tablecloth—his conductor's hands were never truly still. "Then she canceled everything. In December, she moved into a flat near the Rubin Academy in Tel Aviv and has been practicing fourteen hours a day."

"Fifteen," Lisa corrected gently. "The night guard says she never leaves before midnight."

Tanya's analytical mind cut to the heart of things. "So, she plays for this, for your orchestra of impossibilities. And she plays the work of a young composer no one has heard of."

"She plays for peace," Ari said simply, though the word carried the weight of mountains. "She recognized something in the score. Something about the necessity of beauty in broken places." He stopped, overcome for a moment by the memory. "The way she plays the cadenza, it's as if she's speaking directly to God. Not pleading, not demanding. Witnessing."

"Who is this unknown composer?" Jacob asked.

"Remember Noah, my friend from Interlochen? Well, it was through his father, who's a violinist for the New York Philharmonic. Mr. Templos attended our final concert at the kibbutz. He was impressed with our orchestra and sent Professor Friedmann the score of a symphony he had heard played at Juilliard. That turned out to be *A Testament to Wind and Stone*. Even the title fits the land of Israel."

They all agreed on the serendipity of it all—Noah's friend's father sending a new piece of music to a colleague at a music school that falls into the hands of Ari to conduct. "Archer Mueller is the composer; he's my age and a Juilliard graduate. He will be here for our final rehearsals as well as the concert. I can't wait to meet him and finally shake the hand of the man who wrote something that perfectly encapsulates the struggle of Israel."

A silence followed, everyone thinking of the musical choice and its meaning—political, intimate, and vast. Ari broke the silence and tried to explain to his grandmother, "The first time I conducted a full rehearsal of the music with the People's Orchestra, I saw the whole history of this land written on my musicians' faces." He paused. "Third-chair violin Sarah Brodsky, who still flinches at sudden noises after surviving Bergen-Belsen by humming Mendelssohn in her head, sat next to Khalil, whose fingers bear the calluses of both olive harvests and oud strings and whose grandfather's house in Ramallah still holds the key to their lost home in Jaffa. Some of them have studied at the greatest schools in their old, now destroyed, homelands; others have only heard the music. But all of them were overwhelmed with the piece's musical connection to the Middle East and its history. And all those musicians, they want to play for me. The whole thing, it's all very humbling." As he spoke, his hands moved in minute conducting gestures, as if the music lived in his very sinews now. "The percussion section includes a Moroccan Jew who plays his grandfather's darbuka, sitting beside a Bedouin who learned rhythm from desert winds and wedding celebrations. They found a shared language in syncopation that transcends the barriers of spoken tongue."

Yacov set down his wine glass with deliberate care. "Like the technical teams at Suez," he observed quietly. "The same look in their eyes when something finally clicks into place."

"Yes," Ari seized on the parallel. "The symphony itself is structured like a conversation between worlds. Mr. Mueller—he's done something I've never encountered before. The first movement opens with a theme that could have been written by Mahler, all European sophistication and complexity. But then," his hands rose, again conducting phantom musicians, "then it fragments, like a mirror shattering. Each piece reflects something different—Sephardic prayers, Arabic maqams, the rhythms of Yemenite wedding songs. They clash, argue, speak over each other."

"Like the people at the negotiating table," Hiram murmured, the historian in him recognizing patterns.

"Exactly," Ari nodded, his eyes distant with the memory of the score. "The second movement, that's where the miracle happens. The theme returns, but transformed. The oud doesn't just weave through the Western strings—it teaches them a new way to speak. The violin learns to bend notes like a mother's lament, while the oud adopts the violin's precise articulation. It's not fusion," he emphasized, echoing his earlier point, "it's conversation. Recognition. Revelation."

Rabbi Goldfarb asked, "And the final movement?"

"That's the most daring part," Lisa answered. "It remains unresolved. The harmony is there, but it's conditional, tenuous. Like the agreements themselves." She looked at Hiram as she said this, acknowledging his intimate understanding of such precarious progress.

"The last three minutes feature a stunning cadenza for Karolina." Ari shook his head in disbelief. "The piano becomes every voice at once—European orchestra, Middle Eastern soul, all speaking together but maintaining their distinct identities. It shouldn't work. By every rule of composition, it shouldn't work."

"It sounds like Israel itself," Tanya observed dryly. "A proposition that shouldn't work, and yet does."

"The orchestra itself is proof," Ari's voice took on an almost prophetic quality. "We have members who've lost family to each other's armies, who live on opposite sides of walls and checkpoints. But in the rehearsal room ... there's a moment in the second movement where everything drops away except a duet between violin and arghul. Rachel and Ibrahim play it. The first time we rehearsed it, they couldn't look at each other. Now ... " he smiled, a private, wondering expression, "now they argue over phrasing like family."

Tanya watched her grandson across the candlelit table with

the practiced eye of one who had spent decades reading the subtle tells of boardroom adversaries. Here was Ari, animated in a way she had never seen back in Texas, his hands painting pictures in the air as he spoke of his orchestra, his music, his Israel. Gone was the boy who used to stand at the edges of Rosenbaum family gatherings, a wineglass clutched like a shield, eyes always seeking something just beyond the horizon. Gone was the restless energy that had propelled him through endless piano lessons, violin tutorials, conductor's workshops—all excellent yet all somehow insufficient.

The transformation struck her with the force of prophecy fulfilled. In Texas, Ari acted like a sentence missing its punctuation. Here, in this ancient land of stone and mystery, he'd found his exclamation point, his reason for being. The irony of it twisted in her chest like a knife—that he should find his true belonging in a place built on the very question of belonging, just as she prepared to upend everything he thought he knew about his own identity. Tanya felt the weight of Daniel James's impending arrival like a stone in her pocket. Soon he would come with his briefcase full of papers, his lawyer's way of meticulously laying out unpalatable truths. Soon she would have to tell Ari that the sense of disconnection he'd always felt in Texas had roots deeper than culture or geography—that it was the blood running through his veins that carried different memories, different songs.

AFTER DINNER, YACOV SUGGESTED A WALK THROUGH THE OLD City. They emerged into the Jerusalem night, the stones beneath their feet still holding the day's heat. Hiram assumed his professor's role with elegant ease, pointing out architectural features that spanned millennia—Byzantine arches, Mamluk decorations, Ottoman windows. "Each stone," he explained, "tells multiple stories, depending on who's doing the reading."

Tanya barely heard him. She watched Ari's profile in the glow of the streetlights, searching for traces of his birth parents in the line of his jaw, the set of his shoulders. She didn't approve of his beard and shaggy long hair, which was now contained in a ponytail. Still, her grandson had grown into a handsome man, and she couldn't help but think that perhaps King David, who was also drawn to music, would have looked like her Ari.

She shook her head and came back to the present. What would Ari see, she wondered, when he looked in the mirror after learning the truth? Would it explain things to him, or merely replace old questions with new ones?

When they paused at a viewpoint overlooking the Old City, the evening air carrying the faintest hint of desert, Lisa said, "Tomorrow, we will take you all to the Makhtesh Ramon crater in the Eilat region, where Ari proposed to me."

Ruth mentioned their family trips to Palo Duro Canyon and how the canyon was such a special location for them all. "The red rocks there always make me imagine biblical lands." She glanced at Ari. "Remember how you used to sit on the cliff edge at sunset? Just watching?"

Ari's response came slowly, weighted with the consideration of a man comparing two versions of himself. "We went to Eilat last month. There was a moment there, standing between those ancient walls—"

"The light," Lisa interjected softly, her hand finding its habitual place on his arm. "The way it changes the rock from red to gold to purple."

"Just like in Palo Duro," Ruth offered.

"Yes and no," Ari said. "The colors are the same, perhaps. The geology might be similar. But in Palo Duro, I always felt like a visitor. An observer. In Eilat ... " His voice trailed off, heavy with implication.

Tanya caught the subtle flinch in Ruth's features—the almost imperceptible recognition of what her son was really saying. The Texas canyon had been a place to visit; the Israeli one felt like coming home.

Once again, the irony of it caught in Tanya's throat like a stone. Her grandson finally belonged to a foreign land just as she prepared to tell him he had always been, in some sense, foreign to them all.

Ari continued. "The Bedouin say the Red Canyon was carved by the tears of angels. In Palo Duro, we learned about limestone and erosion patterns." He smiled. "Both true, perhaps. Just different ways of reading the same stone."

Yacov might have launched into a comparative geological analysis, but something in Tanya's expression made him hold his peace. The silence that followed was filled with the evening calls to prayer, drifting across the city like threads of gold in the gathering dark.

They passed the Western Wall, its massive stones glowing golden in the artificial light. A few late-night supplicants still rocked in prayer, their whispered hopes merging with the evening breeze. Tanya touched the ancient stones, cool now under her fingers, and felt the weight of her secret pressing against her chest. How many prayers had these stones absorbed?

Ahead of her, Ari was explaining something to Ruth about the acoustics of the narrow streets, his voice animated with discovery and ownership. Tanya watched him—this grandson who was and wasn't hers by blood—and wondered if love could be enough to bridge the chasm that truth would open between them.

For now, however, in these eternal streets, Tanya let herself be just a grandmother watching her grandson in love with his life, his music, his chosen home. The truth would come soon enough, carried on the morning wind that even now was beginning to stir the banners above the Damascus Gate.

25

DANIEL AND KAROLINA

The tall windows of the Dan Tel Aviv Hotel's dining room cast a warm glow across the Mediterranean-style breakfast spread. The hotel, a modernist landmark on HaYarkon Street overlooking the sea, had become Tel Aviv's premier accommodation since its opening in 1953. Archer, Barbara, and his parents occupied a round table near the windows, the breeze carrying the salt air through the open terrace doors. The table was laden with a traditional Israeli breakfast: fresh tomatoes and cucumbers diced into a colorful salad, plates of soft white cheese and labneh, pickled herring, hard-boiled eggs, and warm bread straight from the kitchen. A bowl of olives sat centrally placed, alongside small plates of honeycomb and fig jam.

"The shakshuka here is incredible," Barbara said, breaking the yellow yolk with a piece of challah bread. "Though I have to say, nothing beats my grandmother's."

Nancy, still adjusting to the local breakfast customs, carefully spread labneh on her bread. "It's certainly different from our usual bacon and eggs back on the ranch. But I have to say, the salt air makes everything taste better. I still can't believe they chose your symphony for the celebration, Archer. It's truly a miracle. Your music being played in a country so very different from our own, but yet the music speaks to them."

"When's the rehearsal today, son?" Joe Bob asked, reaching for the coffee pot.

Before Archer could answer, Barbara jumped in. "Four o'clock. But first, we're heading to Jaffa. I want to show everyone the ancient port. The history there is incredible."

Just then, Daniel and Elaine arrived and joined the Muellers at the table.

"My God, Archer, what a coup for you, son, to have your music chosen for this!" Daniel said. Thank you so much for inviting us. I am truly humbled to be here."

Elaine poured their coffee and looked enthusiastically at the food. "Where's Seraphina?"

"Taking her time getting around, I suppose," Nancy said. "We walked through the flea market yesterday. The artifacts they're selling there—some pieces must be thousands of years old."

Barbara's eyes lit up, "My family is so thrilled I am finally here. It's such a momentous time in history. The Sinai Interim Agreement is groundbreaking. It's the first time since 1948 that Israel's given up territory in exchange for peace."

Nancy leaned forward. "You must forgive my ignorance, Barbara. I know it's important, but the fact that Archer's symphony was chosen to mark this moment—what does it mean, this celebration?"

"Well," Barbara began, warming to her subject, "after the Yom Kippur War, Kissinger helped broker this agreement. It's a huge step toward normalization with Egypt, especially after what happened in the Six Day War in '67 with Egypt, then Israel's withdrawing from the strategic Mitla and Gidi passes in the Sinai and from the Abu Rudeis oil fields. We're on the verge of peace at last."

"I read about the Yom Kippur War, even in Texas. It must have had such an impact on this part of the world," Nancy said. "And now, in two days, we'll hear Archer's symphony to cele- brate the peace that has been achieved."

Barbara squeezed Archer's hand proudly. "The rehearsal today will be his first time working with the People's Orchestra in person. It's truly an amazing accomplishment on the part of the young conductor, who is bringing together Arabs and Jews to play for Rabin in celebration of the peace that has been achieved. I am really looking forward to meeting him."

"Oh!" Elaine suddenly straightened in her chair. "That reminds me—Karolina and Dr. Brewer are joining us for dinner this evening. Perhaps you'd all like to join us. I still can't believe she is the star of the concert. That's quite an accomplishment.."

At this Daniel looked over at Archer; the young man needed to be told about his birth mother. But he had to speak to Karolina first. He hoped that he could make that happen before the two met. But then he realized that perhaps she had already met Ari, since she had been in rehearsals for weeks and Archer had arrived two days ago. Daniel set down his coffee. "Yes, having Karolina agree to perform in the symphony was quite a coup. But it's her partner, Dr. Brewer, who I'm excited for you all to meet. He's from Amarillo, too; he's been a mentor to me and a dear friend. He now works with international charities helping women deliver babies. He and Karolina live in London now, but Dr. Tom will welcome some time with Texans again, I'm sure."

Joe Bob appeared thoughtful. "So, the great Karolina Strapovic will be at the rehearsal this afternoon?"

"Yes," Archer spoke up finally. "She's been in rehearsals for weeks here, with the orchestra before the premiere. The piano part is, well, challenging is putting it mildly. But if anyone can bring out the dialogue between hope and history I was trying to capture, it's her."

Daniel studied Archer's face. The boy couldn't have known that the woman he'd just spoken of, the most famous pianist in the world, was his birth mother. Daniel took a deep breath and stared out the window; the Mediterranean glittered in the morning sun, and the sounds of the city beginning its day drifted up from the street below. A waiter appeared with a fresh platter of hot pita bread, and the conversation turned to their plans for exploring the city's famous Bauhaus architecture before the afternoon rehearsal. But Daniel knew he had to visit with Karolina alone sooner rather than later.

THE BAR AT THE DAN TEL AVIV HOTEL WAS QUIET IN THE LATE evening. Karolina sat at a corner table, sipping a glass of mineral water. When Daniel James approached, she stood to greet him with the practiced grace of someone accustomed to performing.

"Thank you for meeting with me, Karolina," Daniel said, settling into the chair across from her. "I know you will be practicing early in the morning, so I appreciate this."

"Of course. You said it was important. And a bit mysterious, calling me here like this, especially since we just had dinner together."

Daniel ordered a single-malt Scotch from the bartender. "What I'm about to tell you is going to come as quite a shock. It's about the twins, the two babies you gave up for adoption, the ones you sent letters to on their birthday every year." He pulled out a bundle of letters from his briefcase, her letters to her babies.

The color drained from her face and her fingers tightened around her glass. "The babies? My twins?"

"Yes. Through what can only be described as an extraordinary coincidence, they're both here. In Israel. In fact," Daniel paused, "one of them is Archer Mueller, the composer whose symphony you'll be performing, the young man who joined us for dinner."

The glass slipped from Karolina's hands, but she caught it before it could fall. "Archer? The composer? He's *my* son?" Her voice trembled. "I have two sons, and both are here? Who is the other one? Archer is my son?" Her beautiful chiseled face had a look Daniel had never seen before.

"Yes. Archer came to me last summer asking about his birth parents. As the lawyer who handled the adoption, I'm reaching out to all parties involved. If everyone agrees, I can release that information to Archer as well as the other twin, if he chooses to know."

Tears welled in Karolina's eyes. "This is … this is a miracle. God's hand must be in this. To bring us together like this, for music that Archer wrote with his own hand, a symphony celebrating peace." She pressed her hands to her heart. "He is a musician—my God, my wish came true."

Daniel smiled, wryly, but said. "I agree, this was meant to be." He took a deep sip of whiskey. "I have some papers here. If you're willing to allow your identity to be revealed, I'll need your signature."

"Of course, of course," she said, reaching for the papers with shaking hands. "But Daniel, what about his brother?"

"We're approaching that carefully," Daniel explained, handing her a pen. "We'll need everyone's agreement before any introductions can be made. He has not signed yet, because he doesn't know he's adopted. It's a delicate matter"

She nodded thoughtfully, "Those letters, you brought them, for Archer to read, then he will know, that I never, not once, stopped thinking of him, of both of them. Thank you. Thank you, Daniel, for keeping them all these years." Karolina turned her beautiful face to the wall, wiping away tears Daniel knew would not stop.

He recalled his conversation with Tanya and Jacob and Ruth a couple of weeks before, when they signed their own agreements, permitting the disclosure. Jacob and Ruth agreed that Tanya would be the one to tell Ari after they arrived in Israel. Tanya was struggling with the idea of broaching the issue with him before the symphony, but she knew it had to be done. Daniel hoped that Ari would be able to absorb the cataclysmic truth before such a big performance.

After she signed, Karolina sat back, dabbing at her eyes with a napkin. Daniel cleared his throat. "There's one more thing. Archer asked about his heritage, specifically if he has any Jewish ancestry. His fiancée's family are Jewish, and her grandmother wants her granddaughter to marry a Jew. So he's curious, hence me asking you. I am sorry, I know how hard this must be for you."

Karolina went still. Her face, already emotional, took on a guarded expression. "The father, he never knew about the pregnancy. He can never know, Daniel. It would destroy his marriage, his reputation."

"I understand," Daniel said gently. "But for the boys' sakes, could you at least confirm—"

A soft, sad smile crossed Karolina's face as memories seemed to wash over her. She thought of Dr. Isaac Rosen, how his eyes had lit up during her performances, how passionately he'd spoken about music and his faith. "Yes," she said finally. "Their father is Jewish. That much I can tell them. But please, that must be all. Promise me."

"Of course," Daniel assured her. "We'll proceed exactly as you wish." He gathered the paperwork and returned it to his briefcase.

The next evening, Karolina would be at the final rehearsal,

playing the piano part in her son's symphony. But for now, she sat in silence, her heart full and her mind boggled with the serendipity of it all.

26

ARCHER

The light spilled across the hotel's terrace, turning the Mediterranean into a sheet of hammered gold. Archer and Barbara sat close together at a corner table, their breakfast mostly untouched, watching the play of light on the sea and the beach. They were discussing Karolina Strapovic, and the fact they had dined with her and her partner last night.

"Her hands," Barbara marveled "When she reached for the bread, I noticed her hands. Such delicate fingers, yet you could see the strength in them."

Archer nodded, his composer's mind still processing one of the most memorable evenings in his young life. "The way she talked about the cadenza," he said. "No grand pronouncements about interpretation or artistic vision. Just ... understanding. As if she'd found something in the music that I'd hidden there without knowing it myself. The dissonance in the third movement," he added. "When she demonstrated how she'll resolve it

..." Archer paused, remembering the moment Karolina had hummed the passage, her fingers moving in the air like birds in flight.

They fell silent as Archer's godfather approached with careful precision, his briefcase dark against his light summer suit. "Good morning," Daniel said, settling into the chair opposite them. A waiter materialized with coffee, then dissolved back into the morning light.

Archer had been waiting for months for the truth, and now, he would finally learn who his mother was. He'd been puzzled when Daniel suggested they meet in Israel to discuss the latest updates, and he didn't want to wait a moment longer, "Let's have it," Archer said, his hands flat on the table. "I'm ready."

Daniel's briefcase opened with a soft click. The papers, when he laid them out, seemed too ordinary to carry such weight. He offered Archer a pen—a substantive thing of silver and certainty.

Archer signed the papers without hesitation, his signature flowing across the page like a musical phrase. Then he looked up, his face set. "Who is she? My mother?"

Daniel sighed. "Her name is ... Karolina Strapovic."

The sea breeze seemed to pause; the waves below held their rhythm for a moment too long. Barbara's hand found Archer's under the table.

"It can't be!" Barbara's voice carried disbelief tinged with wonder. "We just had dinner with her. Last night. Does she know?"

"I met with her after your dinner," Daniel measured his words. "She knows now."

Archer sat perfectly still, the stillness of the moment before the first note is played. His mind raced through the previous evening—every gesture, every glance, every note she'd hummed taking on new significance.

"There's more," Daniel continued, realizing the next revelation would be even more impactful. He cleared his throat. "Karolina had twins. You are a twin. You have a brother."

Barbara's hand tightened on Archer's as tears welled in his eyes. He could not speak, so she asked, "The brother," she managed to keep her voice steady where Archer's would not have been. "Does he know?"

"He will soon." Daniel's eyes met hers with professional compassion. "Oddly enough, he, too, is here in Israel. But you need to speak with your birth mother first. She's at the rehearsal space at the university this morning."

Archer stood abruptly, scraping his chair against the terrace tiles and moving before either Barbara or Daniel could respond, leaving his breakfast growing cold and the morning light painting the sea in colors of revelation. Barbara watched him go, her heart aching for him, after discovering not only who his mother was, but also that he was someone's brother, someone's twin. She sensed the immense consequences of what she'd set in motion and wondered if it was worth it. "It's because of me, isn't it? He would never have known about it at all if I hadn't pushed him."

"Don't worry, Barbara. I have struggled knowing this truth the whole of Archer's life. I talked at length with Nancy and Joe Bob, and they agreed he could handle all the truth. It was time."

"But why is this all happening here, now?"

Daniel thought about this before answering. "I'm a lawyer, a methodical thinker, and a factual person, but when I realized that Karolina was coming here to play Archer's music, I had to pause and think that maybe, just maybe, there is a higher hand at work. Perhaps it's truly about the power of love and the power of music."

The two of them were silent as they looked out to the Mediterranean Sea, which remained indifferent to the human drama playing out on its shore.

～

IN THE LARGEST REHEARSAL ROOM AT THE RUBIN ACADEMY, Karolina sat at the Steinway, her fingers hovering above the keys without touching them, as if she was afraid to disturb a sacred object. The instrument waited, patient and knowing, while outside Tel Aviv stirred to life. As usual, she had arrived hours before the orchestra, before the bustling chaos of musicians tuning their instruments and shuffling sheet music. In the quiet hours, when she had the giant space all to herself, she'd sit at this very piano, working through passages with the methodical precision that made her legendary.

The door opened with a soft click. Karolina looked up to see Archer standing frozen in the doorway. The light streaming through the room's high windows caught the silver in her hair, and for a moment, neither took a breath.

Archer took two steps into the room, his movements deliberate, as if in a dream. "Is it true?" The words came out barely above a whisper. "It's you? You are my mother?"

"I am." Her voice, usually so commanding, was soft and fragile. "I am, and you are such a beautiful boy. My son. My boy." She rose slowly from the bench, reaching out with trembling hands.

He took them in his own, noting how they shared the same long fingers, the same musical hands. This woman had given him more than just genetics—she had given him music itself. It flowed through his veins like a secret language, a code written in his DNA that had shaped his entire existence. Even now, he could hear it in the subtle rhythm of the air conditioning, the distant sound of traffic forming an urban ostinato, the mourning doves outside weaving their melodies into the fabric of the morning.

They stood there, mother and son, separated by decades of silence yet connected by something deeper than words.

"Who is the other one, my twin?" Archer asked finally. "Do you know?"

"No, because, well," she squeezed his hands gently, "he doesn't know yet. Once he signs the papers, then we can all know each other. You were the catalyst in this, so I thank you for that. But my other baby, he doesn't know he was adopted. Daniel told me that you knew, all along. And after meeting your parents last night, I know that you are loved. You cannot know how that fills my heart. That you are loved and had music." She took a deep breath and stared again into her son's eyes, her eyes. "Your brother will need some time to process this, all of it."

The silence between them was filled with unspoken questions, but Karolina broke it first. "Your symphony—it's remarkable. The way you've structured the second movement is genius." She paused, studying his face. "Tell me about your music."

Archer's tension eased slightly as he began to speak the language they both understood best. "From the beginning, for me, there was always music. Nancy—my mother—she is a musician herself, and she saw it in me. She let me explore every instrument, but the piano," he glanced at the Steinway, "the piano was home."

Karolina's smile held recognition, pride, and a touch of pain. Her genes, her gift, living on in this child she had never known.

"Playing the piano is one of my first memories, but then, in high school, I was injured." He flexed his left hand unconsciously. "I couldn't play, not like before." His eyes grew distant. "But then I discovered writing music. Composing showed me a different way to hear it all. The music is everywhere—in the wind passing over canyon walls, in the rhythm of bus wheels in the city, in the space between our words. Once I hear a note with every sound, I add it to a movement, I add it to a beat. It's all-consuming at times."

Karolina marveled at this, that her son thought about music

the way she did. She wanted to know everything about him, every moment she missed, every second of every day. The questions danced on her lips, but she refrained from asking him, knowing they would have time for that. So, they stood together, two musicians reunited in blood and talent and love.

27

ARI

THE SUN HUNG HIGH OVER THE MAKHTESH RAMON, CASTING shadows that carved the ancient walls into sharp relief. The tour group had moved ahead, their voices carrying back on the desert air like distant music. Tanya found herself slowing, her fingers trailing against the warm stone as if seeking support from the earth itself. She noticed Ari murmuring something to Lisa before turning back toward her.

"Bubbe?" His footsteps were sure on the uneven ground, a climber's grace in his movements. "Let me walk with you." Ari's hand found her elbow. The others disappeared around a bend in the canyon, leaving Tanya and Ari alone with the wind and stone.

"I proposed to Lisa right there," he said suddenly, gesturing to a natural stone shelf overlooking the canyon's sweep. "There's something about this place." He paused. "It echoes Palo Duro, yes, but it's more than that. There, I was always looking for something. Here," his free hand gestured at the towering walls, "I found it."

Tanya felt each word like a physical blow. The irony of his seeking, his finding, when all along they had kept from him the very thing he had been searching for. Her fingers pressed against the rough stone beside her.

"We should rest a moment," Ari said, misreading her hesitation as fatigue.

"No." The word came out sharper than she intended. She stopped walking, turning to face him fully. The canyon walls rose around them like witnesses. "Ari, there's something you need to know."

He must have heard it in her voice—that same tone from their walk in Jerusalem the night before. His hand dropped from her elbow. "Bubbe, are you okay?"

"Ari, there is something I must say. You were …" She faltered, the words feeling like stones in her mouth. "You were chosen. Chosen and loved. So loved." The rehearsed speech dissolved in her throat. "Your parents … we … You were adopted, Ari."

The wind whispered through the canyon, stirring loose sand. Ari stood still, the stillness of a conductor in the moment before the first note.

"What?" The word dropped between them like a pebble from the canyon rim.

"We thought … I thought … it would be easier if you didn't know. Your parents wanted to tell you when you were older, but I …" She reached for him, but he stepped back, his shoulder brushing the canyon wall. "It was my decision. And now I am telling you, because your mother said it was my place to tell you since she never agreed with me about not telling you."

"You tell me this, now. On the eve of the biggest event in my life." His voice cracked. "Why now?"

"Well, it's complicated. You see, Mr. James, Daniel, he isn't just here as a family friend and guest; he's here to get us to sign some papers." Her words tumbled out now, unstoppable. "He has papers with information. About your birth mother."

Ari pressed his forehead against the ancient stone. "All this time," he whispered. "All this searching. This feeling of being untethered." His hand curled into a fist against the rock. "Who is she?"

"We don't know yet. But Ari," Tanya forced herself to continue. "There's more. You have a twin. A twin brother who has been searching for his birth parents. He doesn't know yet about you, but he wants to know his mother. So that is why Daniel wants everyone to know and sign some papers so it's all legal and proper."

The silence that followed was absolute. Even the wind seemed to hold its breath. Ari's shoulders went rigid, his spine straightening as if he'd been struck. Without taking a breath, without speaking, he began to walk away, his steps mechanical, unseeing. The canyon walls threw back the sound of his footsteps, multiplying them until it seemed like many people walking away, not just one.

"Ari!" Tanya called after him, but he didn't turn. She watched him disappear around the bend, his figure blurring through her tears. The red walls of the canyon stood impassive, having witnessed countless human dramas in their ancient span, adding this one to their eternal memory.

REALIZING ARI AND TANYA HAD FALLEN BEHIND, LISA TURNED around and traced her steps back through the canyon. She found Tanya leaning against a canyon wall, one hand pressed to her mouth, tears tracking silently down her face. The sight was so incongruous—this titan of industry, this stoic woman, crying in a canyon—Lisa stopped short.

"Mrs. Rosenbaum?" Her voice was soft, uncertain. "Where's Ari?"

Tanya gestured vaguely down the canyon path, her usual precision abandoned. "Go to him," she managed, her voice rough with emotion. "He needs you now. He's—" She shook her head, unable to continue.

Lisa hesitated only a moment before hurrying in the direction Tanya had indicated. The canyon walls rose around her like silent guardians as she followed the path, her mind racing through possibilities. In all their time together, she had never heard Ari speak ill of his family. If anything, his relationship with them had always seemed almost idealized—the successful grandmother who supported his music, the parents who always supported his choices, the extended family who welcomed her so warmly.

She found him on a natural stone balcony overlooking the vast sweep of the canyon. He sat with his knees drawn up, shoulders shaking slightly, and her heart contracted at the sight. This young man who could command an orchestra with a gesture, who could shape sound into emotion, looked suddenly very young and lost.

"Ari?" She approached him cautiously, the way one might approach a wounded bird.

He turned at her voice, and she saw his face was wet with tears. Without a word, he reached for her, and she went to him, settling beside him on the sun-warmed stone. His arms went around her with desperate strength.

"Lisa, oh, Lisa, she told me … she told me … that I'm adopted," he said into her hair, the words muffled but clear. "And I have a twin brother. Somewhere out there, I have another mother and a brother. And I never knew. But … but … maybe I did? I don't know what to think."

Lisa sat still, letting the magnitude of this revelation settle between them. The desert wind riffled through her hair. Below them, the canyon stretched away like a wound in the earth, beautiful and raw. Her answer to him would set the tone of how Ari handled this. He always looked to her to help him with hard decisions, knowing her fortitude and strength equaled his grandmother's. She had to choose her words carefully.

"You have two families, Ari," she said finally, her voice gentle. "It's a blessing, isn't it? Another mother to know, a brother to meet."

She felt him shake his head against her shoulder. "All my life, I've felt like I was watching everything from the outside. Like I was searching for something I couldn't name." His hands tightened on her arms. "It wasn't just the shock of learning I'm adopted. It's him. My twin. A part of me I never knew was missing."

The sun shifted, casting different shadows on the canyon walls. Ari straightened, energy coursing through him like an electric current. "Daniel James," he said, his voice taking on an urgent edge. "He has the papers, the information. Everything." He stood, pulling Lisa up with him. "Meet me at the hotel. I need to know. All of it. Now."

Before she could respond, he was running down the canyon path, his footsteps sure and purposeful on the uneven ground. Lisa watched him go, his figure growing smaller against the red stone walls, moving with the desperate energy of a man racing toward answers he had spent a lifetime unknowingly seeking.

THE HOTEL BAR HELD THE PARTICULAR HUSH OF EMPTY PLACES IN the early afternoon, all dark wood and filtered desert light. Daniel sat with Dr. Tom at a table near the bar, their conversation suspended in the cool air between them, when Ari burst through the door like a desert storm personified. Red dust still clung to his clothes, to his hair, painting him in the colors of revelation.

"Mr. James!" The name came out raw, desperate.

Dr. Tom, reading the gravity in the air, gathered himself with practiced efficiency. "I'll leave you to it," he said.

Ari rushed over to the bar, the desert air palpable with the scent of his sweat. His hair was damp, and his pale face flushed with emotion. Daniel motioned to Tom's empty seat. "Sit down, Ari." His voice had the measured calm of a man who had delivered life-changing news many times before. He caught the bartender's eye. "A double Macallan, neat." Then, studying the young man's dust-covered face: "And water with lots of ice." When the bartender returned with the whiskey, he said, "Take a drink, son."

Ari's hands shook slightly as he sipped his drink.

Daniel watched him, noting how the amber liquid caught the late-afternoon light.

"Is it true, Mr. James? Really? I'm adopted and I have a twin?" Ari's clear brown eyes were rimmed with red, but they were eager.

"Yes," Daniel said. "You were adopted. Your birth mother couldn't keep a baby, let alone twins. It simply wasn't tenable. Every check was made, every precaution taken to ensure you went to a loving home."

"I know, I know. Of course, I know my parents and my Bubbe love me," Ari agreed, his voice rough from the whiskey and emotion. "But ... " He stared into his glass as if reading futures in the remaining drops. "Something was always missing. But now I know that it was a someone."

Daniel reached into his briefcase, the leather creaking softly. The papers, when he laid them out, seemed too ordinary to carry such weight. He explained their contents. "Your parents have given me permission to reveal the information about your adoption, and your grandmother has blessed that decision. If you do not wish to know, that's fine; you can sign this page. But if you do want to find out about your birth mother and your brother, please sign this document. Then I will tell you what I can."

The pieces were almost in place, the symphony of truth ready to play its final movement. Ari's hand steadied as he took the pen and reached for the second set of documents. Daniel watched him sign, thinking of the other signatures he had collected—Karolina's elegant scrawl, Archer's bold strokes, the names of the four adoptive parents who loved their sons beyond measure.

He opened his mouth to speak, to reveal the miracle of mother and twins united for the performance, but a sudden movement at the bar's entrance caught his attention.

"Ari." The voice was familiar to Ari from rehearsals—the man who spoke was Tom Brewer, Karolina's constant companion and protector. "There's someone who would like to meet you."

Ari rose, automatic courtesy carrying him through the moment. Their hands met in the formal greeting of recent acquaintances. "May I have the honor of introducing you to your mother," Tom said.

And there behind Tom stood Karolina Strapovic, an apparition made flesh. The late afternoon light outlined her profile, highlighting the arch of her brow, the set of her jaw, features that found their echo in the young man before her.

Mother and son stood frozen, separated by meters of expensive carpet and decades.

"You?" Ari couldn't breathe. This was his mother? The great pianist Karolina Strapovic?

"My God, you are my son. You have music, you *are* music. You are such a genius. I can't believe it's you." Karolina enormous blue eyes stared at her son's face.

Dr. Tom reached for Daniel's shoulders, the two men witnessing the miracle.

Karolina took Ari's face in her hands and stared at him. "You are exactly the same. Identical as your brother. I can't believe I didn't notice that earlier. Even with the beard, I see now that you look just like him." She kept gazing at him, her eyes brimming with tears.

"You mean, my twin, we are identical? The same?"

"So alike, so alike."

Ari was overwhelmed. Here was his mother, a mother he never knew about. A mother who was a world-renowned pianist, a musical genius. And he had a brother.

"Who is he, where is he? I want to meet him." Ari felt a longing that was both familiar and strange. He had a brother.

"You will, you will. But for now, we must prepare for our final rehearsal. Then all will be revealed. I know what life-changing information does to one when we have to perform, believe me. I had to play a full house at the Chicago Symphony when I found out about you. It was the hardest thing I ever did. But the music comes first."

Ari had momentarily forgotten about the final rehearsal. How would he perform? How would he be able to hold it together?

From across the bar he saw his grandmother walk in with Lisa. His Lisa, his bright beautiful light. She would be there for him, sitting first chair with her uncompromising violin. She would be his rock. He looked to his grandmother and saw concern, doubt, and fear—three expressions he'd never seen on her face before. He went to her and embraced her, whispering, "It's okay, Bubbe. It's okay. I will someday understand why you decided not to tell me. But for now, it's okay. Please don't be afraid."

Tanya Rosenbaum, who hadn't cried so much in years, cried for the second time that day.

28

THE BROTHERS

At the end of that final rehearsal that evening, the last note hung in the air like a prayer. Ari's hands remained suspended, holding the silence that followed—that precious moment when music becomes memory. The People's Orchestra for Peace made the music come alive this evening in ways he'd only dreamed possible. That moment when Mahler-like sophistication had shattered into fragments of Sephardic prayers and Arabic maqams—it transcended every previous rehearsal.

When Karolina played the cadenza, she had found something in those impossible harmonies that spoke of both loss and homecoming. The way she had played those three final minutes, her hands becoming every voice at once—European orchestra, Middle Eastern soul, all speaking together yet maintaining their distinct identities—it was as if she had reached into his very being and pulled out the music that would be a testament to Rabin, to the peace he was forging, and to all of the Middle East.

Lisa's violin and Khalil's oud had achieved that impossible

duet in the second movement, their instruments teaching each other new ways to speak. The violin had bent its notes like a mother's lament while the oud echoed its plaintive melody. The Moroccan darbuka and Bedouin drums had found their shared heartbeat, driving the piece forward with the rhythm of ancient truths finally spoken.

Ari had somehow found the grace to set aside the incredible revelations about his adoption, his mother being the woman he'd just conducted, and the fact that he had a twin brother. There was no way he could have gotten the People's Orchestra to this place, to sound like this, if he hadn't been able to tamp it all deep down for the last rehearsal. Every time the questions he had crept into his mind, he focused his attention on Lisa, on her violin, her hands, and her neck. She was there for him, keeping time and holding his gaze. Now that it was over, he had to resist the urge to flee the stage and pepper Karolina with all the questions. Who was his brother? Why had she given him up? Who was his father? They had so many years to catch up on, so many memories to share. Ari had seen Karolina speaking to his grandmother and parents in the lobby before the rehearsal. When Tanya hugged Karolina, it split his heart in two. He had two families now. And a brother. But who was he?

The silence held, perfect and complete. All the instruments stilled, the musicians reveling in the power of the symphony they had just performed, together.

When Karolina rose from the piano, her presence commanding even in the stillness, her voice carried easily through the hushed hall. "Ari, may I invite someone to join us on stage?"

Ari's heart quickened. Archer Mueller must be here at last—the genius who had written this impossible, beautiful piece that spoke of belonging and separation, of harmony found in unlikely places. In all of the revelations of the day, he'd forgotten how much he wanted to meet this genius.

"Of course." He lowered his hands.

Karolina's eyes shone with something more than the stage lights as she turned toward the wings. "Please, Archer," she called softly, "come meet your brother."

The word hit Ari like a physical blow. Brother. Not just composer. Brother.

A figure emerged from the shadows of stage left, and Ari felt the world tilt on its axis. It was like looking into a mirror, but one that moved independently of his own reflection. The same slight stoop to his shoulders, the same way of carrying his head as if constantly listening for distant music. The same floppy bit of hair in his eyes. And his hands—conductor's hands, composer's hands—hanging loosely at his sides.

The orchestra stirred, whispers rippling throughout as understanding dawned. Lisa's bow slipped from her fingers, the small sound echoing in the charged air. Even Khalil, usually so composed, let out a soft exclamation in Arabic.

Archer Mueller—the composer whose music had felt like memories Ari had somehow forgotten, whose phrases had called to him like a voice he should have known—walked onto the stage and their eyes met across the space where minutes before, music had woven its spell of unity and understanding.

It was uncanny. They had the same nose, the same arch of the brow that Ari saw every morning in his mirror. The same way of blinking when overwhelmed, the same unconscious gesture of running fingers through hair that fell the same way on both their heads. Even their height was identical, their bearing a perfect match, as if they had been cast from the same mold and separated only by circumstance and geography.

The silence in the hall deepened, became something else entirely. Karolina stood between them, her hands clasped tightly together, watching her sons see themselves in each other for the first time since birth. In their faces, she could see her own features reflected twice over—the way she held her head when listening to music, the slight furrow between the brows that appeared when processing deep emotion.

Somewhere in the back of the hall, a door opened and closed softly, a sound that broke the spell. Ari took one step forward, then another. Archer moved as well, their steps unconsciously matching rhythm, a synchronized movement they had never practiced yet performed perfectly. Two sets of identical eyes met, each reading in the other's face the answers to a lifetime of unasked questions.

Karolina took both boys by their elbows. "Follow me, please. We need to talk."

Her private rehearsal room door closed behind them. The twins stood side by side, their identical faces a mirror of anticipation.

"How?" Ari gestured between himself and Archer. "We're exactly the same."

Karolina sank onto the piano bench, her hands trembling slightly. "Please, sit down. Both of you."

The boys settled into nearby chairs, leaning forward instinctively.

"A little over twenty-three years ago," Karolina began, her voice barely above a whisper, "I was touring all over the world. I had no husband, no home—just a suitcase and a different city every month."

"You gave us up. And we were split up? Why, why not keep us?" Ari asked.

Karolina nodded, tears welling in her eyes. "I was alone, on a tour through the United States and found myself pregnant. I was so scared, but someone told me about Dr. Tom Brewer, who was from the Texas Panhandle. I called him and he took care of me, such good care. Part of his promise was that he would find loving homes for you both. But no one wanted two babies; it was too much. He made sure you were both wanted by good families." She reached for her bag on the piano bench. "But I never forgot. Not for a single day."

She withdrew a bundle of letters, bound with a red ribbon. "I wrote to you. Every birthday. Every year." She held them out with trembling hands. "Daniel James kept them safe, waiting for this moment. So you'd know—you'd understand—that I never stopped thinking of you."

Archer untied the ribbon, and the letters spilled into his lap like memories set free. "Uncle Daniel had these all this time?"

Ari touched the letters gently. "All these years ... "

"Daniel was sworn to secrecy, my boys. It was a closed adoption."

Both boys took the letters, scanning their contents, their faces filled with wonder and love. She had never forgotten them.

"But our father," Archer interrupted the moment, his voice catching in his throat. "Who is he?"

Karolina gripped the edge of the bench, steadying herself. "I ... I never told him. He was a devoted fan, followed me throughout my tour of the East Coast. But his name—I promised myself I'd never say it."

"Did he—" Ari hesitated. "Did he hurt you?"

"No, no," Karolina said quickly. "Nothing like that. He was very much enamored of me. And I of him, but our lives, well, let's just say, we couldn't be together. But there is something you should know." She looked at Archer. "Your fiancée asked about Jewish ancestry, didn't she?"

Archer's eyes widened. "Yes. Barbara's grandmother, who fled Vienna's Kristallnacht and never saw her family again, wanted to know. Do we have a Jewish father?"

"Your father was of the Jewish faith, yes." Karolina said softly. "That heritage runs in your blood, both of you."

Silence filled the room. Archer was overjoyed for Barbara and her family to know this now. Ari grappled with the realization that his faith and his commitment to it had not been a choice—it was in his blood. For him, this information was truly the icing on the cake.

Karolina reached out, touching each of their hands. "We have found each other. And now…" Her voice broke. "We three are going to finally play music together. It's been my one desire for you both to have music in your life, and now, look at us. One a conductor, who chose the music his composer brother wrote, to be performed in a country he'd never been to, and for their mother to play a part of. It's not just a miracle. I'd say it was actually meant to be."

29

A TESTAMENT TO WIND AND STONE

Tel Aviv, Israel
January 1976

The Fredric R. Mann Auditorium in Tel Aviv thrummed with anticipation. In the front row, Barbara's grandmother and parents sat to her left; Archer sat between Barbara and his father, while Nancy and Seraphina filled out the row. Archer's hands clasped Barbara's. Behind them, Ari's family sat with Lisa's parents next to Professor Friedmann and Zubin Mehta. The stage before them held Ari's People's Orchestra for Peace—a testament to unity itself, with musicians from across Israel and her neighboring nations arranged in a perfect crescent.

At the podium, Ari's hands trembled slightly as he raised his baton. The gravity of the moment pressed against his chest—Tel Aviv's most prestigious auditorium, Prime Minister Rabin himself in attendance, and his own mother at the piano. His mother. The thought still caught him off guard, even now.

Ari signaled the downbeat, and as the first notes rose from the orchestra, he felt that familiar terror—the fear that had haunted him since his first conducting position in Interlochen nearly seven years ago. But then he caught Lisa's eye in the first chair of the violins. She gave him that look, the one that had carried him through countless performances. Her slight nod said everything: "You've got this. We've got this." His hands steadied.

As a lone ney, a Middle Eastern flute, entered with its haunting melody, Ari dared to glance at Karolina, who sat poised at the piano, waiting for her entrance. For a second, Ari lost his momentum as he realized again that he was conducting his mother. Then his eyes found Lisa. She was his anchor, her bow moving with absolute precision, her presence grounding him in the present.

The first movement then grew with a whisper of wind instruments—Western flutes intertwining with the mournful call of the ney, their combined voice speaking of ancient deserts and shared skies. Traditional violins conversed with the Arabian oud, creating a harmony that transcended borders. When Karolina's piano entered, her notes fell like rain on stone, each droplet precise and purposeful.

Behind Archer, Tanya Rosenbaum leaned forward, her hand warm on his shoulder. "Well done," she whispered, her voice thick with emotion. Archer closed his eyes, feeling the weight of history in her touch. This was his brother's grandmother, a proud woman, a strong woman, and a Jewish woman, whose family had also fled and died from the horrors of the war just as Barbara's grandmother had done. Archer had not realized that when he wrote his symphony, he was writing the soundtrack for a country longing for peace. He thought he was writing for America and all of her foibles and losses, but it was really a testament to her daring to hope. Music truly could transcend worlds. Especially with his brother conducting. An immense sense of pride and awe filled Archer.

Prime Minister Yitzhak Rabin sat with his wife, Leah, in the diplomatic box. As the music swelled—the sound of peace itself given voice through instruments both familiar and foreign—tears gathered in Rabin's eyes. His face, usually stern with a head of state's burden of leadership, softened. He watched as Khalil's oud exchanged melodic phrases with the Jewish violinist, their music weaving together like a prayer. The music was the agreement. Never in his life did he think that Arabs and Israelis would hold a stage together and be able to play in congruence like the sound of angels. He bowed his head to hide the tears forming.

The second movement erupted with percussion—the thunderous voice of the Middle Eastern darbuka drums joining with traditional timpani, creating rhythms that spoke of heartbeats, of war, of peace, of life itself. In the audience, children of different faiths swayed to the same rhythm, their parents watching in wonder.

The final movement began with Karolina's piano solo, a melody that seemed to carry all the weight of history, all the promise of tomorrow. Ari conducted with his whole body, drawing forth not just music but hope from his orchestra. The theme built and built, layers of harmony stacking like the ancient stones of Jerusalem, until the entire auditorium vibrated with sound.

Backstage, Daniel and Elaine stood with Dr. Tom, all three transfixed. Tom, who usually maintained his composure, felt his heart clench. He had delivered those two boys. It was beyond rare to ever know what happened to the children he had placed into homes. Of course, he had always wondered. But he had trusted his due diligence in each placing, knowing he made the right choice. But seeing Karolina's twins reunited like this—playing each other's music, their birth mother on the stage—reignited in him the awe of witnessing miracles. He said a silent prayer thanking God for letting him see His hand at work.

Once the final notes faded in a gentle diminuendo like a desert wind at sunset, silence held the audience captive for three heartbeats. Then Archer rose to his feet, and the entire auditorium followed. The applause was deafening, a standing ovation that shook the very foundations of the building.

In the orchestra, Muslim and Jewish musicians embraced. Ari's parents wept openly, clinging to each other as their son stood proudly on the podium, his baton finally lowered. Tanya applauded, sending up her own prayer of gratitude for the blessings of this day. Prime Minister Rabin and his wife stood, applauding with a vigor that spoke of more than mere appreciation—it was acknowledgment of music's power to unite, to heal, to bridge the unbridgeable.

Karolina remained at the Steinway, her hands still hovering over the keys, as tears streamed down her face.

Ari stepped down from his podium and approached her. "Join me?" he asked, offering his hand to help her rise. As they turned toward the audience, Ari signaled to stage left, and Archer strode out to take Karolina's other hand, and as the three of them bowed in unison, the roar of the crowd crescendoed.

This was more than a symphony. It was a prayer for peace, a testament to the power of harmony over discord, of love over fear, and of a mother and her sons, reunited.

30

DANIEL AND DR. TOM

Tel Aviv, Israel
January 1976

The hotel bar had emptied out, leaving only Daniel and Tom in a corner booth, with a half-empty bottle of single malt standing between them like a silent mediator.

"I still can't quite believe it," Tom said, swirling his glass. "The music, the twins, Karolina ... all of it coming together like that."

Daniel took a measured sip. "The symphony was extraordinary. Archer told me so much as he wrote the music, how it was inspired by a bus trip from New York to the Panhandle. He saw so much pain, destitution, poverty, homelessness. Our soldiers living in the street, coming home from a war no one wants. Archer was moved to write about all the oppositions of the United States. But then he went to Palo Duro Canyon and heard how that struggle was also found in nature, and it was beautiful. He has a brilliant mind, that boy." Daniel looked up at the ceiling, remembering the sound of the instruments. "And Ari, his conducting was extraordinary."

"Extraordinary?" Tom laughed softly. "All of it was more than extraordinary. Let's call it what it was—a miracle, Daniel. A real-life miracle." He leaned. "You know what keeps running through my mind? What if Barbara hadn't asked that question about Jewish ancestry? What if she hadn't pushed Archer to look?"

"The two boys would have found each other eventually," Daniel said, his voice steady. "The music world isn't that big, not at their level. And they are both Panhandle kids. Sooner or later someone would have noticed their looks and put two and two together, don't you think?"

"Two musical geniuses, both from the Panhandle, who look alike?" Tom nodded slowly. "Yes, perhaps. But would it have been in time for this? For Karolina to play one son's composition while the other conducted? And to celebrate Rabin's hopeful attempt at a true peace?"

The ice in Daniel's glass clinked as he set it down. "The timing was significant."

Tom's voice grew more contemplative. "You know, there was a time in my life—a long time—when I didn't believe in miracles or God. I'd lost my faith completely after Ruth was taken from me; it shook me to my core. Science and medicine, those became my articles of faith." He traced the rim of his glass with one finger. "All those babies I delivered, all those families I helped create—I thought I was the one making things happen."

Daniel studied his old friend, saying nothing.

"But this." Tom's voice cracked slightly. "Watching Archer's music come to life, seeing Ari conduct, knowing their mother was at that piano. Daniel, how can anyone witness something like that and not see the hand of God?"

The silence stretched between them, comfortable yet heavy with meaning.

"All these years," Tom continued, "all the twists and turns my life has taken. The choices I made, the secrets I kept. I thought I was steering the ship, but now ... " He took another sip of whiskey. "Now I wonder if I was just following a current I couldn't see."

Daniel nodded, thinking to himself what he'd known all along—that God's presence had been there from the beginning, orchestrating this symphony of lives with infinite patience and grace. But he kept this thought private, understanding that some revelations need to be discovered rather than told.

"Faith," Tom said finally, raising his glass. "Not in what we can prove, but in what we can feel. In what we can hear when the music plays."

"To faith," Daniel replied, lifting his own glass. "And to miracles."

THE PRICE OF PEACE: THE STORY BEHIND THE STORY

I am a Christian who fell in love with Israel. The first draft of this novel was sent to a friendly editor on March 3, 2022, long before the horrors that unfolded on October 7, 2023, in what is now known as the Israel-Hamas War. *A Testament to Wind and Stone* concludes with a time in Israel's history that has shaped my life. What follows explains.

The story is a gift from the muses who originated from my life as a husband, a father, an educator, a lawyer, and a Christian. Many working parts formed this story about the power of love, the power of peace, and the power of music, whispers from my muses that had to be put on a page.

A large part of the story I so desperately needed to tell was rooted in my experience as a young lawyer handling private adoptions in the Texas Panhandle. Like Daniel James, I carried unnamed babies to approved couples in hospital parking lots. My experience was guided by a doctor who handled the births and founded and vetted those families. That man has always warranted my respect, and I hope I have captured him in the character of Dr. Tom Brewer.

I've never been able to reconcile handing over a child to a

wanting couple and then never knowing what happened to that baby. When our son and his wife had two sets of identical twin girls, I couldn't help but wonder even more what happened to those children I placed in good homes. The story of Ari and Archer was a way for me to resolve those questions. Writing about twins was also a way to explore the unique relationship between identical twins. It is a miracle they even exist, and their relationship to each other is one that is like no other in life.

Of course, the main muse in my life was my wife, Gene Alice. One of the greatest gifts of my life, if not the greatest, was being her husband. Genie was so many things to so many people, but with this story, I wanted to honor her extraordinary gift for music and the power that music had in her life and the lives of those she touched. She was a true teacher and resounding feminist; but it was her passion for music that lifted her up so high. Being her husband taught me more about the power of love and the power of music than anything else in my life.

Placing Ari in a Jewish family was also my attempt put into words the profound experience I had in visiting the Holy Land, for first time in 1976 and again in 1993. At the time of those trips, I had no idea that Israel's struggle and her elusive path to peace would be something that would shape me for years through my love for the Jewish people. Israel itself and its path to peace through the man Yitzhak Rabin became another one of my muses. So much of what I learned, experienced, and came to believe as a fundamental truth, I found in Israel and its people.

In 1976, an accidental trip to Israel, when Genie and I were stand-ins for Texas State Senator Babe Schwartz and his wife, Marilyn, cemented my love for Israel. Yad Vashem, the World Holocaust Remembrance Center in Jerusalem, is Israel's memorial to the victims of the Holocaust. When Genie and I visited, we planted trees on a nearby hill and stood in silence at the Eternal Flame in the Hall of Remembrance. After that first visit, we sat outside for most of the night at our kibbutz hotel, reflecting on our experience of being in the almost-smoldering remains of war. We have photos of our group sitting around kitchen tables at the kibbutz with several of the young new settlers. Because Genie and I were so much younger than the others in our group, our visits to the kibbutz were longer and more personal. They shared hopes and dreams with us, reminding us of the young people who settled the barren high plains of the Texas Panhandle, our home.

That same trip gifted me with one of my favorite memories of Gene Alice. As part of the U.S. delegation, we were guests of honor at the Israel Philharmonic Orchestra. We were seated in the first two rows, just below the conductor, the legendary Zubin Mehta. Genie and I were in the two end seats on the right aisle of the second row. At the intermission, we scattered to the restrooms. As the lights started to dim, Genie had not returned. She rushed back to the auditorium door, which closed just seconds before she reached it.

"When I arrived at the door, a young Israeli soldier stepped in front of me and lifted his AK-47 across his chest to block the entrance," she told me later. "I looked him straight in the eye and confidently said, 'It is important that I get to my seat.'" He didn't know whether to shoot me or let me in. He opened the door."

Mehta was poised, like Batman over Gotham, with his baton raised to strike the first note of Gustav Mahler's Symphony No. 2, *Resurrection*. At that moment, he must have noticed the door open and a stunning thirty-seven-year-old blonde gliding down the aisle, unabashed and unhurried. Mehta then lowered his baton, turned graciously to allow the elegant, golden-gowned beauty to take her seat. Beside me. I am convinced I saw him and Genie nod to each other as whispers came from the audience.

"Who is that?"

"Is she a Scandinavian princess?"

"Could she be the wife of one of the governors?"

Mehta then returned the baton to its poised position, and music filled the hall.

Gene Alice Wienbroer Sherman knew exactly who she was. Always did.

When our son, Lynn, and I went to Israel with a small party in 1993, we returned to Yad Vashem. Our trees had grown. We entered a very modernistic building, then walked slowly in near total darkness by holding onto a rail to enter a room with a vast domed sky. We were inside the Children's Memorial, built in 1987, where five candles are multiplied exponentially with the use of mirrors to reflect thousands of stars. A voice sounded the names, ages, and countries of the 1.5 million children murdered in those killing fields.

On this trip, we were allowed to visit a kibbutz that had been off limits in 1976—Kibbutz Manara, located in the Upper Galilee adjacent to the Lebanese border. It was established in 1943, five years before Israel achieved statehood, by members of the HaNoar HaOved VeHaLomed youth group and other young immigrants from Germany and Poland.

Our small group was invited to sit down and visit with residents in the bunkers that were part of almost every home. As the quasi chair of our group, I asked if we could meet Rachel Rabin-Ya'akov, a founding member of that kibbutz and the sister of then prime minister, Yitzhak Rabin. Our hosts made it very clear that she did not give interviews. However, as we were eating our meal, a young woman tapped me on my shoulder and asked if I would come with her. Ms. Ya'akov agreed to see me, but not the group. I asked if my son could go with me. She looked at Lynn and said, "I think that will be okay."

We were led behind a curtain in a far corner of the dining room, then down a hall to another building. There we met Rachel Rabin-Ya'akov. She reminded me of my mother—petite, barely five feet tall. She cradled a newly born grandchild in her arms. We made small talk about the things we had seen this trip. She made a few suggestions for how to use the rest of our visit to Manara. Then with a seriousness to her voice, she said, "Obviously, this is not why you asked to meet with me."

"No. Not really," I confessed. "Ever since we have been in Israel, the headline of every newspaper gives daily accounts of your brother's efforts to negotiate a peace treaty with Palestine. From what I read, it is quite possible he will be successful. If that happens, the chances are almost certain that the land for this kibbutz or some part of it will be returned to Syria. It is difficult for me to ask, but is that possible? Would you support your brother and that element of a peace treaty?"

This beautiful, elegant, gray-haired woman, holding a grand-child born recently in that kibbutz, looked intently into my eyes. "If it will bring peace, we will do it." Tears were streaming down her cheeks, as they did for me and Lynn. It is a moment not recorded, but not forgotten.

On September 13, 1993, Rabin signed the Oslo Accords, securing a long peace process aimed at achieving a treaty resulting in both the recognition of Israel by the Palestine Liberation Organization and the recognition by Israel of the PLO as the representative of the Palestinian people and as a partner in bilateral negotiations. The following year, Rabin was awarded the Nobel Peace Prize, along with Shimon Peres and Yasser Arafat.

Those peace efforts were cut short when Rabin was assassinated on November 4, 1995, following a peace rally in Tel Aviv, pierced by three bullets aimed in hatred. The peace Israel so desperately wanted and needed is a piece of history that is yet to be written; with Rabin's assassination, it fell apart.

At Rabin's last speech, minutes before history was robbed of a true hero, the Kings of Israel Square pulsed with the energy of more than one hundred thousand people, mostly young, their voices rising in unison: "Rabin! Rabin! Rabin!" A call that carried hope on its wings, hope that had seemed impossible just years before. For those who knew him well, something was different about Yitzhak Rabin that night. The usually stern-faced soldier-turned-peacemaker smiled, even sang—a rare sight that his colleague Shimon Peres would later recall with poignant clarity: "We knew each other a very long time. He never embraced me. I never heard him sing. And there he was embracing, happy, singing. That was the greatest day of his life."

As Rabin left the platform to go to his car, a Jewish assassin fired three bullets into his back. Yitzhak Rabin passed away at Ichilov Hospital, after all attempts by doctors to save him had failed. Everyone was shocked. One observer said, "The whole place was full of young girls and boys, crying like babies, and the whole nation was crying."

At 11:15 p.m., Eitan Haber, Rabin's communications adviser, walked out of the hospital to face the television cameras and announced Rabin's death to the media:

> The government of Israel announces in consternation, in great sadness, and in deep sorrow, the death of prime minister and minister of defense Yitzhak Rabin, who was murdered by an assassin, tonight in Tel Aviv. The government shall convene in one hour for a mourning session in Tel Aviv. Blessed be his memory.

In Rabin's pocket was a blood-stained sheet of paper with the lyrics to the well-known Israeli song "Shir LaShalom" ("Song for Peace"), which was sung at the rally. It dwells on the impossibility of bringing a dead person back to life and, therefore, the need for peace.

Just two years earlier, on that same soil where young Israelis gathered to support peace and cheer Rabin, I had walked those same streets, choked with protesters—settlers and their families who opposed any concession of land, any step toward compromise. The geography of peace, like the geography of war, came down to mere miles: Tel Aviv to Cairo was shorter than Amarillo to Dallas, yet the distance between opposing views seemed insurmountable.

Rabin's words, his person, his leadership, all need to be studied and committed to memory and action. With his loss, the world gained what seems to be a never-ending fight for a peace that could have been.

In Rabin's speech accepting the Nobel Peace Prize, delivered just months before his murder, he delivered what I deem to be not only one of the greatest speeches ever given on peace, but also something of a prophecy.

Max Sherman
Austin, Texas
November 2025

YITZHAK RABIN'S NOBEL
PEACE PRIZE SPEECH

Oslo, Norway
December 10, 1994

Your Majesty the King,
Your Royal Highness,
Esteemed Members of the Norwegian Nobel Committee,
Honorable Prime Minister Madame Gro Harlem Brundtland,
Ministers,
Members of the Parliament and Ambassadors,
Fellow Laureates,
Distinguished Guests,
Friends,
Ladies and Gentlemen,

At an age when most youngsters are struggling to unravel the secrets of mathematics and the mysteries of the Bible; at an age when first love blooms; at the tender age of sixteen, I was handed a rifle so that I could defend myself—and also, unfortunately, so that I could kill in an hour of danger.

That was not my dream. I wanted to be a water engineer. I

studied in an agricultural school, and I thought that being a water engineer was an important profession in the parched Middle East. I still think so today. However, I was compelled to resort to the gun.

I served in the military for decades. Under my command, young men and women who wanted to live, wanted to love, went to their deaths instead. Under my command, they killed the enemy's men who had been sent out to kill us.

LADIES AND GENTLEMEN,

In my current position, I have ample opportunity to fly over the State of Israel, and lately over other parts of the Middle East, as well. The view from the plane is breathtaking: deep-blue lakes, dark-green fields, dun-colored deserts, stone-gray mountains, and the entire countryside peppered with white-washed, red-roofed houses.

And cemeteries. Graves as far as the eye can see.

Hundreds of cemeteries in our part of the Middle East—in our home in Israel—but also in Egypt, in Syria, Jordan, Lebanon, and Iraq. From the plane's window, from thousands of feet above them, the countless tombstones are silent. But the sound of their outcry has carried from the Middle East throughout the world for decades.

Standing here today, I wish to salute loved ones—and foes. I wish to salute all the fallen of all the countries in all the wars; the members of their families who bear the enduring burden of bereavement; the disabled whose scars will never heal. Tonight I wish to pay tribute to each and every one of them, for this important prize is theirs, and theirs alone.

LADIES AND GENTLEMEN,

I was a young man who has now grown fully in years. And of

all the memories I have stored up in my seventy-two years, what I shall remember most, to my last day, are the silences.

The heavy silence of the moment after, and the terrifying silence of the moment before.

As a military man, as a commander, I issued orders for dozens, probably hundreds of military operations. And together with the joy of victory and grief of bereavement, I shall always remember the moment just after making the decision to mount an action: the hush as senior officers or cabinet ministers slowly rise from their seats; the sight of their receding backs; the sound of the closing door; and then the silence in which I remain alone.

That is the moment you grasp that as a result of the decision just made, people will be going to their deaths. People from my nation, people from other nations. And they still don't know it.

At that hour, they are still laughing and weeping; still weaving plans and dreaming about love; still musing about planting a garden or building a house—and they have no idea these are their last hours on earth. Which of them is fated to die? Whose picture will appear in a black border in tomorrow's newspaper? Whose mother will soon be in mourning? Whose world will crumble under the weight of the loss?

As a former military man, I will also forever remember the silence of the moment before: the hush when the hands of the clock seem to be spinning forward, when time is running out, and in another hour, another minute, the inferno will erupt.

In that moment of great tension just before the finger pulls the trigger, just before the fuse begins to burn; in the terrible quiet of that moment, there's still time to wonder, alone: Is it really imperative to act? Is there no other choice? No other way?

And then the order is given, and the inferno begins.

"God takes pity on kindergarteners," wrote the poet Yehuda Amichai, who is here with us tonight.

God takes pity on kindergarteners,
Less so on schoolchildren,
And will no longer pity their elders,
Leaving them to their own.
And sometimes they will have to crawl on all fours
Through the burning sand
To reach the casualty station
Bleeding.

For decades God has not taken pity on the kindergarteners in the Middle East, or the schoolchildren, or their elders. There has been no pity in the Middle East for generations.

LADIES AND GENTLEMEN,

I was a young man who has now grown fully in years. And of all the memories I have stored up in my seventy-two years, I now recall the hopes.

Our peoples have chosen us to give them life. Terrible as it is to say, their lives are in our hands. Tonight, their eyes are upon us, and their hearts are asking: How is the authority vested in these men and women being used? What will they decide? What kind of morning will we rise to tomorrow? A day of peace? Of war? Of laughter or of tears?

A child is born into an utterly undemocratic world. He cannot choose his father and mother. He cannot pick his sex or color, his religion, nationality, or homeland. Whether he is born in a manor or a manger, whether he lives under a despotic or democratic regime, it is not his choice. From the moment he comes, close-fisted, into the world, his fate lies in the hands of his nation's leaders. It is they who will decide whether he lives in comfort or despair, in security or in fear. His fate is given to us to resolve—to the presidents and prime ministers of countries, democratic or otherwise.

LADIES AND GENTLEMEN,

Just as no two fingerprints are identical, so no two people are alike, and every country has its own laws and culture, traditions, and leaders. But there is one universal message which can embrace the entire world, one precept which can be common to different regimes, to races which bear no resemblance, to cultures alien to each other.

It is a message which the Jewish people has [*sic*] borne for thousands of years, a message found in the Book of Books, which my people has [*sic*] bequeathed to all civilized men: "*V'nishmartem me'od Inafshoteichem*," in the words in Deuteronomy: "Therefore take good heed to yourselves." Or, in contemporary terms, the message of the Sanctity of Life.

The leaders of nations must provide their peoples with the conditions—the "infrastructure," if you will—which enables them to enjoy life: freedom of speech and of movement; food and shelter; and most important of all: life itself. A man cannot enjoy his rights if he is not among the living. And so every country must protect and preserve the key element in its national ethos: the lives of its citizens.

To defend those lives, we call upon our citizens to enlist in the army. And to defend the lives of our citizens serving in the army, we invest huge sums in planes, and tanks, in armored plating and concrete fortifications. Yet despite it all, we fail to protect the lives of our citizens and soldiers. Military cemeteries in every corner of the world are silent testimony to the failure of national leaders to sanctify human life.

There is only one radical means of sanctifying human lives. Not armored plating, or tanks, or planes, or concrete fortifications.

The one radical solution is peace.

LADIES AND GENTLEMEN,

The profession of soldiering embraces a certain paradox. We take the best and bravest of our young men into the army. We supply them with equipment which costs a virtual fortune. We rigorously train them for the day when they must do their duty—and we expect them to do it well. Yet we fervently pray that that day will never come—that the planes will never take flight, the tanks will never move forward, the soldiers will never mount the attacks for which they have been trained so well.

We pray it will never happen because of the Sanctity of Life.

History as a whole, and modern history in particular, has known harrowing times when national leaders turned their citizens into cannon fodder in the name of wicked doctrines: vicious Fascism and fiendish Nazism. Pictures of children marching to the slaughter, photos of terrified women at the gates of crematoria must loom before the eyes of every leader in our generation, and the generations to come. They must serve as a warning to all who wield power:

Almost all the regimes which did not place Man and the Sanctity of Life at the heart of their worldview, all those regimes have collapsed and are no more. You can see it for yourselves in our own day.

Yet this is not the whole picture. To preserve the Sanctity of Life, we must sometimes risk it. Sometimes there is no other way to defend our citizens than to fight for their lives, for their safety and sovereignty. This is the creed of every democratic state.

LADIES AND GENTLEMEN,

In the State of Israel, from which I come today; in the Israel Defense Forces, which I have had the privilege to command, we have always viewed the Sanctity of Life as a supreme value. We have gone to war only when a fearful sword was poised to cut us down.

The history of the State of Israel, the annals of the Israel Defense Forces are filled with thousands of stories of soldiers who sacrificed themselves—who died while trying to save wounded comrades; who gave their lives to avoid causing harm to innocent people on the enemy's side.

In the coming days, a special Commission of the Israel Defense Forces will finish drafting a Code of Conduct for our soldiers. The formulation regarding human life will read as follows, and I quote:

> In recognition of its supreme importance, the soldier will preserve human life in every way possible and endanger himself, or others, only to the extent deemed necessary to fulfill this mission.
>
> The Sanctity of Life, in the view of the soldiers of the Israel Defense Forces, will find expression in all their actions; in considered and precise planning; in intelligent and safety-minded training and in judicious implementation, in accordance with their mission; in taking the professionally proper degree of risk and degree of caution; and in the constant effort to limit casualties to the scope required to achieve the objective.

For many years ahead—even if wars come to an end, after peace comes to our land—these words will remain a pillar of fire which goes before our camp, a guiding light for our people. And we take pride in that.

LADIES AND GENTLEMEN,

We are in the midst of building the peace. The architects and engineers of this enterprise are engaged in their work even as we gather here tonight, building the peace layer by layer, brick by brick, beam by beam. The job is difficult, complex, trying. Mistakes could topple the whole structure and bring disaster down upon us.

And so we are determined to do the job well—despite the toll of murderous terrorism, despite fanatic and scheming enemies.

We will pursue the course of peace with determination and fortitude.

We will not let up.

We will not give in.

Peace will triumph over all our enemies, because the alternative is grim for us all.

And we will prevail.

We will prevail because we regard the building of peace as a great blessing for us, and for our children after us. We regard it as a blessing for our neighbors on all sides, and for our partners in this enterprise—the United States, Russia, Norway, and all mankind.

We wake up every morning, now, as different people. Suddenly, peace. We see the hope in our children's eyes. We see the light in our soldiers' faces, in the streets, in the buses, in the fields.

We must not let them down.

We will not let them down.

I do not stand here alone, today, on this small rostrum in Oslo. I am the emissary of generations of Israelis, of the shepherds of Israel, just as King David was a shepherd; of the herdsmen and dressers of sycamore trees, as the Prophet Amos was; of the rebels against the establishment, like the Prophet Jeremiah; and of men who go down to the sea, like the Prophet Jonah.

I am the emissary of the poets and of those who dreamed of an end to war, like the Prophet Isaiah.

I am also the emissary of sons of the Jewish people like Albert Einstein and Baruch Spinoza; like Maimonides, Sigmund Freud, and Franz Kafka.

And I am the emissary of the millions who perished in the Holocaust, among whom were surely many Einsteins and Freuds who were lost to us, and to humanity, in the flames of the crematoria.

I am here as the emissary of Jerusalem, at whose gates I fought in days of siege; Jerusalem which has always been, and is today, the eternal capital of the State of Israel and the heart of the Jewish people, who pray toward it three times a day.

And I am also the emissary of the children who drew their visions of peace and of the immigrants from Saint Petersburg and Addis Ababa.

I stand here mainly for the generations to come, so that we may all be deemed worthy of the medallion which you have bestowed on me today.

I stand here as the emissary of our neighbors who were our enemies. I stand here as the emissary of the soaring hopes of a people which has endured the worst that history has to offer and nevertheless made its mark—not just on the chronicles of the Jewish people but on all mankind.

With me here are five million citizens of Israel—Jews and Arabs, Druze and Circassians—five million hearts beating for peace—and five million pairs of eyes, which look to us with such great expectations for peace.

LADIES AND GENTLEMEN,

I wish to thank, first and foremost, those citizens of the State of Israel, of all generations and political persuasions, whose sacrifices and relentless struggle for peace bring us steadier closer to our goal.

I wish to thank our partners—the Egyptians, Jordanians,

Palestinians, and the Chairman of the Palestinian Liberation Organization, Mr. Yasser Arafat, with whom we share this Nobel Prize—who have chosen the path of peace and are writing a new page in the annals of the Middle East.

I wish to thank the members of the Israeli government and above all my colleague Mr. Shimon Peres, whose energy and devotion to the cause of peace are an example to us all.

I wish to thank my family for their support.

And, of course, I wish to thank the members of the Nobel Committee and the courageous Norwegian people for bestowing this illustrious honor on my colleagues and myself.

LADIES AND GENTLEMEN,

Allow me to close by sharing with you a traditional Jewish blessing which has been recited by my people, in good times and in bad, from time immemorial, as a token of their deepest longing:

"The Lord will give strength to his people; the Lord will bless his people—all of us—with peace."

THE TEAM FOR MY FIRST NOVEL

As I mentioned in "The Price of Peace: The Story Behind the Story," this book was inspired by my beloved wife, Gene Alice, as well as the two sets of identical twins in our family. It was also based on my own experience as a young attorney in the Texas Panhandle handling adoptions in conjunction with Dr. Early B. Lokey, who inspired the character of Dr. Thomas Brewer.

I had no idea that I had a novel in me until the end of July 2021, when my good friend and, as she says, "protégé" Stacey Abrams sent me a copy of her new novel. I read it in three days. Two weeks later I was asked to give a talk on twins that Gene Alice had prepared for Open Forum here in Austin.

Those two events inspired me to step up to the plate and write my first novel.

Once I got started, my longtime friend Betty Sue Flowers emailed me in February 2023 and asked if I was writing another book, to which I replied: "You are probably not surprised that yes, I have written another book, a novel put together in less than twelve months." Betty Sue, as always, kindly reviewed that rough draft and made several thoughtful suggestions.

Now it is, two and a half years later, and I finally have a novel that I am proud of.

As I went through the writing process, I realized that this book is the product of a team effort. Here are many of the people who have massaged and recommended many of the changes that turned my initial draft into a polished first novel that I am proud of.

I would like to thank my editors, Cyndi Hughes of Booktique Consulting and Katherine Moore, for their guidance and assistance in shaping my initial draft into a true novel. It was a long process, but seeing the book come to life has been magical.

I also want to thank several people for providing thoughtful feedback on the early drafts:

Rabbi Brian Strauss, Senior Rabbi at Congregation Beth Yeshurun, Houston, Texas, reviewed and clarified my interpretations of the Jewish faith.

Joanna Hitchcock, the former director of the University of Texas Press and a past president of the Association of American University Presses, was my mentor for my book *Barbara Jordan: Speaking the Truth with Eloquent Thunder* and also one of my early readers for this novel.

Gregg Ramshaw, the former producer for PBS's *The MacNeil/Lehrer NewsHour,* which eventually became the *PBS NewHour,* also offered suggestions that helped improve the book.

I also want to thank three new friends with whom I dined most every Monday night here at our senior living complex: Dina Milman, Juanita Silberstein, and Irene Wyde Parker, all of whom knew I was writing a novel with a major component based on Judaism. They generously shared their families' stories, ranging from a young boy being conscripted in the czar's army to coming to America via Ellis Island and Galveston, Texas, then to the mines of Colorado and migrating to the Texas Panhandle. Their stories intertwined with my own research from the many books written about Jews in Texas. These and other family stories found in the archives of many synagogues inspired the Rosenbaums.

As I approached my ninetieth birthday, the encouragement of my family, our son and daughter, six granddaughters, and their significant others was so important: "How's the novel coming along? Are you about through? When will I be able to read it?"

And I could see Zubin Mehta nod to my Gene Alice as she whispers in my ear, "Max, you can do this."

Top: Max and Gene Alice in 1965

Middle: Max and Gene Alice with their twin granddaughters Mary Alice and Hattie in 1993

Bottom: The Sherman family, including both sets of identical-twin granddaughters

"RELEASING THE BUTTERFLY" EXCERPT

MAX SHERMAN'S PREVIOUS BOOK, RELEASING THE BUTTERFLY IS A love story that follows the decades-long relationship of a couple who met as teenagers by happenstance at a jail in the Texas Panhandle and find happiness in all situations—including Alzheimer's.

These descendants of blue-collar parents, raised in a tradition steeped in education and faith, became friends through a shared love of literature, theater, film, and music. Having come of age in the 1950s, they would have to negotiate the terms of their relationship to ensure a wholly equal partnership. They would learn how to navigate a life together, find fulfillment, and, ultimately, confront a heartbreaking challenge that threatened to upend their happiness and their own self-identities.

By a caregiver for caregivers, **Releasing the Butterfly** *offers a glimpse of hope and resilience through Alzheimer's.*

"I did not set out to write a self-help book about coping with a spouse who has Alzheimer's Disease. But in writing this book about my journey with my beloved Gene Alice, I helped myself."

CHAPTER 1

I love a low-key evening. No excitement, no surprises. That's the kind of evening Gene Alice and I were having when it took an unexpected turn. I did not see it coming, perhaps because the evening had unfolded in the most spectacularly ordinary way.

We were in the apartment and had just watched a rerun of one of *Mission Impossible,* one of our favorite old-time TV shows, running in syndication. I had slipped off my shoes, exposing a new pair of yellow-and-blue argyle socks. They were loud, but they will make Gene Alice smile, I thought. And she did when she glanced over at them.

Red-stained napkins and plates holding pizza crust still sat on the table, the remains of a simple but tasty dinner. I didn't care about the mess. We were nestled in a pair of recliners in the living room, side by side, close enough that we could clink our wine goblets. We were enjoying a robust Chianti, a Classico Gran Selezione. It was perfect. I wanted to make Gene Alice happy, and when the wine expert steered me to this bottle in his shop, I probably spent a little too much. But Gene Alice always said she wanted a "good Chianti" with her pizza, and, I told myself, she was worth the splurge.

I looked over at her, relaxing in her chair, feet up, the pale blue light of the TV illuminating her delicate profile. It was nearly mid-night, and I was tired. The dishes can wait, I told myself. I stood and looked back at Gene Alice. "Let me put the dishes in the sink," I said. "And then let's go to bed." The words were hardly out of my mouth when Gene Alice jumped up and glared at me in fury. She opened her mouth, and I could see her teeth as she started shouting. My first thought was of a lion that had once locked eyes on me before emitting a startling roar at a zoo in Colorado. Then shock. And fear.

"You are not my husband," she screamed. "You have to leave right now. If you don't, I will call the police. I want you to get the hell out of my house, right now!"

She dashed to the door and unlocked it. I ran to her, my mind racing as fast as my heart was thumping. What had set her off? Was it the mention of bed? Was she going to push me out the door or run out instead? I reached for her arm, but she flung me off. She opened the door a few inches. I managed to slam it shut before she could escape. She then tried to push me away with her leg, and I watched in growing astonishment as she summoned the strength of that mother who lifted a car pinning her small child. Gene Alice was determined to get away from me.

This is dangerous and can't happen again, I told myself. Perhaps I had been living in denial, too willing to suppress warning signs that arrived like a flash flood but quickly receded.

I realized now I was up to my knees in uncharted waters, and they were drawing me in, deeper and deeper. Clearly, it was time to act, maybe even past time. I made a plan, executed it, and unwittingly set the stage for the awful accident that would change everything.

It came just a few nights later in the exact spot where Gene Alice and I had scuffled. I was reduced to lying on the floor of the apartment, writhing in pain, and asking myself: How did we get to this sad, scary place?

CHAPTER 2

I met Gene Alice at the Hutchinson County Jail in 1953. The jail is in Stinnett, which is in the Texas Panhandle, about fifty-five miles from the Oklahoma border and fifteen miles from Phillips, the town where I grew up.

I was the child of a single mother, Eva Davenport Sherman, whose husband divorced her midway through her pregnancy with me. I don't think he even noticed she was carrying me; I am not mentioned at all in the divorce decree. My father took my five-year-old sister, Billie, to live with him, and when I was just two weeks old, my mom carried me away from the hills of Viola, Arkansas, to the flat oil patch of West Texas. She already had family in Hutchinson County. Her three surviving sisters were brought there by their great-aunt Mary and great-uncle J. O., who raised them. Mom's family toiled as grocers and store owners. Like them, we arrived dreaming of a life better than the hardscrabble existence that had defined the Davenport family's time in the Ozarks. Uncle J. O. was probably the wealthiest man in town, before he let drink and gambling become his boss.

Phillips was in what would be considered a godforsaken scab on the high plains but for the 1921 discovery of oil and gas in Hutchinson County. In fact, the entire Texas Panhandle would not have had a city or a large town had it not been for the petroleum bonanza that started a decade before our arrival. Before oil, those expansive plains were populated by cowboys and the few merchants who supplied agricultural and other goods to the sprawling ranches and their occupants. The new oil and gas economy changed everything. It birthed the first railroads, which proved to be the salvation of the cattle industry as it opened up a national market for beef. It also attracted waves of newcomers, many of whom were down on their luck, like Mom and me.

Our adopted county had been primed for a boom. By 1926, the population of Hutchinson County's new town of Borger was estimated to be between 40,000 and 50,000. The vast majority of its residents lived in tents and shacks spread over the rough, unforgiving landscape, pocked by a few barren hills and crooked crevasses. But opportunity permeated the town and fed everyone's ambitions. Almost overnight, Borger had become home to oilmen, prospectors, roughnecks, panhandlers, fortune seekers, card sharks, bootleggers, prostitutes, and dope peddlers. Not surprisingly, the town's somewhat seedy reputation also made it a haven for criminals and fugitives. Before long, the town government was firmly in the hands of an organized crime syndicate. The Texas Rangers were called in to bring order.

Gene Alice was from Borger.

By today's standards, the less-exciting town of Phillips might have been a prime example of industrial socialism. Everyone lived in a company house. Everyone had a job with Phillips Petroleum Company. Everyone was white. The company owned the hospital, and the doctors were company employees. The public school had one taxpayer, Phillips Petroleum.

As a Phillips student, I never had to pay for anything. If the band needed a new oboe, petroleum tax dollars bought it. If our winning football team needed new helmets or uniforms, which it did when I was on the roster, plenty of industry-supplied tax money sat in the school system's coffers, waiting to be spent. The Phillips High School Field House had the first whirlpool and electric stimulating equipment for sports injuries of any high school in Texas and, quite likely, before any college in the state. Teachers made almost 30 percent more than others in the region because the money was there. And, let's face it, the dry, windswept plains were not a pleasant place to put down stakes. The oil boom made the town more upper class.

My mother had taught school in Arkansas, but her credential didn't qualify her to teach in Texas. She needed money now and decided she could make a healthy living by operating a beauty salon. That also was not without sacrifice. Mom had to take a fifty-mile trip to Amarillo every Sunday night to attend the region's only beauty school. Late on Fridays, she would return home where we lived with her oldest sister, my aunt Ann. My aunt and I shared the same birthdate, January 19, and she was a kindly surrogate mother during the week. She worked as a checkout clerk in a grocery store and was married to Jonsie, but that marriage was on life support, and he was not around for long. They had no children, nor did my other aunts.

After Mom graduated from beauty school, she opened Eva's Beauty Shop on Main Street in Old Phillips, which had been named Whittenburg before the oil boom. My great-uncle Walter Goodwin owned almost every building in Old Phillips.

With my mother's new-found financial independence, she and I moved into a one-room stucco shack with a tiny kitchen and a concrete shower. She worked all the time, fixing other women's hair in her beauty shop and cleaning our small home in the few spare moments she had. Going to church did not become a habit for her until long after I left home. But Mom was religious in the faith of her fathers, distinctly Southern Baptist. When I was a baby, she would hold me in her arms as we went to bed and teach me to pray. "Now I lay me down to sleep, I pray the Lord my soul to keep. If I should die before I wake, I pray the Lord my soul to take." That was my first class in theology.

Mom slept on a double bed in the corner by the shower. I slept on a cot near the front door. When I was four, Billie came to live with us after the father I never knew died from injuries he suffered in a car wreck. Our little house was spartan, but it was blessed, literally, because it sat in the shadow of Phillips Southern Baptist Church, a huge influence on my childhood and adolescence. Aunt Ann was the one who taught me to not ever miss Sunday school. When we lived with her, she scrubbed me, dressed me in my finest clothes, and ushered me through the wire gate into the alley and off to church. I did not miss a single Sunday of that routine through my first grade in public school, after which I continued the tradition on my own in the little house Mom and I **[Wasn't Billie with you then?]** shared. As an eight-year-old, I qualified for the "Perfect Attendance Bible," given to those who never missed Sunday school.

Just before my twelfth birthday, I gained a wonderful stepfa-ther, John Crupper. We lived with him in an 800-square-foot Phillips company house for a little less than six years, when he tragically died of a heart attack. Death was a part of my life from an early age, but my faith assured me we would one day meet again.

Religious faith was the reason I was at the jail the day I crossed paths with Gene Alice Wienbroer. I was one of four high school boys who held a church service every Sunday after-noon at the jail. I officiated, carrying with me the perfect-atten-dance Bible I had earned. Everyone at the jail called me Pastor Max, which is funny, because I wasn't really a pastor. I was barely eighteen and had been running the service for nearly two years.

On this momentous Sunday, we invited a quartet of guy friends to sing during the service. They brought a beautiful fifteen-year-old girl to accompany them on an old army fold-up field organ. As she was working to unfold it, I noticed her elegant ankles. She was wearing a long skirt patterned with soft yellow horses and light-pink flowers. When she sat, the skirt dipped down to her lower calves, revealing a lovely patch of alabaster. Unlike most of the girls in my high school, she wore leather loafers without white ankle socks. She did not need any embellishment. My eyes were immediately drawn to the smooth skin just above her proper loafers. Her finely chiseled ankles were a work of art,

Gene Alice's loosely curled auburn hair, accented by notes of ginger, framed her radiant face. My heart skipped a beat when she tilted her head to smile at me. I noticed then she was still struggling to unfold the organ.

Instinctively, I asked, "May I help you?"

"No thank you," came the quick reply. "I can do it myself."

Releasing the Butterfly is now available as an ebook, paperback, large-print paperback on Amazon or as an ebook at Audible. Proceeds from the book will go to the Austin Presbyterian Theological Seminary's program in sacred music, which was always important to Gene Alice.

For more, please visit the Releasing the Butterfly website or contact Max Sherman at maxshermanauthor@gmail.com

ABOUT THE AUTHOR

Max Sherman tells people, "I'm a lawyer by training, a politician by practice, and an academic (and writer) by accident." He is professor emeritus and former dean of the Lyndon B. Johnson School of Public Affairs at the University of Texas at Austin. He also served as the president of West Texas State University (now West Texas A&M University) in Canyon, Texas. Sherman was a Texas state senator from 1971 to 1977, and he was named one of the state's best legislators multiple times by *Texas Monthly*.

His first book was *Barbara Jordan: Speaking the Truth with Eloquent Thunder*, published by the University of Texas Press in 2007. Sherman was Barbara Jordan's friend and colleague for twenty-five years, first in the Texas Senate and later at the LBJ School. A follow-up book of Barbara Jordan's speeches and lectures is being reviewed for copyright permissions.

His second book, *Releasing the Butterfly: A Love Affair in Four*

Acts (2020), is a memoir about his decades-long love story with his wife, Gene Alice, and how they found happiness in all situations, including Alzheimer's. *Releasing the Butterfly* is being promoted in partnership with Alzheimer's Texas (please visit releasingthebutterflybook.com for more details).

Throughout his distinguished career, Sherman has served on various boards and committees, including vice president of the Harry S. Truman Scholarship Foundation (current), president of the National Association of Schools of Public Affairs, the Austin Presbyterian Theological Seminary, the Presbyterian Church USA Committee on Theological Education, the Federation of State Humanities Councils, and the Schreiner University Board of Trustees.

His business affiliations include serving on the board of directors for Transport Life Insurance Company and the board of directors of Corporate Systems.

Sherman has a J.D. degree from the University of Texas at Austin and a B.A. in history from Baylor University. He lives in Austin, Texas.

To contact Max Sherman, please email him at maxshermanauthor@gmail.com.